PUPPY BENEATH THE BEAM

B S Jha

MINERVA PRESS
NEW DELHI
MIAMI LONDON

PUPPY BENEATH THE BEAM

ISBN 81 7662 206 0

First Published 2001 by
MINERVA PRESS
13 Palam Marg
Vasant Vihar
New Delhi – 110 057

Printed & bound in India
for Minerva Press India Pvt. Ltd.

PUPPY BENEATH THE BEAM

For my Father, Mother and Gurudev

ACKNOWLEDGEMENTS

After the Almighty and my parents, who are the reasons of my being, I am deeply beholden to my wife, Vibha, daughters, Ekta and Annie for their sacrifice and encouragement to make this book possible.

This book would not have made its journey to the world without the help of the Minerva family. I am also indebted to my Editor for his support.

ABOUT THE AUTHOR

Capt. B S Jha, is an ex-army officer, who was commissioned into the Armoured Corps. After a short spell with the Indian Army, he opted out and ventured for a career on civic street.

Contents

Chapter I

PUPPY AND THE CHILD

It was a serene winter night in a small village, in the month of January. People had gone to slumber, and very few of them astir to hear the wail of a child. He had to be drowned in the pond located east of the village, for reasons best known to his father. Very few of the lights could be seen fluctuating in the slight wind. The atmosphere was full of noise made by the water insects, cicadas, cockchafer and grasshoppers that made their living in the grass on the edge of the pond. All the palm trees that ringed around the pond, made the sound of dangling leaves due to the wind that chilled everyone's heart. One can't see the water hyacinth, lying on the edge of the pond, that had been uprooted along with the movement of the buffaloes that went into the pond everyday and came out late in the evening. One can hear the coughing of the elders having their last spell of hookah before going to sleep. Many of them suffer from whooping cough and sleep once they have the extra dose of tobacco from their hookah. It makes a typical sound of air bubbles that pass through the water before entering one's lungs, thus making a permanent scar inside. Some of the elders do not sleep and sit in a semicircle around the fire burning in an earthen pot, that is known as *Borsi* in the local lingo. The embers in it retain a slight heat even after the flames have been put off. It is put under the beds of the old ones to make them warm and have a peaceful sleep without disturbing others with their coughing.

The boy, Chotu as his parents called him, didn't know

what was happening to his mother and him. All he heard from his father was, 'We don't need a child who is good for nothing and has become a nuisance for the village and the family'. Mother had been begging for his life and tried desperately to save him from drowning. It was a pitch-dark night. Hardly has night set in but it seems as if the village has no living soul and is totally deserted.

In any case, people in this village hit the sack very early, as they have nothing better to do. All they have are radios, that too belonging to only a few people working in the government department as clerks or primary school teachers. In the whole village, we had a few radios, hence it had a social status attached to it. Every evening, people gathered outside the houses having these sets to hear the regional news. *'Ye Akashwani hai, ab ap Anant Kumar se Pradeshik Samachar Suniye.'* This was All India Radio, Bhagalpur. There is pin drop silence. No one is allowed to talk, save the teacher or the clerk. Once the news is over, many of them clarify their doubts, from the primary school teacher or the clerk, as they are the ultimate in knowledge and they can't be disputed. No polemic is allowed. Whatever comes from their mouth – good, bad or ugly – is taken by the villagers as sacrosanct or the gospel truth. They are the privileged class of the village. They can afford to have their evening tea in a cup and saucer. Everyone else is also sometimes, offered a cup of tea prepared with jaggery. They have this in metal tumblers. The teacher or the clerks have their tea in cups and saucers prepared with sugar drawn from the government control shop. They also stay in houses made of bricks, half concrete and other half mud. Some of them also boast about their radio, and how good it is. 'It is a National Panasonic make and can catch many stations including BBC and Ceylon. We can also hear *Binaca Geet Mala* (a famous programme based on the top Hindi songs of the week).' Most of them had received these radios, Sun Raleigh cycles and Seiko wristwatches in dowry. This proved their pre-eminence over other families in the village, as other didn't have any other such source of income besides agriculture. Every father dreamed of getting his offspring married to a family that could afford to provide a National Panasonic radio, a Seiko watch and a Sun Raleigh cycle to them in dowry.

Parents never allowed their sons of marriageable age - which was as low as fourteen to sixteen years - to move out of the village, especially during the marriage season, as many of the upper caste boys were forcibly married by the relatives and friends of the girl's family. They generally eyed the boys, who had relatively better status in the village. This system was a means to counter the dowry system that prevailed in the village.

Many girls' families couldn't even afford to pay the dowry that was in vogue at the village and they had to suffer the sarcasm and scoffing of the society if their daughter crossed the age of fifteen or sixteen. It was very difficult for the parents of the girls who had attained the age of sixteen to get them married, and at times they thought of eliminating them. People cursed the birth of a girl child and a female. Daughters-in-law, not able to give birth to a son were tortured or had to deliver virtually every year until they delivered a boy.

Many of the parents of such girls resorted to getting their daughter married through this route. Once the marriage was solemnised it was not possible to get rid of such a marriage and it had social sanction as well.

Parents of the young boys, remained under constant fear and threat from such groups, mainly because they didn't want to get deprived of the radio set of National Panasonic, UK – made Sun Raleigh cycle and a Seiko watch.

Every youth in the village dreamt of becoming a teacher or a clerk, as they could not think beyond that and also because they had a gala time in the village. There was nobody to check as to what time they reported to the school or to the office. Most of the time they spent in their houses. In any case, primary teachers of schools had many holidays, summer vacation or rainy-season vacation, other than the national holidays entitled to any Government employee.

These people have contributed considerably to the population of this village. Some of them had retired from the same school that they had joined at the beginning. They faced no transfer or separations from their families at all, throughout their career.

Most of the teachers or the clerks had large families, mainly because the infant mortality rates in the village were quite high. They felt that by the time the children grew up, some of them were sure to die, and then they would have at least a few of them who would survive. Moreover, there was no electricity and people went to sleep very early. The only sources of entertainment were women and sex. Literacy rate in the men was low and amongst the women, zero. There were no age gaps between the children. The health of the women was affected very badly and many of them lost their lives due to old method of terminating pregnancy or childbirth.

Fornication is a quite common affair in the village as people stay in a joint family and have smaller houses. They also take baths in the open and go outside for nature's calls or morning ablutions. People in the villages are quite used to seeing the defecating bottoms of girls and women, but this action plays a very significant role in their lives. Most of the sexual intercourses materialise when they are out on the fields for ablutions in twilight - real or fictitious - especially in winter, when the crop of maize or sugarcane stands tall in the fields awaiting harvesting. People were generally aware of the 'quickies' that took place in the fields and they ogled at girls and women out for defecating, to hook their prey.

Many young girls would become pregnant due to their own close relatives and would then be eliminated by poisoning or by other methods to keep the honour, prestige and image of the family.

There was also no source of entertainment, like newspapers, library or any such facility.

People didn't pay any heed to the death of women, as men had a condescending attitude towards them and got a new wife immediately, with new dowry. This had contributed in a big way to the population of the village as well as the nation.

The mother had been running helter-skelter, with a hurricane lantern in her hand, to save her son from the hands of her husband. She caught his feet and pleaded for clemency, 'Please forgive him and don't throw him into the pond that might end his life. He is not even six and doesn't know how to swim. He is sure to die, as the water is very cold. There are many water snakes and other poisonous insects that may bite him. I have only one child please forgive him.'

He pushed her with the full force of his feet. She was thrown many feet away from him. She was broken and sure that she wouldn't be able to save the life of her child and resorted to wailing loudly for help.

There are many hovels of the lower caste, the 'Dusadhs', on the outskirts of the village, quite close to the pond. She finally yelled for Parmeshwar Paswan, hereinafter referred as Parmeshra, the most trusted lieutenant of the house, a swarthy skinned person with a, bulrush and scraggy beard willing to do anything for the family at the drop of a hat. He too is a Dusadh. He was attached to the house from the day he was born. His father had taken loan from the child's – Chotu's – great grandfather; some cash and grains for the marriage of his sister, that they hadn't been able to repay. Ever since they had been attached to this family. They were also given some part of the land to construct a house, along with some agricultural land for their livelihood, to grow crops for their survival. These lands are still in the name of Chotu's great grandfather and they could be thrown out any time. They dare not work for others either in their house or in the fields. Chotu's family had exclusive rights on them and their offspring. They were totally at our mercy.

I don't want to hide my identity anymore. Yes, it's me. Mama calls me Chotu with love. The wailing of my mother and my cries reached the ears of Parmeshra and he ran out to know the reasons for my cries. Many other villagers, mostly Dusadhs, arrived along with Parmeshra. Even many members of our Brahmin community arrived to watch the fun. Many of them got a new story to talk about and discuss for the next few weeks. This incident would be discussed not only in our village but also with other relatives in many other villages.

Before Parmeshra could reach us, and while mother lay on the ground, I was plunged into the pond, in the six-feet deep chilled water. My feet got stuck in the hyacinth, commonly known as *Jalkumbhi* in the local lingo. I was trying desperately to keep myself afloat and was clinging to the bulbs of hyacinth, very firmly with my little fingers. Mama tried her best to locate me in the water, but she was blinded due to the reflection of the light of the hurricane lantern she was holding above the water. She put the lantern on the ground and was about to jump into the pond to save me. In the meantime, Parmeshra arrived and jumped into the water before Mama could. I caught hold of his neck very firmly. I didn't know what was happening to me. My feet were trembling. I couldn't stand on my feet. Parmeshra tried his best to put me on to the ground but I didn't leave him. Once again, father tried to separate me from him and throw me back into the pond. Mama resisted, as did Parmeshra. He took me away to his small hamlet.

He put me down. I couldn't stand on my feet, I winced and squirmed, more due to the shock and to some extent due to the cold. He wiped me with his *gamcha,* a locally woven towel used by the locals in our village. The villagers generally use this *gamcha* either on their shoulders or tie it around their waist. He wiped himself as well. He also covered me with the old torn bedsheet given to him by my grandmother, hereinafter referred as 'Ma'. In the meantime, Mama arrived with my clothes and towel. She once again wiped me after putting all my clothes down. She cleaned my *Phu*, as we referred to our genitals then, it had shrunk inside, along with my testicles that had become very hard due to the cold. She made me put on my clothes and took me in her lap. She wiped my tears and started back for home. I once again started crying and refused to return due to the fear of father. I caught hold of Parmeshra's lungi and requested him to save me and keep me at his place. On seeing my plight, and my fear of father, he offered to come along with us to assuage the anger of Ma and father.

'Malik, ek to bacha hai usko bhi maar daliye, Apko pata nahi hai App kya kar rahe hai or Kiske liye kar rahe hai bad main bahut pachtayenge,' Parmeshra added painstakingly. Ma couldn't tolerate such words from him and rebuffed, 'You keep your mouth shut else you will regret. What is your problem? Can't you see this brat has made my life miserable as hell.'

'Do what you want,' he sneered and added in calmer tone, and walked out angrily. Parmeshra's presence and comments gave a fillip to father's anger.

We found father still murmuring in anger, as was Ma. I hid behind Mama's sari and peeked. Ma cursed Parmeshra for wiping me with his *gamcha* and offering me his bedsheet. She ordered Mama, 'Give him a proper bath, change his clothes before taking him inside the house.'

'It seems both of you have decided to kill him, he will die of cold,' murmured Mama deprecatingly. It was very cold and my hands and feet were already numb. But father's anger was much more fearful than to have a bath. I left myself to Ma's mercy for the moment. I was once again given a bath outside the house and made to put on a different set of clothes. I was shivering. Ma kept cursing me for my deeds. Mama took me inside and offered me hot milk and *roti*. My lips were swollen, my jaws were paining and I did not feel like eating. Mama was trying to feed me with her hands, quietly cursing father and Ma for our condition. Father could see that Mama had been trying to feed me with her own hands. I was very tired and didn't feel like eating at all. I wanted to sleep snuggled in the warmth of my mother. I embraced her and leaned on her lap. In the meantime, father, to take out his frustration, came and picked up the pot of the milk and *roti* and forced down my throat as much as he could. I almost choked and vomited, whatever little I had in my tummy. Mama once again cleaned off my whole body as the pot, full of milk and *roti* was smeared on my body, soiling my clothes. She took me inside and put me to sleep on the cot inside the room and covered me with multiple quilts. I was sobbing and couldn't sleep as the hiccups kept coming, an after-effect of long crying and the ordeal.

After sometime, Mama came to the bed with a pot of hot mustard oil and applied it thoroughly on my body and feet. She kept murmuring and cursing Ma for our predicament. She wiped my cheeks with the pure mustard oil and a burning sensation swept through my face as the cheeks were sore due to strong winter winds.

The reason for our ordeal was an accusation from Ma about Mama and me. Ma was a widow, an orthodox, not allowed to eat non-vegetarian, not even vegetarian food cooked with onions and garlic. She was also not allowed to dress up in coloured clothes or wear any makeup on her face. Those were the traditions followed by the Brahmin widows in the village.

One morning, she had left home for an unrevealed destination without any information. She had kept all her clothes ready in the night itself, tied in an old bedsheet. Lucky, the official watchman appointed by the Government by an organisation *Gram Raksha Dal,* arrived every witching hour and Ma and he had a long chat with her on his routine round of the village. They also shared the tobacco pipe, hookah or bidi. Ma always slept outside the house in the open as she felt very hot in summer, and had long sessions with Lucky on his nocturnal visits. Lucky had suffered a paralytic attack and Ma had helped him financially for his treatment, but he didn't recover. Ma shared all the information with Lucky about the village. He was given a few acres of land by the government to cultivate in lieu of his salary. He was the only person who was aware of Ma's plans to move to Deoghar, without informing anyone.

That morning was a usual morning in all respects for us, other than the fact that Ma didn't return after morning ablutions, even when the cows were about to be milked by Matra, a cowhand, and a Yadav by caste. He looked after all the cows, buffaloes, goats of the Brahmins and other upper castes of the whole village and took the entire lot out for grazing in a meadow across the river, throughout the year. In lieu, he received a few kilos of grains from all the houses with cows, buffaloes and goats every month.

Matra had arrived and was waiting for Ma to release the calves, to go to their respective mothers to tug or suck the nipple before milking. Matra always deceived the cows by tying the calves in the rear leg before milking. Initially, Mama took it lightly and asked Matra if he had seen Ma anywhere. He denied. Matra left after the daily ritual of milking the cows.

The sun rose in the sky. Mama became restive and worried about Ma. She asked me to check, first at Babu's place and subsequently in the neighbours' houses to ascertain about Ma. Many a time, whenever she became upset she used to leave for Babu's place and had most of her meals with them till Mama apologised and got her back. I looked for her in every nook and cranny of the village and the houses in the neighbourhood, especially at Babu's place but couldn't find any clue of Ma. I returned and informed Mama. She panicked and could smell a rat. She immediately summoned Parmeshra and asked him to find out about Ma. He left; she remained upset and kept cursing me for touching Ma's food plates after touching an untouchable. She had apprehensions that Ma might have left for her daughter's place.

Her daughter, Nirupama, was married to a clerk working at Deoghar Collectorate. Ma had quietly left for Deoghar, earlier on one such occasion, when she had some scuffle with Mama. Mama had briefed Parmeshra properly, to look for Ma everywhere, including the place from where the one and only bus left for Deoghar everyday, with the passengers of twenty odd villages packed like sardines. Parmeshra came back after a few hours with the concrete information that Ma had indeed boarded a bus that had left in the morning for Deoghar. The bus boarding point was miles away from our village and one had to cross many agricultural canals and a river existing in the area. Mama knew it was not very safe to travel alone, that too early in the morning. Ma was seen going towards the bus boarding point by couple of villagers and they, in turn, informed Parmeshra.

Everyone started inquiring about Ma. The news of Ma's departure spread like wild fire in the whole village. Mama broke down several times, and was in tears replying to everyone about Ma. Many of the ladies, especially the mothers-in-law cursed her for not being able to look after her mother-in-law properly and keep her happy. Everyone blamed her for what was not her fault. She didn't cook food and kept thinking of Ma. I walked up to her and wiped her tears. She cried louder for a while, after embracing me in her arms. It remained a matter of talk in the whole village for a long time. The whole village taunted and made scathing remarks about Mama and me and gossiped.

Mama sent Parmeshra the very next day, to give this message to father and also reconfirmed whether Ma had arrived at Deoghar or not. Father was very upset to know about Ma and sent Parmeshra back to the village. He too, travelled to Deoghar to meet Ma. He was informed of some distorted and exaggerated stories by Ma and Nirupama. He surmised it to be true and was furious and decided to take both of us to task on arrival. He, in any case, was an irascible, ornery and erratic person and didn't heed any value to women.

The culture of the village was totally different. It was a male-dominated society where women had not a vestige of importance or say in it. All they had to do was to stay under the *ghunghat*, cover of their saris. They dare not speak a word in the affairs of men. Every man in the village was given importance according to his ability to dominate. Excesses or cruelties on women were synonymous to the dominating status.

After a few weeks, father arrived at the village with Ma in the evening. Instead of coming to the house, at the instance of Ma, both of them first went to the house of Babu, where once again Babu and his wife beguiled him and informed him with exaggerated and made-up stories.

Babu also admonished father and said, 'You are unable to look after your widowed mother. You take away your family with you and let Ma stay at the village peacefully.'

This added fuel to the burning heart of father. He was very upset and their words poisoned his mind further and stimulated him to take drastic action against Mama and me. Ma agreed to come home only when father promised her that he would take both of us to task and also ensure that it was not repeated in future.

That was the fateful night. As soon as he arrived home, he caught hold of Mama and started beating her. Mama kept whimpering to him to listen to her version of the facts, but that made no difference to his plan of action. He didn't bother to listen to her and thrashed her very badly. It was heart-rending for me. I ran towards Mama and cried loudly after catching her sari. He left Mama and caught hold of me in order to throw me into the pond.

What was the reason for our impasse? Why did the whole village curse Mama for not being able to look after Ma? The basic reason was very different. But the reason for what Ma had blamed us was a puppy.

All I had done was to bring a puppy in the house. I had seen a very small, puny puppy in a paddy field, stuck in the mud and badly injured. I cleaned all the mud and brought it home. I knew Ma wouldn't allow me to keep it anywhere near the house. I made a small house of bricks, stacked for the construction of our house. It didn't want to stay there and made helluva noise to come out. It was too weak to walk and seemingly hungry. I brought a pot full of milk for it. After having milk, it stayed in its house. It became a routine and I used to pilfer rice and milk to feed him everyday. Somehow, it remained quiet in the daytime but it didn't want to stay alone in its house at night. It made helluva noise. I looked for a solution. We had a beam that was stored in the corridor of the house. It was meant for the construction of the ceiling support for the rear part of our house. I sneaked in the puppy everyday before dark, wrapped it in a rag and hid it beneath the beam. It was a small little puppy, brownish with white patches all over its body like a Dalmatian. The patches over its body made it more cute than other puppies.

One thing that bugged me was to ascertain whether it was a boy or a girl, not male or female. I didn't have the concept of male or female. I showed it to one of my village friends who was little older to me. He too couldn't tell me whether it was a boy or a girl. I didn't know the difference between a male and a female puppy. I was happy as long as it was a cute looking one. I played with it alone for hours together. It licked my cheeks whenever I lifted it on my lap. We shared our happiness many times a day, talking and trying to understand each other. I almost understood all its gestures as it scratched my hands and body with its front paws. He hid his face in the cleavage between my arm and body. We were in love and wished to spend most of our time together. At times it did *Phoo*, as we referred to urinating then, on my lap but I never scolded it. It didn't talk but conveyed most of the things by gestures.

This continued until one day while stealing milk and rice, Ma caught me. She yelled at me. I froze. I hid the rice in my tiny pocket, and even poured the milk that I was carrying in a small glass, into it. I was well aware of Ma's anger and didn't want to take any chance and poured the milk into the pocket, being oblivious to the fact that milk was leaking from the pocket. I very innocently confessed, 'I am hungry and wished to eat'. She slapped me lightly and took my knickers and threw all the rice mixed with milk on to the floor of the courtyard. All the sparrows had a good time whereas my puppy starved. I thanked God for saving me from Ma's anger.

I went up to the puppy and complained about Ma. I explained to him all I had gone through. It licked my fingers soiled in rice and milk as it could get the smell of the food that it ate everyday. It was fidgeting and wanted me to put food into the pot. I had nothing to put. I tried once again to communicate what I had gone through, but it couldn't understand and kept licking. It even showed its anger and scratched my thigh with its tiny paw, making a ticklish sensation. I waited for Ma to go out of the house so that I could manage something for it. I was very restless. We generally had supper very early at about eleven or so, and had nothing that could be given to the puppy. I was very depressed as my friend was hungry.

Finally, Ma left on her routine visit to Babu's house. She spent every afternoon, at that place for a tête-a-tête with Babu and his wife. One of the topics of their gossip remained Mama and me. They always offered Ma something sweet to eat and Ma enjoyed it, oblivious of her being a diabetic. One of the reasons for her scuffle with Mama was that she never allowed Ma to eat anything that would harm her, like sweets, potatoes and rice. On the contrary, Babu's wife offered her the cheap quality sweets made by the local *Bania* that satisfied Ma. She always brought sugar or sweet from the village *Bania* and hid it in her 'Gandhi Charkha'. She had a nice box where she stored her thread weaving manual machine, popularly known as Gandhi Charkha in the village. At times, she even offered me some sweets after taking it out from her Gandhi Charkha. Ma was not aware of their motive of offering her the food that was prohibited for her. Even the doctors had advised her not to eat sweets, potatoes or rice.

Mama tried her best to ensure that Ma didn't eat potatoes, sugar and rice. But she always misinterpreted these intentions of mother and ate all those things restricted for her at Babu's place. She was completely oblivious to the fact that it was hastening her death. Many times she complained to others that Mama didn't allow her to eat food in the house but she felt hungry mainly due to being a diabetic.

Babu and his wife, had a different motive to keep Ma happy as she kept all her money and gold ornaments with them. Ma had lot of savings from the agricultural income. She looked after the whole agricultural affair and didn't tolerate any interference in it. She kept all her savings with Babu and his wife. She never trusted Mama. That was the reason they always instigated Ma against Mama to ensure that we left the village and stayed where father served in a Government office.

No sooner did Ma move out of the house, I rushed inside to collect a lot of rice and milk and gave it to my puppy to eat. It ate and relished everything and looked cylindrical. Probably, it thought thereafter it might not get food and hogged the full thing in one go. In the evening, before Ma could have entered the house for puja, I put my puppy beneath the beam, after wrapping it with a rag.

We always had our meal sitting on the floor in the walkway of the corridor near the beam. Ma couldn't see in the night properly, more so when the lantern used to hang at its place in the corridor. At night, while we were having our dinner sitting near the beam in the corridor, the puppy came out on smelling the food. I hid it behind my back and put it back in its place with a small piece of *roti*. I thought, perhaps, I had somehow managed to save it from Ma's eye. But no! Ma could make out what I was up to and asked me to own up. 'What are you hiding at the back?' she asked.

I panicked. In a hurry I hadn't been able to hide it properly and it once again sneaked out of the beam before Ma. In the low intensity of the light of lantern, Ma was not able to see it properly but as I tried to hide it, it was hurt inadvertently, by my leg and whimpered. My heart sank. Ma's eyebrows went up. Mama was in trouble. She tried to protect me from Ma's anger by scolding me and telling me not to repeat and touch the puppy ever, but Ma was not satisfied. She took out her bamboo stick and dragged the puppy out of the house. It cried continuously. Its cry pierced my heart. It was thrown from the veranda to the ground, four steps down. It ran towards the house I had made for it. I cried more than it did, but was helpless. My puppy was my best friend. It never complained of anything, I shared all my feelings with it for hours together and it too made faces as if it understood everything that I discussed with it. Once it was thrown out, it was my turn to get my share. I hid behind Mama but Ma didn't spare me and caned me too. 'If you bring this *kutte ka bacha,* I will hang you upside down,' she admonished. 'Don't ever bring the puppy inside the house again, as it is an untouchable,' she cautioned. She ordered Mama to wash my feet and hands before allowing me to bed. She took a bucket full of water and washed the whole area wherever it was either dragged or had walked.

Ma slept in a different room. She ordered me to go to bed. I had no sleep in my eyes and kept thinking of my friend. After sometime, it came up and started crying for me to let it in. Right from day one, it had a habit of sleeping beneath the beam. That was its first house. How could someone take away its house? It was damn upset and kept crying. I quietly got off my bed and went near the door. I bent on the floor to look at it through the slot of the door. It could sense my breath and smell, as I put my face down near the slot. I knew it must have taken a lot of pain first to negotiate the door and second to climb the four steps to the veranda with its tiny feet. I put my cheek near the slot between the door and the floor; it could sense the nearness between us and pleaded with me to open the door. I was too small to reach the shutter of the door. I couldn't help at all. I put my little finger towards it through the gap, it licked it and developed a lot of hope of getting in. It became quite confident of winning but was oblivious of my plight. No sooner did I remove my finger from the slot, it whined louder and louder resulting in awaking Ma from her sleep. She once again got up to sort it out. I returned to my bed. This time Ma was more upset than before and hit it very hard. I clutched the corner of the quilt firmly in my hands and kept hearing the cries of my friend but couldn't help it at all. It was totally outrageous on her part. I knew. But I couldn't help the puppy. The cries waned after sometime. Perhaps Ma took it outside the boundary wall of the house and drove it away. I kept thinking of my puppy. How it must be suffering in the extreme cold of winter! I cried for sometime and fell asleep.

At midnight, I awoke with the thought of my puppy. I couldn't sleep properly, and got up very early in the morning, before I could hear the moo of the calves and their mothers, to let them out. I was waiting for Mama to get up so that she could open the main door. I lied to her that I had developed loose motions and wished to go out.

She admonished, 'I have told you several times not to eat fried *Chana Dal*, as that must have upset your stomach.' I liked eating fried gram before grinding to convert it into powder or *Sattu*. I came out of the house and felt as if I had been freed from a cage. I ran out to look for my friend in the little house I had made for it, but it was not there. After a long search, I could locate it in a ditch quite far away from our house. Before Ma could have got up, I brought it and hid it in its house. It felt safe and relieved.

For a few days, we had a good time once again. I had very cleverly found another place for my puppy so that it couldn't come out on smelling the food. It was the other end of the beam. But it couldn't resist the smell of the food and travelled from one end to the other, beneath the beam and waited for our dinner. While we were having our dinner, once again, my friend came out. I hid it behind me. I was having dinner in the same plate with Ma. I had touched her pot, glass and even the food after touching the puppy. I was more worried about my friend and wasn't eating at all. She asked me to fetch the milk pot for her. I took a little time to get up and cradled the puppy on my lap. Perhaps, I could take advantage of Ma's old age and the low intensity light of the lantern. But no, I was not fortunate enough to get the advantage of anything. Ma could see the puppy on my lap. It was the end of everything. She threw the puppy out of the house with the stick, washed the whole area took the pot of water and pretended to vomit the food she had had. She cursed me and wished for my death or at least that I suffer from leprosy. Mama couldn't tolerate such words from Ma about her child and objected to such words. Mama also pleaded on my behalf to forgive me, but Ma wasn't in the mood for compromise, as her *dharma* was broken. All the blessings of the Almighty she had earned throughout her life were diminished with this act of mine. Ma had a great altercation with Mama for a long time. Mama pleaded, 'Ma, please forgive him and forget it, I assure you, that I'll ensure that the puppy is not allowed in the house.' Ma didn't budge and was adamant and even abused her.

Three things were highly untouchables for the Brahmins, especially widows. They couldn't reconcile with the sins earned by touching an untouchable, unless they underwent *Prayashchit*. *Prayashchit,* for the sin that they committed by touching an untouchable or having the food and water in a pot touched by someone after touching an untouchable. That could only be purged once they worshipped a virgin cow, drank its urine and had its dung for a few days. Besides, they also would have to offer food to eleven Brahmins on one of the auspicious days after worshipping a virgin cow and the rituals associated with it.

These three things were Muslims, the lower caste and the dog. These three things were totally prohibited in the house of Brahmins and the upper caste. I remember that every house of the Brahmins had separate enamel pots, plates and mugs for the use by the Muslims and the lower castes. Whenever any Muslim or the lower caste visited the house, they were offered the food or water in those pots separately kept for the above categories to use it, wash it and replace it at its place outside the house.

The Muslims on *Batai* cultivated most of our lands. *Batai* is a system still prevailing or in vogue at the village, wherein the landlord gets fifty per cent of the total harvest in the land given to him for cultivation. Whenever any Muslim *raiyat* cultivating our land visited us, they were not allowed to sit on any of the furniture or enter the house. They always sat on the floor and discussed the issue with Ma, that too outside the house. Mama was not allowed to interfere in Ma's affairs. Most of the time, they had water after pouring it on to their hands, without touching the pot or were given in the enamel mug exclusively kept for this purpose.

I remember Azim, the mason who worked for the construction of our house, was exclusively given a brand new set of enamel pots and mug to be used by him. That used to be handled by the labourers, mainly, Dusadhs every time Azim used it for food, tea or water.

Once, Ma had seen Kusmi, Parmeshra's wife eating and sharing the chutney, of rats with Azim, the mason. The rats were burnt in the fire, crushed and mixed with salt, chilly and pepper. She was very upset and had thrown her out of the house. Mostly the lower castes, Dusadhs and Mushahars ate the rats in the village. I had seen Kusmi catching rats a number of times. After the paddy crops were cut and removed from the fields, they even ate the small babies of rats, without eyes, after frying them. That used to be a delicacy for them. They also ate snails and the fish that looked like snakes known as *kuchia* fish in the village. Ma hated them, with a vengeance for eating these creatures. Ma also hated dogs because they fed on carcass, so also the

Chamars, a lower caste in the village, who ate dead cows after skinning them.

How could Ma have reconciled with a puppy in the house? That too, I had touched her food plates, water pots after touching an untouchable, although it was the last in order of the merit of the untouchables. Lower caste and the Muslims preceded it.

These were the reasons why Ma had left the house early morning after that incident. Though Mama was quite worried when Ma had left home, I had immense fun. Firstly, I could play and feed my puppy without any hassles and secondly, I was not aware and worried about the forthcoming ordeal that waited for Mama and me. I had absolutely no restrictions to play with my puppy and putting it under the beam in the night.

The day Mama had sent me to look for Ma, I had not been able to locate Ma but I had found my puppy, before I went to Babu and the neighbour's house to look for Ma.

We had a good time together as long as Ma was at Deoghar. My puppy had grown sideways, as I didn't have to steal the rice and milk for it. Everyday, it had its stomach full of food. I overfed it till Ma arrived with father. My puppy was not aware of the problems that Mama and I had gone through, while it lay snoring to glory, every afternoon beneath the beam. The passage beneath the beam was becoming small for my puppy. It had grown bigger, and whenever it entered beneath the beam it got stuck under it. It could neither come back in reverse gear nor move forward and come out from the other end. Even though it got stuck, it didn't leave its first home and habit of entering inside. It was totally attached to the beam. When it grew big and couldn't enter at all, it used to put its mouth beneath the beam to have the feeling of entering beneath the beam.

Everyone is attached to its home but as one grows, one has to sacrifice and act accordingly. But the puppy was adamant and didn't want to leave the beam. Whenever it was taken away from the beam it cried for a long time. It always wished to stay beneath the beam. I knew how difficult it was to leave one's first home. It was too attached to the beam. Whenever it got stuck under the beam I took the help of Azim and Kusmi to take it out. In the process one day Azim called it *kutia*. I had got my answer that always bugged me to ascertain whether it was a girl or a boy. I could make out it was a girl, not a boy. It wouldn't be able to rub its *Phu*, against the pillow or with the small little finger and enjoy the pleasing sensations. Ma was not at home. We were not bothered about her, as she was the hurdle between us. We had a good time together as long as Ma stayed out.

One of the major and main raison d'être of our ordeal, was the complaint from Ma to father apropos infringement into her Dharma by me, resulting in paving a path of hell for her. Mother, obviously, could have defended her child, but would have got stuck in an argument with Ma. How could a young daughter-in-law win against her mother-in-law in Indian culture? After all, it was the house of Ma's son and husband first. It was she who came to this house first. She had been staying in that house for almost forty years or so. Earlier it was a *kuchha* house with a thatched roof; she had struggled hard with her son to bring it to the level of half-concrete with a thatched roof. It was her husband's house first. He had died after leaving an infant in her lap. She had brought up her son all alone, sent him to a school, which was five miles away across the agricultural canals and rivers from the village. She herself used to drop him everyday to school to ensure his safety. She was very close to her son. They loved each other and any intrusion in their love wouldn't be tolerated. She had been helping her son financially, for the construction of the house. She sold the grain and put up the money for construction.

There were many other reasons for our ordeal. The village politics also played a big role in the whole affair. Babu played the lead role and fired the gun from Ma's shoulder. Before I go into the depth of village politics and the ordeal of mother and me, I must introduce all the characters in the game.

By now you know who Parmeshra is. Though he had played a very important and crucial role in our life and even saved my life, he is not of much significance. I have been seeing him from the day I had opened my eyes on this planet or was a nascent. He was a part of our family in all the ups and downs in life. He had seen my grandfather dying of dehydration after diarrhoea. He was the person who used to take my grandfather to school where he taught as a primary teacher. He never slept and left the house until asked by my grandfather. He was the most trusted lieutenant of the family. I remember that as a child, he carried me piggyback many times right from the bus stop to our home, which was a distance of more than five miles. Mama and I were highly obliged to him, but in the eyes of upper castes he was just one of the lower castes. He is of no significance in this story, because he is a lower caste. He is meant for that. God had sent him to this mother earth to serve the Brahmins. His sacrifices for the family were totally ignored. It was his duty. It was not a big deal if he had served the Brahmins all his life. He had done nothing great. He was supposed to do all that he had done for the family. After all, his hamlet was on our great grandfather's land. He and his family survived on the food or crops that he cultivated from the lands given to him by my grandfather. He had nothing of his own, probably, not even the child he claimed to be his. Then how could he live for himself?

He started his day at our field, where he went everyday to work, very early in the morning to ensure the crops were not dried or had sufficient water to survive. His wife Kusmi reported at the house almost at the same time her husband reported to the field. She cleaned the cowshed, gathered all the cowdung that had been littered in the night by the cows, and made cakes out of it that would be used for cooking. She took all the clothes for washing that was put into caustic soda powder the previous evening. She sometimes requested mother for the toilet soap. She wanted to impress the upper caste youths, who all adored her beauty. Mama would hand her over the broken pieces of 501 bar used for washing the clothes. She would wash her hair. Once, she finished all this work, she joined the construction labourers and pushed them to work faster. She had the feeling of belongingness to our family. She belonged to this house, while other labourers would leave soon as the construction work was over. Both the wife and husband were quite loyal to the family. Still they do not play a significant role in the family.

Kusmi sometimes got green grams from the field, peeled them off and handed them to me. I used to fill them up till the top of my tiny pockets of the readymade shorts that my father bought for me. In the village, the other children wore shorts tailored by the village tailor. It didn't have buttons. They tied it with the threaded ropes. Kusmi sometimes fondled me with love. She made me put on clothes and pulled my *Phu* while making me put on my shorts. I used to laugh and pull her nose while she pulled my scrotum. I complained about it to Ma and Mama at times.

Construction of the house was in full swing. Ma always stood at the site to ensure that work moved smoothly and none of the labourers were idle. Mama was not allowed to come to the site and only came out to distribute the food to the labourers. After Azim the mason had his bath, Kusmi collected his food and offered it to him. Kusmi washed his plates. All the other labourers went out to have their food and relax under the trees. They had two hours break before they resumed their work. Mama went away after distributing the sattu, the powder of gram and barley, to the labourers.

I never slept in the afternoon, as that was the only time I had the freedom to play with my puppy with no one to disturb us. That was the time I could openly play in the sand, making lovely houses for my puppy, hiding it and confusing it by putting it inside the house made of sand. I also climbed the lintel quietly, as Ma might wake up and take me to task. I jumped off the lintel once, twice and thrice… and got tired. I climbed on the lintel, walked over it for sometime, as I had discovered a new game of walking on the lintel, a narrow walkway. That gave me a feeling, as if I had grown big and could do the things that elders could do. While doing so, I saw Kusmi climbing on Azim in one of the rooms. I couldn't understand the game they were playing. What game was it? I quietly sat on the lintel while they played the game and I watched. I was utterly confused to see Azim profusely sweating and even touching Kusmi's *Pupu* as then we referred to the breasts of women. Kusmi was biting Azim's cheek. Her sari covered half of the body of Azim and made a circle around him with the frill of her petticoat. I kept watching the game for quite sometime but couldn't understand the logic of the game. But while I was watching the game something was happening to me, a different feeling that made me watch more and more. I liked watching this game more than any other games that I played with my friends. I had discovered another reason for not sleeping in the afternoons. I watched everyday as Kusmi first massaged Azim's leg, body, his *Phu* before she climbed over him and rode him like a horse. Maybe they played

Ghoda-Ghoda, as we referred to the game of Horse-Horse, that we children played amongst ourselves.

It was seemingly a very popular game amongst all the age groups of people in the village. Earlier, I thought only the children played this game with the parents or among themselves. One day, I was about to ask Kusmi the name of the game played by her in the afternoon, while all the other labourers went out to relax in the recess, but couldn't get the opportunity. This continued until one day, I found Azim riding her and Kusmi had become a horse. I burst into laughter to see her legs facing the sky. My eyes met hers. She could see me sitting on to the lintel like a monkey. They hurriedly got up. I sat at the same place and continued laughing. Both of them were shocked.

They asked me, 'What did you see?'

I replied, '*App Ghoda-Ghoda har roj kheltae ho to main dekhta houn.*'

She became pale and asked me, '*Har roj?*'

I replied, 'Yes'.

She panicked, whereas Azim went out, piddled like a donkey in the open, for a long time and once again lay dead on the place he played *Ghoda-Ghoda*. She requested me not to speak to anyone, especially Ma, that they played *Ghoda-Ghoda*. I was confused. What was there to hide and not to speak to Ma? I thought, perhaps they too are scared of playing in the afternoon as I was. I once again climbed on to the lintel to watch the afternoon game, but it was not being played. Azim just talked, whereas Kusmi massaged him.

After that incident, I could make out the difference in their behaviour towards me. They refused to help me in taking out my puppy stuck under the beam. I cried before they did. They had entered into a quid-pro-quo arrangement with me. They asked me not to climb on to the lintel in the afternoon if I wanted them to help me out to take out the puppy, stuck under the beam. I happily agreed, as I liked my puppy more than watching the game of *Ghoda-Ghoda*. Their afternoon game continued, while I played with my puppy on the clean white sand used for the construction purpose. I made big castles for the puppy that she broke with her front paw. This game of *Ghoda-Ghoda* and making castles continued till Ma arrived back with father and we had to go through such an ordeal.

All the villagers and Babu upbraided and blamed father for not looking after his widowed mother and also for the cruelty meted out to her by Mama. There was a meeting organised by Babu in our house to discuss the issue relating to Ma's dissatisfaction with us, especially with Mama. Mama knew the outcome of the meeting, as we were aware that Babu had vested interest in it and would be able to easily delude father and Ma. Rightly so. Mama was blamed for the whole episode. I was branded as an impudent and the naughtiest child having no control of mother on me. Father was asked to take his family away with him to the place he worked. Mama tried her best to explain things to father but he didn't budge at all. Mama was not given any chance to do so. He too, blamed her for the crisis in the family. Ma was quite happy with the outcome. She could manipulate things, as she desired.

After the verdict was given, father threatened Mama with divorce and thrashed her badly. I hid behind the door of the room where we shared our bed. It was comparatively darker than the other room as it had only one small window. Mama fell at his feet, imploring. He was not satisfied and dragged her before Babu and other elders sitting in the veranda. She was treated worse than an animal. Her sari came off her face, everyone could see the welts on her face and she almost died of humiliation. I cried and shivered in my room but couldn't help Mama, who I loved the most. Before this, I always slept with Ma, but after this incident I refused to oblige her and slept with Mama. I had developed a fear of Ma, if she could do that with mother she would not spare me. Moreover, I had come to know the fact of that fateful night. Though Mama always encouraged me to sleep with Ma, I was scared and avoided her.

Mama, being a primary school teacher, had a fair knowledge and awareness about the problems Ma suffered, besides the poisoning of her mind by Babu's family. She was asked to leave her job by her father after she joined her in laws' place. The system in the village was quite different and a girl only joined her in-laws, once a second marriage ceremony, *Gauna* was organised, which usually took place only after five years of their marriage.

Mama always advised Ma not to eat sugar, sweet, potatoes and rice or any other rich diet that would have had a detrimental effect or harmed Ma. Ma could never understand mother's feeling and blamed her for the restrictions that she had imposed on her. Ma used to eat the things disallowed to her at Babu's place and cursed Mama for stopping her from doing so and living a normal life. Moreover, Ma was too simple to understand the motives and shenanigans of Babu, and his other family members for keeping her happy at all cost. Mama had informed father regarding the money and jewellery that Ma kept with Babu's wife. But father always blamed Mama for being absurd and suspicious. Mama also tried to explain to him about the losses that our family incurred every year in the agricultural income due to Babu and his wife. 'Either you are blinded by Babu or scared of him,' Mama said. He could not accept the truth and hit mother very hard with his sandal. She cried in isolation. She was too decent a lady and didn't want to make an issue of it. She didn't wish to discuss the issue any further and withdrew. Even after these incidents, Mama never showed any resentment or an indifferent attitude towards Ma. She remained the same for her and always applied oil and massaged her feet before she retired for the day. Ma didn't do any work in the house, and everyday, after her supper, she left for Babu's house for the afternoon gossip sessions.

It was time for father to resume his duty at the place of work. Before leaving he pleaded to Babu to grant him a little more time before he could shift his family to the place of work. Mama knew it was just to please Babu. He never wanted to take us to the place he worked. He handed over some money to Ma for the on going construction work. Ma had developed a different relation with Babu's family, as we never stayed at the village. Now it was difficult for Ma to break that relationship overnight. Moreover, Ma didn't trust Mama with her cash and jewellery.

Ma perhaps, had the wrong impression that Mama might not return her gold ornaments and money, that she had gathered over a period of time and had deposited with Babu's wife. Ma still continued depositing all our agricultural income with Babu. Mama tried several times to make her understand the realities but she didn't believe her. Babu and his wife had poisoned Ma very deeply against mother. Ma had grown older, and as her memory weakened, she couldn't keep the account of the money that she had deposited with them. Babu and his wife took advantage of Ma's age and considered Mama as a potential threat to their recurring income. Ma being alone, had even deposited all her ornaments with them due to fear of theft. Now it was difficult for her to withdraw her ornaments, as that would have strained her relations with them. She had a couple of gold coins with an inscription of Viceroy's parliament that was given to my Mama by my granny. That too was kept with them. Mama was more worried for those pure gold coins bought during the British rule by my granny. Mama was really concerned and worried for the few gold coins given to her by her parents.

I had seen her on a couple of occasions wearing those necklaces with *asarfees* woven in red thread. She wore it last when she had gone for 'Butsavitri Puja'. That day, all the Hindu ladies worshipped the Banyan tree, for the long life of their husbands. Her great grandmother gave those coins to my granny and it was passed down to my mother. My mother had brought many things in the dowry besides the *asarfees*. She had also got five cows, two buffaloes and lots of big brass and bronze pots and plates. One of them was a brass pot commonly known as *Kalas*. It was an antique piece and mother had a lot of attachment to it, as that was passed in dowry from generation to generation. Her mother had given it to my granny. It also had their names inscribed on it. Mama was in tears when she discovered that Ma had presented that *kalas* to Babu's daughter at her wedding. The *kalas* had a long neck with flowers designed and inscribed on it. Mama had requested many times not to hand over the *kalas* to Babu's family but Ma was adamant. These were the reasons Babu and his family members didn't like the presence of mother at the village. They were apprehensive that if mother would come to know the modus operandi, it would expose their motive and Ma would be forced not only to break the relationship but also demand the deposits lying with them.

As long as father stayed at home, my puppy and I had a tough time. It missed the beam and I missed it every night. It had to remain hungry and missed its meal many times as long as father stayed at home. I was not allowed to move out of the house until and unless asked by Ma or mother. I was not allowed to go out and play with other children. I had kept my puppy inside the house made of bricks. As and when I got a chance to come out of the house, I had a look at it and also fed it sugar and rice. I couldn't have taken a chance to go for milk, as that would have exposed the motive. I quietly used to put rice in my tiny pocket and add sugar to feed it. Once father left, I could offer food and meet it freely but I was not allowed to bring it anywhere near the house. It was gradually getting used to the place outside the house.

On one of the afternoons, while I relaxed with Mama, she asked me whether I had really touched some dirty clothes kept in a hole at the school wall near Matra's house. I couldn't understand what Mama was referring to. Once again she clarified and said, 'Did you touch a cloth kept by the wife of Matra, the milker, in a hole of the school wall?'

I remembered and confessed the truth to Mama and said, 'Yes, I did!'

She lost her temper and slapped me on my left cheek. I cried and told her the whole story.

It was the day when Matra didn't turn up for milking the cow. Mama remembered, as she only had sent me to look for Matra.

I narrated to her, 'When I reached his house she, the wife of Matra was hiding something in the wall of the school building, which was the inner wall of her court yard. I could see blood clots on the floor of the courtyard as well. I thought something had gone wrong and as soon as she moved out to call Matra, I took the clothes out from the hole with a stick lying on the floor. As soon as I took out the cloth, I was horrified to see the blood on to it. It was almost soaked in the fresh blood with bloodclots over it. I got scared and ran back to return home. I was so petrified that I couldn't put the cloth back and ran leaving the cloth on the ground itself before she returned.'

That cloth soaked in blood remained in my mind for a long time. I couldn't speak as my voice got choked with the mere memory of the cloth. Mama cried for a while after hearing my story, as she could read the innocent look and feeling in my eyes. She embraced me on her lap; both of us cried for a while, she wiped my tears with the corner of her sari as well as hers. She also whispered, 'Son, you are too small to understand what it was. Never ever touch any such dirty clothes with bloodstains else you might get infected with some disease.'

She opened her steel trunk and handed me a candy. I didn't enjoy the candy. Once again, I was reminded of the cloth with bloodstains. The cloth with bloodstains was one of the reasons for the punishment awarded to Mama and me by father. The mystery of the cloth with bloodstains remained in my mind until I grew young and learned things about girls or ladies in my own way. It was the first time I had seen so much of blood on one single cloth and was really dumbfounded.

I hadn't forgotten how Ma had punished me that fateful day of this incident. No sooner did I return home after leaving the cloth with bloodstains on the floor, Matra and his wife had followed me. They complained to Ma about my taking out the clothes from the hole. His wife spoke something to Ma that I couldn't understand. Ma caned me badly at the back followed by a bath. I had not been able to understand what had gone wrong. After seeing the bloodclot on the floor I wanted to know who was hurt so that I could be of some help to Matra's wife. That was my intention. I was utterly confused to see Ma's behaviour. What wrong had I done? Why did Ma beat me black and blue with a cane? What had Matra's wife told Ma? Would someone explain to me the reasons of my punishment? I had cried for a long time sitting on a wall at the rear of the house. The stains of tears remained on my face for a long time till Mama wiped it in the evening with the corner of her sari.

I was not able to understand the reason why Mama had once again asked me about that cloth with bloodstains. I had a great fear in my mind and was sure that whatever I had done was something drastically wrong, otherwise Mama wouldn't have asked me once again. I went back to Mama and caught both my ears and promised not to repeat it ever in my life. One thing was very clear in my mind that I had done something that was wrong and uncalled for, but what was it? I also promised Mama that I wouldn't do anything that might create problems for her. I cried for a long time. She could make out that I was deeply hurt. She hugged me and took me out to show me the baby lamb at the neighbour's house to divert my attention. I kept sulking and cried.

She once again changed the topic and wished to see my puppy and its house that I had made behind the wall. I was thrilled, for the very first time one of the family members had shown a desire to look at my puppy. She asked, 'Where is it, and from where have you brought it?'

I told her, 'It was lying in a ditch.'

She asked me to collect food for it. I was very happy. I hugged Mama and kissed her on her cheek. I took a bowl of milk and rice and walked ahead of Mama holding her hand, to the house of the puppy to feed it. She also asked me to collect food for the puppy everyday when Ma left for her bath. That gave me immense pleasure. Thereafter, I didn't have to steal the rice and milk anymore. As soon as I put the food before it, it devoured it all within no time. Its tummy bulged out on either side and it looked very bulky. We came back and slept on the cot, Mama made a pillow of my body and slept on me. I laughed with the ticklish feeling her long hair on my tummy. I hugged her, played with her and climbed on her. I made a pony of her and caught all her hair in my little hands. She had very thick hair coming down to her waist.

One day, once again I took Mama to show my puppy. She had grown big and, of course, sideways. She informed me it was a girl. By now the puppy had grown big and could even recognise my mother. Now, she used to go out of the premises and return by herself. I had become a little carefree about her, as at least now, no one would steal her. Earlier, I always worried that someone might take away my puppy. She could scurry much faster than before. She could climb on to the veranda in one go and jump off it as well. I was very thrilled to see her playing and jumping around. She could put both her front legs onto my shirt and soil it with mud. As and when Ma left the house, she used to climb onto the veranda and reach the beam and tried to enter beneath the beam. Mama scared her at times and she ran away jumping over the four steps directly from the veranda. It was great to see her jumping and running so fast as she had become much agile and faster than Ma was. It was not possible for Ma to catch her or cane her anymore. She looked very healthy, her coat shone and looked very attractive with brown and white patches all over her body.

Chapter II

BABU

The day we arrived at our village from the town, we had seen Babu, a tall middle-aged, well-built, scruffy-looking human with an extra lump of flesh at the bottom of the left ear. I first saw him, on our way to the village. We were dropped off with all our luggage, miles away from our village by a truck. Our village was not motorable and after a point everyone had to depend upon the bullock cart. We had also hired a couple of them to reach the village with all our luggage including the furniture. I loved to travel on the bullock cart as it moved without any tension. The bullocks raised dust with their feet. It could navigate the track and negotiate the turns in the night, without any light and could cross the canal waterways without any problems. The commands given to the bullocks by their master was full of grace as it encouraged them to climb on to the heights without hitting. We had arrived very early in the morning near the village. I found father touching the feet of a person holding a *lota* – a pot made of mixed metal meant for carrying water. Perhaps he was out for his morning rituals. Mama pulled her sari down and covered her face completely and greeted him, touching his feet thrice with the corner of the sari. This was the system that prevailed in the village, to greet elders. He was the younger brother of my grandfather. He had many children, therefore, his liability was much more than my father. My father was the only son of his father and inherited all the property without sharing with anyone.

Babu asked him about the goats tied at the rear of one of the carts. He informed, 'Doctor has advised to feed goat's milk to him,' pointing towards me. Since then the mother goat and its baby were a part of our family. We also narrated to him the story that took place on the way. Both these goats were put on the roof of the truck and tied properly right over the driver's seat. While on the move, the goats had urinated and it had leaked on to the driver's head. The driver was upset and wished to know what was leaking. Before Mama could have said anything, father informed him that they had some bottle of medicines and the holy water of the Ganges that had perhaps broken on the way had leaked on to his head. The driver replied, 'But it is stinking.' Father said, 'It would, as the water of the Ganges must have got mixed with the medicine, hence the smell.' The driver was fully convinced and satisfied with the answer.

We reached our home, which was under construction. Ma bought *jalebees* for me from the *Bania*. She also proudly introduced me to all the elders of the village. I was smarter than any other child of the village. At least I had seen motor vehicles, steam engines and trains.

For a few months, we enjoyed our life in the village, as we had plenty of nice fruits and vegetables, curd and milk to eat. Subsequently, things started deteriorating. For everything that we wished to do, we had to ask Babu's family. Mama didn't like to go for everything to them and her behaviour was not appreciated. Things gradually became from bad to worse, as Babu hadn't been able to make a house of concrete of his own. Father, being a next generation, could afford to construct a house, a fact that Babu was not able to digest. He was also envious, as father had a government job whereas all his children survived on the income that came out of agriculture. It was not sufficient for the entire joint family. He had gradually started poisoning Ma against my mother so that he could manipulate the agricultural income in his own way. Babu dominated not only the Brahmin lot but also had very high influence on the lower castes. Most of the Brahmins feared him because his family was the custodian of the *Kuldevta* the family God. In each of the festivals, the rituals started from his house. He personally carried the boxes of the God studded in gold to all the houses and brought them back to his house. Many people made donations of gold, silver and cash to God and that automatically became the earnings of his family. We also had a system of sacrificing goats in a couple of festivals, wherein he himself carried the divine sword with him to sacrifice the dumb animals in all the houses of the village. Everyone sent some part of the sacrificed goat to his house as *Prasada*. Every Brahmin had non-vegetarian food. Babu never allowed anyone to touch the divine sword of the God used for slaughtering the dumb animals, to ensure that the booty of sacrificed animal were sent to his house by everyone without fail.

No one could raise their voice against him, as his words were almost the words from the custodian of the God's family. Most of the family disputes, viz., marriage, death and birth including the estates and properties used to be presided over by him and settled.

It was the time of winter. Many people had gathered near the outhouse, commonly known as *Dwar* in the local lingo where Babu relaxed in the afternoons and nights. He was sitting on a *charpoy,* whereas many male members of the village stood all around to see the fun. Even many ladies and the children gathered all around. Every lady had covered her face with her sari and was watching the fun, and at times they passed their opinion to others on the incident. No one was allowed to talk. Two men cowered writhing around on the ground, with both their hands tied at the rear of their body, their faces abraded and swollen. The sticks had left welts on their body, as they were being caned on them. They didn't speak at all and were totally at the mercy of Babu and a couple of other Brahmin elders of the village.

It was a first time that Mama and I had seen something. Like this. She was very scared to even allow me to go near the front and was holding me tight with both her hands. I wasn't allowed to go on to the crowd. Everyone was quiet other than Babu. He kept talking impassively about the incident and the probable action that was to be taken against them. I couldn't understand the reason for such silence. In the meantime, the entire crowd turned towards the cries that were coming from outside the circle of the crowd. One of the men was almost being dragged towards the crowd while three or four children and a couple of ladies followed them wailing. It was pathetic to see the children, wife and other ladies related to them, putting their head down on the feet of the upper caste elders sitting on the sagging *charpoy* and imploring them. They pleaded, bowing obsequiously, to spare their father and husband, but no one had any mercy for them. He was thrashed in front of his wife and children. Babu himself got off from his seat and caned him impassively till he got tired. The fellow at the receiving end kept pleading and finally collapsed on the ground. The other two fellows whimpered continually. Mama felt very bad about treating a human worse than an animal. None of the lower caste gathered, had the spunk to even raise a word against the diktat of Babu.

What was the reason for all this drama? Why were three humans being tortured worse than animals? What crime had they committed? It was a bit too much for the petty thefts that take place in the village, for which every time these people were harassed and tortured. All three of them were suspected of stealing and selling a cow along with its calf to a Muslim, in the neighbouring village. They were just suspects of the crime. Their ordeal continued for three days but nothing came of it. Finally, they were set free but the scar and the hatred for the Brahmins remained in their heart for life. Respect for them was on the ebb. Their wounds were healed but the wounds that were generated in their heart didn't go. As I being a small child, remember the torture they had gone through, I am sure their small children, then watching the ordeal of their father and the memory of themselves pleading and imploring, by putting their head on the feet of elders of upper caste, wouldn't have been able to eradicate and eliminate the discontent from their heart. The seed of hatred was sowed by the upper caste elders on the heart of the elders and the children of the lower castes in the village.

After a few weeks of this incident, the cow and its calf were found in one of the village markets about to be sold by one of the Muslims. They had stolen it. It was not the lower caste of the village as speculated by the upper castes. But the damage was done; no one amongst them even felt a need to call these three fellows and plead forgiveness from them for their irascible behaviour.

On another occasion, a couple of the lower caste were found guilty of catching fish in the pond. The pond was meant for the animals to have water and also for the purpose of irrigation. It was located on government land and none of the people or community members had any exclusive rights over it. But by default, it had become the exclusive property of the upper caste. Whenever they decided to go fishing, they could easily do so for their entertainment or otherwise, but none of the lower caste were allowed to go to the pond for fishing or other reasons. Mostly the buffaloes had a good time in the summer, and in the rainy seasons it was flooded with rainwater gushing in and the fish came out of the pond that climbed against the rain water falling on to the pond. Many of the upper caste people openly went fishing. At times, even the lower caste youth ventured out to the pond, but only at night, although it was not so easy to fish in a pond full of hyacinth and many snakes.

Two of the lower caste boys were reported to have gone fishing in the pond at night. No one was aware how many fish had really been taken out in the night, neither had anyone actually seen them doing so. It was mainly on hearsay.

Both these lower caste boys were quite enterprising, and dexterously made terracotta toys and sold them in the village fair every year, and earned decent money out of it. Their families also had a little better living standard than other lower castes and even some of the upper castes. That was perhaps the reason the upper caste couldn't digest the information and wished to fix them. The upper caste never allowed or wanted the lower caste to grow, as that would reduce their dominance and they would also become a potential risk to their agricultural income. Most of the agricultural work was done by these lower caste in the fields of the upper castes. They wanted the lower caste to be servile to them. Both these boys were brought before Babu for justice. In any case, any lower caste brought before Babu used to be badly beaten by the youths, before they were brought for justice. That used to be an official excuse to punish them. Both of them were once again thrashed by Babu and his associate elders and warned of dire consequences. All the family members of the boys kept pleading before them but it was no good. They remained bedridden for weeks together, and every wound that was made on their body created exponential increase in the hatred for the upper caste amongst the lower caste. The upper castes were oblivious of these facts and had taken things for granted. The lower caste, being so many in number, never ever did anything against the upper caste and took their verdict as gospel truth. No one ever questioned

Babu's decisions. But gradually, things went a bit too far and it was the upper caste who forced them to revolt or look for an option.

Many of the upper caste boys had sex with the girls of the lower caste, working in their fields. It was their right. Even the elders, including Babu at times, boasted of having fathered many children in his lifetime from the women of the lower castes. Many of them were brought before the Babu for justice but were let off just with a warning. Many ladies never complained of the relation that they had with their masters, as they wished to improve the complexion of their offspring like the ones that the Brahmin ladies bore. Many of them had sex with the upper caste of their own wish, either due to fear or for some favours. Many cases of fornication were reported, resulting in the birth of children in the village, every year, from the girls of the lower castes. Many of these girls were either killed or married. That gave birth to the early marriage system in the village, as it would hide the cases of fornication and also eliminate the fear of such incidents being public. Due to the excesses meted out to the lower caste, the control and respect for the upper castes was waning.

One summer afternoon, Mama asked me to call for Ma, as she had to take some decision on sowing of crops as the monsoon was approaching. One of our raiyats, person permitted to cultivate on our fields had come to meet Ma. I left to call for Ma. She was busy talking to Babu's wife in one of the small dark rooms of the huge house made of mud walls. After informing Ma about the arrival of Yusuf, the *raiyat*, I ran behind a cat and was busy playing. The cat went on to the upper floor of the mud house constructed on wooden logs. I quietly sneaked into the dark, thatched room of the upper floor. I found Babu playing *Ghoda-Ghoda* with one of our widowed aunts. He was busy playing *Ghoda-Ghoda*. Children were shit scared of Babu as the elders respected him helluva lot. I ran down and came straight home. Ma hadn't reached till then. Mama asked me, whether I had informed Ma or not. I was very nervous and scared. She could make out there was something wrong. She took me to the room and asked, 'What happened, why are you so scared?'

I confessed and said, 'I climbed on to the first floor room of Babu's house behind a cat, where I found Babu and Madhu auntie playing *Ghoda-Ghoda*.'

She was shocked. I could see the colour of her face changing to red. She half-heartedly asked me to explain who had become a horse. I said, 'the aunt'. She once again took me to the room and asked me not to say anything to Ma or anyone else. I was utterly baffled about this game. Every elder played this game of *Ghoda-Ghoda* but why in isolation? Why not in open, as I played with other children? I even played with Mama, then why the hell people ask me not to speak to anyone about such a lovely game that everyone loves to play? Kusmi and Azim had asked me not to speak to anyone about the game that they played, now even Mama advised me not to open my mouth about the game that Babu and Madhu auntie played. I could make out there was something fishy in this game of *Ghoda-Ghoda*.

Yusuf had come with his small daughter Ajra. She was a very fair and good-looking lassie. Mama asked me to give her the local sweets made by our village sweetshop. I offered her a little bit of it, she enjoyed it sitting on her father's lap. I caught her hands and took her to show my puppy that had grown big. On seeing me, the puppy came running to me, shaking her tail. Ajra was frightened and ran back to her father howling with fear. I once again brought some sweets and gave it to her. She took it from my hands and stopped crying. In the meantime, my puppy arrived. She walked over to the veranda and jumped down. Ma arrived and on seeing my puppy on to the veranda, she pointed her stick, that she mostly carried with her towards it. It ran to save her life on seeing Ma, before Ma could have caned her. Ma had also seen me holding Ajra's hands and offering her sweets and eating with the same hands.

Ma had a detailed discussion with Yusuf. For everything she quoted as the order of the Babu, as if none of the orders or decisions were valid without his stamp on it. For each and every deal of the house his interference was there. Mama didn't like it and said insinuatingly not to unnecessarily mix our things with Babu's affairs. The land cultivated by Yusuf had nothing to do with the Babu or his heir. Ma enunciated very angrily, 'Bahuria,' as she referred Mama, 'Will you keep shut? For god's sake don't butt in my affairs else you will have a tough time ahead. I am still alive.' Mama perhaps thought it was the end of it and hereafter Ma wouldn't raise this topic. Ma finished her talk with Yusuf. No sooner had Yusuf left she took me for a bath to the well. She also sprinkled holy water of the Ganges that was procured from the temple of Babu's house, all over my body, for touching the Muslim child and eating with the same hands.

Next evening, Babu arrived at our house, I was very scared and didn't come out of the house. I thought that perhaps he had come to complain to Ma, as I had seen him playing *Ghoda-Ghoda*. I ran inside and informed Mama about the arrival of Babu. Even she was nervous, the colour of her face changed as she could apprehend the problems and took me along with her to Ma. He gave a malevolent look at Mama and a dirty smile at me. Babu was offered a wooden, high back chair that was used by my grandfather. He sat and started shouting at mother. He ordered me, 'You go and play outside the house.' Mama caught me and asked me to wait. Ma was very pleased and repeated the incident that took place before Yusuf, the previous day. Mama was admonished for her words and was asked not to create rift in a family of high traditions like ours. Mama didn't open her mouth at all and was a patient listener. Once Babu finished his talk, Ma ordered her to get a cup of tea for Babu. I came inside the house with Mama. She cried due to the humiliation suffered in the hands of Ma and Babu. I requested her to be calm and quiet and not to worry. She carried the cup of tea and handed it over to Ma and Babu. She had covered her face with her sari. She was once again warned not to forget and reminded of the things that had happened few months back and said, 'If you repeat this, we would be forced once again to discuss the matter with Chotababu,' as father was referred by them. Mama came inside with me and sat on the ground in the kitchen and cried. Her eyes were in any case full of water, as she had just prepared the tea on the fire made of the cowdung. The smoke raised due to burning of cowdung cakes, used for cooking, goes into the eyes, resulting in watering.

Babu left and Ma walked with him to see him off and returned soon. I didn't talk to her. She was extremely delighted at her victory. Either way it was her loss that she was unable to judge. She made me sit in her lap and fondled my hair with love. I was utterly confused with her show of artificial love. She offered me five paise and said, 'You are a nice boy, go and get the *chiki* made of jaggery from *Bania* and enjoy.' I could make out the purpose of sending me away from the house, as she could admonish and fight with mother once again. I didn't go for the jaggery and was lurking near the rear door of the house to hear the talk that Ma was having with mother. Ma was too rude to Mama. She, in fact, once even threatened to thrash her with a stick if she didn't listen to her. I cried on hearing and seeing Ma's behaviour with Mama. I moved out of the house and sat on the fence wall dangling my feet. It was at the rear of the house and it was my favourite place. Whenever I was hurt I sat there and cried for a long time. I didn't feel like coming inside the house where people had no respect for Mama.

I complained and bleated about the dastardly act of Ma and Babu to all the trees and plants and everyone present out there. I told the clouds, the tiny stars that were about to shine clearly and brightly. I spoke to the birds, retreating to their nests after a whole day's tedious search for food. I also informed the imaginary pictures and the designs on the fence wall, that at times gave the look of different pictures over it, about Ma's behaviour and cried. I was desperate to complain to any person who could help or salvage both of us out of this mess. I prayed and asked for help from the clouds, the Sun and all the supernatural powers to do some magic and edify Ma's mind.

I had that money with me, given by Ma, in my pocket I felt like throwing it in the pond where I was thrown once. I didn't go home and kept sitting at the rear of the house on the half-constructed wall and watched the chameleon feeding on the black ant. Many butterflies flew near the wild flowers without any restriction. It was in the group that probably had its mother, father, and grandparents, as well, together. I wasn't destined to such luck. Mama was humiliated. She didn't utter anything at all either to Babu or to Ma. I was pensive and forgot the place I was sitting and went into a different world of daydreaming.

Mama was a decent, diligent and prudent lady. She loved father, Ma and me. She cared for all, then why was Ma always after her to lay her down? I could hear Mama yelling for me. It was about to be dark. It was time for my dinner. She was used to that and came looking for me. I didn't speak at all. After a long search she located me. As soon as she started moving towards me I put my head down and started crying. She could see the expression on my face and asked, 'What happened?' I didn't speak anything and said everything with my tears. I burst into tears and wailed loudly. She asked me the reason once again, thinking that I didn't know what had happened. I cried disconsolately and said, 'Ma'. She understood what I wished to convey. She embraced me in her arms and took me in her lap. She brought me in and gave me something to eat. I didn't feel like eating. She was such a decent mother and a human being. How could someone hate her? I handed her over the coin of five paise given to me by Ma. She asked me, 'Who gave you this coin?' I told her everything. She once again hugged me and asked me to keep the money with me. I replaced it in the top pocket of my T-shirt.

Ma was not at home. There was no restriction from Mama to give food to my puppy. I rushed out. Mama gave lots of milk and *roti* for my puppy. While I was feeding my puppy, Ma arrived. She asked me to come to her. I rushed inside and hid in the darkest room behind the door. She yelled for Mama and said, 'You make him understand for the last time, that either the *kutia* will be here or me.'

I got scared and came out and pleaded before Ma, 'Please don't leave us and go. Please spare my puppy this time. I wouldn't touch it ever.'

I once again promised her not to touch the puppy. Catching my ears, she took me to the well for washing my hands and feet. While doing so, the coin given by her dropped on the ground. I showed her the coin. I returned it to her. She was shocked and cursed Mama for poisoning the child's mind. I cried, and informed Ma, 'I couldn't go to the *Bania's* shop.' She didn't believe me and took the coin from my hands. I went to bed. I couldn't sleep for a long time. Mama came to the bed and fondled my hair, face and covered me properly. She didn't know that I was awake. Ma requested her to put me on her bed. I became upset and cried. I didn't want to sleep with Ma. Mama was surprised to see me awake. She informed Ma that I was awake and didn't want to go to her bed. She cursed us both and went to her room.

It was summer, the right time for the mangoes to ripen. We had an orchard totally under the control of Babu. It was a joint property, looked after directly by Babu and his children. It was like a festival in the village the day the mangoes were plucked by the owners and handed over to the Muslim brokers. They, in turn, sold it in the town or cities at higher prices. Everyone having mango trees, reached the respective mango groves with food carried in aluminium pots. There was no system of carrying water, as the river was quite close to the grove, and people could go to the river make a small ditch in the river sand and have fresh water to drink. I was very excited. I too wished to accompany her to see the mangoes plucked. Every child had the duty to collect the mangoes that drifted in different direction after falling from the trees. A cot used to be carried for Babu. He sat on it and supervised the operation.

Our share was much larger than Babu's as my father was the only son of his father. Moreover, till now there were none to challenge his authority and ask for the share. It was for the first time that we had arrived and probably Ma might supervise and inform mother about the money that was procured after the sale of mangoes. Ma went and sat with Babu on the cot. The plucking had started right in the morning itself. I could see the heaps of mangoes, under many of the trees, being packed and filled in the sacks by the Muslim brokers. I enjoyed eating and collecting the mellowed ones with other children. In fact, I had carried a small cloth sack to collect the mangoes of my choice and get it home. This continued for a few days before it came to an end. Now it was time for Ma to get the money of our share. She was given very little money in comparison to the mangoes sold on the pretext that some payment was still due from the Muslim brokers. Ma believed him and came back. For the very first time I could see Ma a little worried and concerned about the family and Mama. She went virtually everyday to find out whether the broker made the payment or not. Babu was in the habit of welshing on his promise; he denied it every time. Ma handed over the very little money to Mama, that was given by Babu to her, and became suspicious of their behaviour. Ma gradually started getting her gold ornaments and *asarfees* from Babu's house and gave a few of them to mother and requested her to keep them safely. I saw Mama hiding these *asarfees* in a terracotta pot containing *til* hide it in the place meant for storing the grains. People at the villages were shit scared of the thieves, more so when they had no male members in the family. I was the only male member present with Ma and mother, but was of no good to them.

Ma's relation with Babu and his wife had deteriorated. She missed many afternoon sessions and spent time with us or spent her time weaving the Gandhi Charkha. I enjoyed seeing Ma weaving the charkha while I played the gramophone of HMV, with the spring action. It was told that father had bought it in early fifties when he had got a Government job and drew his first salary. Since then it was a part of our house. I remember, Ma telling us the story of how it was brought to the house by Parmeshra on a bamboo – balanced set used for carrying load, hung from either side of the shoulders with the body as the fulcrum. The whole village had gathered to see the demonstration of the gramophone. My father was the proud owner of the set. He gave the demonstration to all. This message had spread to many of the nearby villages and as and when it was played, many people from other villages too came to see the set. Ma was known in many of the other villages as *Gramophone* Ma. It was no more an item of attraction or exclusive use. Ma never stopped me from playing the gramophone as and when I wished. I had not been able to forget the song that

Mama sang and we had most of the records of the songs of mother's choice. Mama always sang the songs while sweeping the courtyard or the house. One of the famous songs that mother liked the most was *Gam Diye Mustakil Kitna Nazuk Hai Dil Ye Nah Jana, Hye-hye ye zalim zamana and Jab Dil hi Tut gaya.* She also at times sang the song *Samdhan teri Ghodi Chane ke Khet Main... or Chup-Chup Khadi Ho Jarur Koi Baat Hai...*

Our relation with Ma was improving and after a long time we spent many happy afternoons together listening to the stories of the marriage of my mother and even Ma. The story's of Mama's marriage was quite interesting. My father, then a young lad, along with other villagers had gone to attend a wedding of one of his colleagues to a nearby village. In the village, the system of wedding was very different from the ones in urban society. Even now, the *Barat* – relatives and friends that accompany the bridegroom to the bride's house stay for three days and enjoy the hospitality of the bride's family. Those are the only time when villagers get a change to enjoy a VIP status, and don't leave any stone unturned to exploit the opportunity. They demand the best of food to eat and soap to bathe and wash their clothes. Some of them perhaps await for such an opportunity to have a bath with a good soap and even wash their clothes with good washing cake, which is otherwise washed in caustic soda powder.

Father, being the only male child of his parents, was one of the most sought after and eligible lads in the village for marriage. Many parents dreamt of having a bridegroom of his stature. More so, because those days my grandfather was the sole literate individual who worked as a teacher and had a little extra income other then agriculture before he died. Many of his contemporaries were jealous of our family's respect in the society and the dowry that Ma would have got in her son's wedding. Therefore, they wished to deprive her of that pleasure that she would have enjoyed on account of the dowry of her son.

Some of the elders planned to get my father married while he was attending the wedding of his colleagues. Mama's father himself was a teacher and was an infallible and respectable person. He was approached to get his daughter married to the most sought after boy. Mama was then in fifth standard. Though her father initially refused, after a long mulling he agreed to offer his daughter in marriage to my father, quietly. Father was in class tenth and after the wedding, he ran away to one of the relative's house, and didn't reach home, due to the fear of my grandmother. He was not traceable for weeks together. Finally, he was traced and brought home by Ma and Parmeshra.

Mama later joined a primary teacher's training school and became a teacher at a very tender age. Ma initially had accepted and welcomed her even though she was deprived of the radio set and cycle. But my granny did present a Swiss make Westend Watch Company's wristwatch to my father and number of cows, oxen and buffaloes in dowry. But perhaps Ma couldn't reconcile with the fact of being deprived of the radio and cycle and always taunted Mama for this and cribbed.

Ma's story was more ineffable than Mama's was. She was married at the age of five and didn't remember anything of her marriage other than what her parents had told her.

Ma also told me stories of how my father was scared of darkness and could never sleep alone. He was good in football and had played for his district and even the state.

Ma, time and again, followed up for the money that was due from the sale of the mangoes, but Babu ignored her and even at times, spoke very rudely. Ma could make out the intentions of Babu and at times repented for her scurrilous acts with mother. She now wished to at least collect the money that she had deposited with them, over a period of time from the sale of grains and other agricultural products like potatoes and other things. Even that was denied on the pretext that it would be returned at the appropriate time. At times, they returned very petty amounts to her, that piqued and depressed Ma but she had no choice other than brooding for hours.

During that time, the wife of Jawahar the younger son of Babu was pregnant and was shortly due for delivery. It was her first child. In the night, we heard a knock at the door of our house for Ma. Ma opened the door. She was informed that the wife of Jawahar was in terrible pain and child was stuck in the womb. Ma offered her services immediately. Ma tried her best to take out the child but didn't succeed. Finally, in the night itself two of the bullock-carts were placed in the service to shift her to the block hospital, eight miles away from our village. Ma also ordered Mama to pack up a couple of old saris, old clothes and get ready. Our house was located on the outskirts of the village. I declined to stay alone at home without mother. I was also allowed to accompany them and board the bullock-cart. I don't remember the time in the night we started, but we reached the hospital only early in the morning. On the way, I could hear the cry of the poor lady. I was not too sure what had really happened to her. I was utterly confused as a child. What kind of disease did she suffer from? Whole night we kept hearing Ma's voice consoling that lady to bear the pain, as we were about to reach the hospital. On arrival, I found that even my puppy had quietly followed us throughout the route and had reached the hospital. There was no one at the hospital other than a watchman. Ma requested him to call for the doctor immediately. After half an hour or so, an old nurse arrived and made her lie on a stretcher. She was in pain. The doctor arrived only when mother and Babu's wife reached the residence of the doctor to personally explain the trauma the lady was going through. Before the doctor arrived the child was born but was in a bad shape. He was unable to breathe properly. The doctor did something but the child succumbed to the pain after an hour or so.

It was a disturbing sight at the hospital. By that time many of the male members had arrived at the hospital including Babu. Babu lost his temper on all the ladies for killing the child, especially on Ma, being the most experienced lady. The doctor tried his best to convince him that the child was not getting oxygen properly and was stuck in the exit path. No one understood the case and blamed Ma for the whole episode. It was a terrible experience for mother and Ma. The whole night they had travelled with her and brought her to the hospital. Ma had been more worried than anybody else and fought with the nurse and the watchman to call the doctor. Being a lady, she had done the best that she could have done in that situation. The Doctor explained, 'It was too late for the child to survive, you all had taken much time in travelling by bullock-cart.' Perhaps it would have been better if the lady had been carried by the men on the improvised bamboo stretcher used for carrying patients. Ma had suggested it but Babu didn't agree as it was late in the night and they didn't want to take the risk due to irrigation canals and rivers. And so they had followed the longer route taken by the bullock-cart. This had also jolted the body of the pregnant woman, harming her and increasing the complications.

All of us came back to the village. Everyone had come to know about the incident that occurred at the hospital and the whole village blamed Ma for the death of the child. This was the right opportunity for Babu to get Ma into their clutches. Ma remained very upset over the whole episode. She justified her actions to many of the elders of the village but it was of no avail. In any case, relations between Ma and Babu's family had become strained and this episode escalated it further. She couldn't have imagined in her dreams that the family for whom she had sacrificed all her life would take out their grudge in this fashion. She was shocked at their behaviour and it made her blood curdle. All the respect that she had earned amongst the villagers, over a period of time, was diminished after this episode. Worst was still to come.

One fine morning, Ma was called by Babu to have a look at the cow that had stopped giving milk and didn't allow the milker to even touch her nipple. Ma took me along to feel little secure as insecurity haunted her after that episode. Babu waited there for her along with other elders of the village. As soon as she arrived Babu said, 'This cow is in trouble, kindly have a look and cure the cow immediately and spare her from your witchcraft.'

Ma was bemused and surprised and started abusing Babu.

'You hag, if you don't stop your sorcery, I know how to get rid of it.' he said in an intimidating voice.

One of them said, 'The only way to make a sorcerer forget her mantra and diminish her power is to make her eat the human refuse mixed with urine.'

Ma was shocked. She didn't know how to react. Earth moved beneath my feet as by staying in the village, I had become familiar to such talks and could precisely understand what were they talking. 'I won't forgive you for this and ensure that Chotababu takes you to task,' Ma threatened.

'Are, woo to monga hai, woo kya kar lega?' (He is a female, what will he fight with us.) He replied truculently.

Babu was very excited and openly blamed Ma and shouted loudly, 'You witch, we know you took a trial of your witchcraft after killing the child of Jawahar, and now you are taking a trial of your power on a dumb animal.' He added, 'If you don't withdraw your evil witchcraft power, we will take another course of action.'

Babu was utterly unscrupulous in his dealing with Ma. She cried profusely and left immediately. I cried more than she did. She picked me up in her lap, as my knickers were falling time and again, as I wiped my tears with both my hands. Most of the buttons of my knickers had come off and I had stuck it in the *kamar band,* a thread worn by all the Hindu children at the villages at their waist. I kept hitching it up time and again. Ma could she the bumps of my back and picked me up in her lap. Babu had stooped below his dignity, his age, and so also the other upper caste elders sitting out there. I didn't stop crying, as I was fully aware of the repercussions of branding a widow as a sorcerer.

Many people had gathered to watch the fun and none of them had the spunk to speak against Babu. My blood boiled as I understood the whole situation but couldn't help Ma. She returned home crying. 'Bahuria, Babu had the temerity to call me a witch.' she wailed. She was exasperated by his temerity of addressing her as a witch. She narrated the whole story to mother. Mama was shocked at Babu's behaviour and cursed them for inculpating and branding Ma as a witch.

This was the end of the relations that Ma had developed with Babu in the last fifty years. She had seen Babu as a child when she was married to his elder brother and came to the village. She had brought up Babu in her lap. If he could do that to Ma, there was nothing that he couldn't do to others. Mama knew Babu could stoop to any level for his own benefit, but father was not able to understand this simple fact. Right after he joined a job in the city, he hardly visited the village and had left everything on Ma. She, being a lady, had to totally depend on Babu as he helped her in agricultural activities. Moreover, he was the first blood relation of our family. She could never think of any foul play that Babu could commit. Since we stayed in the city, most of the cash crop or the fresh crop used to be used by Babu's family. Ma had never ever asked for the money that came out from the sale of mangoes or jackfruit. They had got used to all these and after we came to the village, obviously such liberty was lost, as Mama objected to all these. That was the reason why Mama was an eyesore for them and gradually even Ma became their target. Father could not understand Babu's deviousness and oppose his verdict as he had his own weaknesses and Babu took advantage of the situation. Moreover, his lackadaisical and ineptitude in handling the household affairs encouraged Babu to take control of all our land and agriculture related activities.

Chapter III

END OF MA'S LIFE

Ma was the kind of human being who had lived all her life independently and never accepted a dictate ever while leading a respectable life all through. She could never spend a few hours in her own house and always served the people of the village in a crisis or otherwise. She couldn't take the personal allegations made by Babu and his family and remained mostly confined at home. The news of her mastery in the art of sorcery, spread to all the neighbouring villages, and even to the villages, where we had our agricultural land and Ma went to supervise. It was too much for Ma. In any case, she was convinced that all her deposits that she had made in her lifetime were at stake. She had no hopes of getting them back. A couple of times, she had tried to recover them from Babu, but instead he had shown his teeth and she was humiliated and insulted publicly. 'We have exposed you as a sorcerer and done a favour to the whole village and now we will brand you as a mad woman as well,' they threatened. Ma was totally broken and frustrated. She felt like killing herself. It was perhaps the saddest day of her life.

One day, she cried hugging Mama for a long time, and informed her about the amount of money she had deposited with them and given as loan to some of the other families in the village. This continued for a few months. Father visited the village and went away but he didn't pay any heed to the shenanigans of Babu. Instead, he tried to pacify Ma to improve relations with Babu's family. Mama tried her best to convince him that Babu had done great injustice to Ma but father didn't want to listen to anything against him. Ma suffered from diabetes and these incidents broke her thoroughly. Though she looked quite healthy and walked straight, but she was dying from within due to the humiliation. She had very sharp features and was quite tall. She looked very pretty at that age and had a pleasing personality.

She restricted her movements and fell ill. She was not keeping well at all and was getting more infirm and emaciated with every passing day. Mama tried her best to look after her and always nursed her. She never allowed her to do any work. Ma was touched by her gestures but didn't want to make Mama feel small by opening her mouth and praising her. Her eyes spoke everything. Father was not really worried for the health of Ma and all he did for her, was to send some money at times to Mama to show her to a village doctor. There were no hospitals in the village and all we had was a Muslim quack. He was contacted and visited us regularly and gave some medicines to Ma. He visited our house on his horse. Ma's condition was deteriorating. She improved at times but didn't recover fully. She looked sickly and pale. The lustre of her skin and glow of her face decreased and was gone forever.

She was more worried about her money than anything else. Though Mama tried her best to convince her and said, 'You forget about the past and stop worrying for the money or ornaments, your son is still earning and would get the things once again.'

She was hurt, as she felt cheated and deceived. She couldn't reconcile with the fact that Babu and his wife could do that to her. She remained in trauma but felt demoralised to share her feelings with mother. Mama tried to find out and ascertain the quantum of money that she had handed over to them, but Ma was not able to give any details. Every time she deposited money with them Babu said, 'You do not have to bother for the accounts part of it, I will take care and ensure that every penny is counted in your account.' Times had changed but she hadn't been able to change with the time. She had blind faith on Babu and could never think that a person whom she had seen right from childhood could betray her. All these thoughts were killing her from within. Moreover, she took this as a personal defeat of her long experience of life. How could she go wrong in judging people? Her health deteriorated and affected her very badly. She, as it was a diabetic patient. She couldn't take it any more and was looking for a shoulder to cry. Mama hadn't changed her attitude towards Ma at all despite so much humiliation by her and that made her feel guiltier. Mama never tried to put across her point or justified who was wrong or right, as that would have stimulated the guilt feeling in Ma. Ma's mind was filled with remorse for having caused so much of social embarrassment to Mama.

I couldn't believe that she was feeling so helpless and meek. She had led all her life with dignity and never gave in to anything. She used to always help the lower caste whatever way she could. She was otherwise a 'terror' and no one could dare go against her wish. Even all the *raiyats* were shit scared of her.

I remembered the day when I had developed toothache and suffered severely. We had no doctors anywhere near the village besides the city, which was ten miles away from our village. Ma couldn't tolerate my pain and took me to a quack on the advice of Parmeshra. No sooner had Ma entered his house, he had greeted Ma and requested her to sit. Ma warned him beforehand and asked, 'Will you be able to do something or not, first, you explain it to me clearly.'

He had treatment for all diseases. The quack did some jugglery, put some herbs in mustard oil and after warming on the fire put a couple of drops into my ear. I screamed with pain. Ma couldn't take it. She warned him of dire consequences in case something went wrong with her grandchild.

The quack was nervous and couldn't satisfy Ma and said. 'He is scared, relax him in your lap for sometime till I prepare some other medicine for the night.'

He moved out, got a few, very small dead insects and mixed it in the oil prepared for the treatment. He very smartly tried to mix the oil with insects with my saliva by putting it into my mouth. While doing so, Ma caught him. He had cheated many of the villagers but couldn't get away from Ma's sharp eyes. I was in pain as he had put a lot of mustard oil into my ear for treating me for toothache. He tried to convince Ma that the insects in the teeth actually hide in the ear and the treatment for toothache had to be started from the ear. Ma was furious. She doubted him and asked Parmeshra to witness the whole treatment and to take him to task. Finally, he couldn't convince Ma. The quack, after mixing the insects in the saliva, tried to confuse Ma and said, 'Rest of the insects would take time to die and that would come out only in due course of time.' He handed over a bottle full of oil boiled with some herbs to be put into my ear at regular intervals. Ma kept watching and hearing his cock-and-bull story that was getting on her nerves. At last, she picked up a stick kept at his house-cum-clinic, and started thrashing him. The more I cried the more she caned him. Many villagers gathered near his house and everyone agreed that the insects lying on the banana leaves in my saliva were the normal insects available in the atmosphere. Everyone's eyes were opened by Ma. That quack had been taking the villagers for a ride for a long time. The lower caste had no education. I was perhaps the last patient he saw in his career of practicing medicine. Ma was a strong lady and never gave in during difficult situations.

After coming to the village, I had once requested Ma to get a small baby goat in the house as I used to play with the baby goats at Parmeshra's house. Ma had purchased a pregnant goat for me so that she delivered in the house and I could play with it. Ma loved us very much.

One afternoon, one of the babies of our goat was taken away by a jackal, as the mother goat had moved out of the premises with the babies for grazing. Ma had called the only tribal family of the village and had tried her best to rescue the baby goat from the jackal but unfortunately, the baby goat was carried on to the mounds by the jackal. She had even slapped Kusmi for not looking after the babies of the goat, as that was exclusively brought for me to play. She was furious and had promised to get me another baby goat once again. I cried for a long time as the baby goat was lifted right before my eyes. I yelled, '*Gidar, Gidar*...' as we referred to jackal in the local lingo, and ran towards Kusmi, but it was too late. I could see the jackal carrying my baby goat from its neck with the face of the baby goat in its mouth. Ma had informed Kusmi not to allow the mother goat to move out of the house until and unless the babies grew.

I always slept with her, and she ensured that I was not awakened as I used to get scared of the noise of the palm trees all around our house. Whenever Lucky, the watchman, arrived she offered him bidi and in lieu, Lucky updated her on the village politics. Our house was located on the outskirts of the village. Ma had ensured that Lucky came and had a round everyday. Ma never got scared and even didn't lock the door or windows of the house. One night, I heard the wail of an old lady and got up. Ma was fast asleep. I was very scared and couldn't sleep. I woke her up and said, 'Ma I do not want to sleep outside in the veranda and want to go inside to mama.' She asked for the reason. I informed her the reason but she didn't believe me and asked me to go back to sleep. She brought me closer to her tummy and covered with the bedsheet.

After sometime, once again the same cry could be heard. This time even Ma could hear it. She was worried for me and immediately called for Mama and put me inside the room on her bed. After I slept with Mama, she ventured out to look for the reason of that cry. Even Mama was scared of the wail of a woman at midnight. One could clearly see the cremation ground from our veranda on full moon nights. Mama used to be scared. After an hour or so, when Ma returned, she informed Mama not to make me sleep ever again in veranda. There was something that Ma didn't wish to share and make us scared. Since that day, even though I insisted to sleep outside with her in summer she didn't allow me. All her life she had slept alone and never got scared of anything.

During the Dushera festival, all the children along with their parents visited the nearby village, where a village fair would be organised every year. Mama, being a *Bahu* of the village was not permitted to visit the fair, but I insisted on visiting with other children. I was too small to be sent with someone else. Ma herself, had accompanied me to the fair and ensured that whatever I wished to have was given to me. I bought a whistle, a motor car, a king and queen and other toys that none of the village children could afford to buy. I could not walk the full route so and she carried me to the fair, and on our return journey she had asked Parmeshra to carry me back to the village, on his shoulders. I was also given different types of sweets that I wished to have as well as other eatables. I had bought a couple of things for Mama as well. Ma not only spent for me, she even spent for the other children, that of Kusmi and Parmeshra. She had also shown me the Bioscope - a kind of movie box that used to show the pictures of the seven wonders of the world, the actors and actresses. This was an expensive item and was not affordable by any children of our village. Even Kusmi requested Ma to allow her to see and Ma paid for the charges. It was great to visit the village fair with Ma. That was the first and last village fair that I could see as thereafter Ma had strained relations with Mama and the distance increased between us.

One afternoon, Mama could see a monitor lizard entering the house, and before she could close the door, it went inside the room where she and I slept. She was scared to even enter the room and requested Ma to call for Parmeshra to drive it out. It made a very scary hissing sound. Mama once again requested Ma to call for Parmeshra and not to enter the room. She didn't listen. She entered the room and dragged the creature out of the house. I jumped on the cot to see the king-size monitor lizard moving out slowly and twisting its tongue and neck all around. It was provoked and at times attacked Ma's stick whenever she pressed its tail gently. As far as Mama and me were concerned, she was our hero and saviour. We fully depended on her for everything. She was no less than a male elder member of our family; she could do everything for us that a male member could do for a family.

She had gone through the rarest hardships of life. Her husband, my grandfather had died at a very young age leaving two small babies - a son and a daughter, Nirupama, in her lap. She looked after all the property and ensured that the things took proper shape till her son had grown big enough to look after the property and help her out. She used to walk down many miles to our fields, to check and verify the crop in the fields. She ensured that all the harvesting took place on time and the money earned was kept for the education of her lone child. She had got him admitted to a school miles away from the village and walked to the school everyday with him. She waited till the school was over and returned with him. It was tough to get children educated in the village like ours, which had no school and no one was even bothered about education of their children. Since her husband, my grandfather himself was a teacher in the primary school where she took my father, she had the dream to make her child too, at least a schoolteacher. Everyone at the school supported her, as her husband had taught as a teacher at the same school before he died.

Her whole life, Ma spent alone and looked after two small babies. She used to tie father to her tummy with a *gamcha* before sleeping, as she was scared and apprehensive of her child's safety and his life. He was the lone heir to the whole property that her husband had left for them. She ensured that her child didn't have any problems and he got everything in that scenario.

She was known as an iron lady and always kept a stick on her bed in the night. Parmeshra was the most trusted lieutenant of Ma and whenever father was to move out of the village, she insisted on taking Parmeshra with him. Before Parmeshra was married to Kusmi and she was inducted to the house for work, Parmeshra's mother worked for Ma and Ma looked after her very well, as she too was a widow and had nothing to fall back upon. In fact, Parmeshra's mother had died in her room. She served Ma till the last day of her life. She ensured that they had no problems of food, clothing and shelter. No one else in the village dared talk to Parmeshra for any work. Not even the Brahmins could dare say anything to Parmeshra, as they knew that he was working for Ma. Ma had sponsored all the expenses of Parmeshra's house whether it was death, birth or marriage. She bore all the expenses for the marriage of his sister. Ma seemingly looked gruff but was very kind-hearted and looked after the poor people of the village, irrespective of their caste or creed. Unlike other upper caste families, our family was liked by the lower caste of the village, mainly because of Ma's concern for them. Moreover, my grandfather was the only person having a government job and earned a salary. Ma had a very comfortable life as long as he lived. They also had a salary besides agricultural income, with hardly any liability.

Once a snake in our field bit Parmeshra. He had gone to ensure the level of water flowing from the nearby canal to all our paddy fields. It was evening. He came running to Ma. It took him ten to fifteen minutes to reach home from the field as it was the rainy season. Kusmi was very worried and didn't know what to do. No one helped him other than Ma. Besides the first aid or the local medicine, herbs were given to him. He had to be taken to the hospital that was miles away. Ma agreed to provide him with assistance for hiring a tractor that was available a few miles from our village. He was taken to the hospital in the night itself. Had he gone on a bullock-cart, perhaps he would have lost his life. But Ma came forward to help him, financially, to hire a tractor that could take him faster than a bullock-cart. He could survive mainly because he could reach on time. He hadn't been able to forget the help Ma had done to him and his family members. There were many people in the village who lost their lives every year due to snakebite. But Ma had ensured that Parmeshra got medical assistance in time.

He was to stay in hospital for a week before he could return home. Ma had even gone to look him up in the hospital and ensure that his dues were cleared and all the medicine prescribed by the doctor was made available to him.

He was in tears on seeing Ma. He knew that it was a rebirth for him, and he had got his second life only because of Ma. He came back and shared all his experiences with the people of his clan and caste. Every Dusadh in the village loved Ma and us, mainly due to Ma's helping attitude towards them.

Like others, even Parmeshra was not unaware of Ma's plight. He openly discussed the matter with Ma and Mama to know the basic reason for her ordeal and the malicious intentions of Babu. Parmeshra's blood boiled and he assured Ma and Mama that he would take care of Babu. But Mama knew Babu's cunning ways very well. She advised Parmeshra to keep out of it. 'It will not be difficult for Babu to implicate and castigate you, or even brand you as a thief or a danger for the Brahmin population and punish you,' she warned. He could make out the truth in Mama's version but wasn't satisfied.

It was not only Ma who was branded as a witch by Babu. There were many other older women, mainly the widows who were branded as sorceress by Babu, just to settle his personal score with their families. No one could raise his voice against him, as he was too powerful for anyone to fight alone. The entire lower caste was against Babu and wished for his downfall, especially the younger generation. They waited for an opportunity to take revenge on Babu's family.

Ma was very worried about her reputation and didn't like to socialise in any of the village functions. She was one of the leading women of the village who donated generously for the Ramlila or *Nautanki* that took place during Dushera. She knew many of the women, branded as a witch, in the village had a tough time. They had to take many precautions to safeguard their own life from the villagers. They avoided talking to a child or loving them. As, if by chance that child fell sick, or something went wrong with him, the woman, branded as witch, loving her or him would have a tough time. She would be asked to cure the sickness by witchcraft. Ma didn't want to take any chance and never spoke to any child or pregnant woman.

Those days, due to the lack of medical care or want of facilities, many women lost their lives or their first child during delivery. In all the delivery deaths, the family of the deceased blamed one of the ladies branded as a sorceress. It was very difficult for the ladies to cope up with the situation once they were branded as a witch. Most of them were firstly a widow and secondly, old and aged. At that stage of their life they desired to have family support and respect from the villagers, rather than insult and personal injury. But even the family members of such ladies didn't show solidarity with such widows and blamed them for their plight. They were not only discarded by the society, but also discarded by their family members to get rid of a bad name to their family. It was pathetic to see their lives in the village. None of them could attend any village function and their food was brought to their respective homes and handed over to them to eat. No one understood their feelings. The villagers treated them worse than animals and their family members thought of them as a burden.

I was damn scared and worried for Ma, so also Mama. How would Ma lead her life? Would things ever be normal for her? Even I used to be called by the boys at school, the grandson of a witch. They teased and asked me to provide them with candy or sweets given to me by my grandmother through witchcraft. Many children pointed out at me and said, '*Ye Dain Ka Pota Hai.*' (He is the grandchild of the sorcerer.) I felt very bad and reacted very badly. Many a time, I complained to Mama but she ignored it. Many a time, I refused to go to the school as everyone called me '*Dain ka Pota*,' meaning, grandson of a witch. It had become a slang or sobriquet for them instead of my name. Even the pregnant and newly married ladies gave me a strange look and pointed, '*Ye ladke ki dadi Dain hai*,' 'The grandmother of this child is a witch,' they said. It used to be very demoralising and hurting for me. I too, started to avoid the group of children and the newly wedded or pregnant ladies. I too had become an untouchable for them.

Ma had become a dumb lady and she hardly spoke with us. She didn't know how to tackle the matter. Mama, many a time, explained to several people about Ma and how decent a lady she was. People heard her and made fun of her later on. '*Dain ne iske uppar bhi jado kar diya hai, jab wo maregi to isko sikha ke jayegi.*' (She had done magic on her as well and once she dies she would pass down her power of witchcraft to her.) All this had a detrimental affect on Ma's health and compounded her discomfiture.

One night, Parmeshra came to our house. It was raining and he was totally wet. He was in a great hurry. Mama opened the door and asked him to explain the problem. 'Kusmi has labour pain *Malkin*, please do something, else she won't survive.' Mama didn't know how to help her out. She was quite apprehensive. *If something went wrong, Ma would be a confirmed witch of the village. Moreover, people will take advantage of the situation and even the lower caste will lose faith in her*, she thought. She was in a dilemma. It was for the first time that someone had come to seek Ma's help after she was branded as a witch. Mama was veiy worried on this account and told Parmeshra to excuse Ma as that might further escalate the problems for her. Parmeshra was in tears. He cried and begged of Ma to help Kusmi out. He came down on his feet and touched Ma's feet. '*Malkin*, please help her, for God's sake, I know villagers are fools and bastards. You are not, and cannot be a witch. You have saved many lives. How can you take some one's life?' he begged. 'If you don't help, in any case my child and even Kusmi would die,' he added.

Ma immediately left with him to ensure the delivery. Earlier, it was a ritual for Ma. None of the women delivered until Ma arrived. At times, people brought the ladies to Ma for delivery to our house. She never touched any lower or upper caste woman delivering, she just directed their relatives to ensure the safe delivery. After ensuring the delivery, she never entered the house until she took a proper bath and sprinkled the holy water of the Ganges over her body. Mama was also worried and she too couldn't sleep. She was fidgeting on the bed, breaking or disturbing my sleep.

It was about to be first light, when Mama heard a knock at the main door. Parmeshra and Ma had come back with good news. Kusmi had delivered a son. It was great news for Ma, Mama and, of course, Parmeshra. They were elated and were gloating. Ma had tears in her eyes. She narrated the whole story to Mama. Kusmi was in deep trouble, and Ma herself was apprehensive about separating the child from her, but Ma's years of long experience came in handy. The outcome was a matter of concern for everyone. This message spread in the whole village, that Kusmi and her child survived mainly due to Ma's experience. In fact, Babu and his family didn't like the outcome of Ma's effort. They commented and remarked, 'People like her and her family had been encouraging the lower caste and due to this reasons the lower caste had been comparing themselves with Brahmin families.' Babu was shaken with this episode as his version of branding Ma as a witch was weakening.

Mama provided Kusmi with many old saris and clothes for the little one. Mama, along with Parmeshra, had decided to revive the lost dignity of Ma and ensure that a cunning and cynic like Babu didn't succeed in his motive. Ma's success gave her a lot of mental satisfaction and to some extent, she could overcome her mental anxiety. Many of the lower castes of the village, Dusadhs, Chamars and others were quite happy with Ma and decided to take her help in all their delivery matters. This incident certainly exonerated her partially from the blame for the death of Babu's grandson and alleviated her mental anxiety. On the one hand, she was totally boycotted by the Brahmins and other upper castes due to fear of Babu, whereas on the other, the lower castes of the villages continued taking advantage of Ma's expertise in delivery of pregnant women. Many of them even gifted us fruits and vegetables, though Ma didn't allow Mama to cook them until they were washed thoroughly.

Within three to four months, Ma had helped a couple of other lower caste women in their successful delivery, whereas one of the Brahmin ladies lost her child during delivery. This created a lot of ill-feeling amongst the Brahmin family and they started realising the value of Ma per se.

A couple of families of pregnant women, gradually started talking to Mama to persuade Ma to help them out during the delivery of their kin. 'She should help us out during delivery, we have nothing against her,' one of the ladies pleaded. It was quite comforting to Mama. She informed Ma that she was approached by a few women to help them out in a crisis. Ma flatly refused to oblige them with any such help as she didn't want to take any chances. 'In case something went wrong during the delivery, I will be blamed once again. They are not the type I should help, they don't deserve it,' she said. Mama nodded and agreed with her. 'It is not so easy to deprive any family of help in case they desired so.' Mama whispered. 'Moreover, in either case you would be blamed or defamed,' she added. 'In case something went wrong while you take them on, or if you don't go to help, once again you would be blamed for doing witchcraft and killing the child,' she continued. Ma agreed with Mama's reasonings and tried to avoid the forthcoming deliveries in the village.

Mama decided to send Ma to Deoghar, to her daughter's place for some time, till things became little normal in the village for her. Ma agreed to her proposal and decided to leave for Deoghar with Parmeshra. Ma couldn't walk to the bus-boarding point, as she had become quite weak and was very depressed. A bullock-cart was arranged to transport her to the bus stop. Parmeshra came back after dropping Ma at Deoghar. He informed Mama that she had fallen sick on the way and hadn't recovered when he returned. Mama remained upset for Ma. She wrote a letter to Nirupama to inform father in case Ma hadn't recovered fully. Ma's health was not improving and was deteriorating everyday. She was an extreme diabetic. That remained under control mainly because Mama used to be very strict with her and always stopped her from eating anything that would have harmed her. At Deoghar, no one really took care of Ma and she was allowed to eat anything she wished. Nirupama herself had three small children to be looked after. Moreover, she didn't want to keep Ma for a long time. Ma could realise that her own daughter was hinting at her to return to the village. She sent a message to Mama. Parmeshra was once again sent to bring her back to the village.

Father was not really worried for either Ma or us. He had got something very precious and important in his life. He stayed with a lady steno working in his office, who was much younger to him. She was an unmarried Bengali female and stayed in the same apartment where father had hired an accommodation. Their relationship had reached a level from where it wasn't possible to return back. They spent nights together. One of the clerks, working in the city where father worked, had informed Mama about the relationship that father had developed with that female, Paromita Bhattacharjee, hereinafter referred as Paromita. Everyone in the village knew Paromita's relationship with father.

Father was informed about Ma's condition. He once again sent some money to Mama, without realising that that money was of no use for Ma, as there were no hospitals or doctor available for consultation in the village. All we had was a quack, who was good for nothing and, in fact, hastened many people's death by prescribing wrong and expired medicines.

Father didn't want to leave his beloved Paromita and look after his mother. Ma returned to the village. She had become much weaker than before. She couldn't walk on her own anymore. Every morning, she used to be helped by Mama to get up and I accompanied her to the nearby fields for her morning ablutions. We had no toilets in the house and everyone at the village went to the riverside for their morning ablutions, including the ladies. Ma didn't like to ease herself in the nearby fields and insisted on going to the place on the bank of the river - she had used all her life. Mama acceded to her request but she could barely walk and subsequently stopped going herself.

It was my duty to take Ma to the riverside every morning and bring her back. She took a lot of time to ease herself. She suffered from constipation and sat for a much longer time than usual. Many a time, Mama had rushed to the place to find out the reasons for our delay as we took a lot of time to return. Mama spent most of her time nursing Ma. Kusmi too spent most of the time in the house nursing.

The doctor had advised giving only *roti* to Ma. Rice was totally prohibited. One day, Mama realised that there was no flour in the house. Parmeshra had gone to another village to inspect the ploughing of fields, related to the preparation of pre-monsoon. Mama had no choice other than sending her beloved child to a village, few miles away, for grinding the wheat. We had a Muslim-dominated village nearby that had a diesel version of a flourmill. I was just about seven. Mama handed me over few kilograms of wheat and asked me to go to the nearby village for grinding it. I left with the wheat. There was a long queue and I, being a small child having very little wheat with me, the owner of the flourmill didn't bother much about me. At last it was ground. I handed him over the money for the grinding work that Mama had given to me. I had the coins in my top pocket of the 'bush-shirt' that I was wearing. I was holding the pocket all along the route to ensure that I didn't lose the money. It was rather difficult to carry the wheat for a few miles – nearly five kilograms of wheat for a seven-year-old child!

When I started back, it was cloudy and about to rain. I rushed towards our village. I ran till my breath reached its peak and couldn't manage to run anymore. Time and again, I intermittently walked and ran to ensure that I reached home before it rained. A very strong wind started to blow. I panicked that the whole flour would get wet and my Ma wouldn't be able to eat *roti* in the night. Moreover, Mama would scold me for not taking proper care of the flour. I ran towards the hut made for the purpose of looking after the mango groves in the summer. I ran as fast as I could to take shelter inside the machan. I hid the flour bag at the rear of my body, against the wind, and kept running towards the hut. It rained cats and dogs and a strong wind blew. Mama was quite worried as she was sure that all the flour must have got wet. I was fully wet, but I had removed my shirt and covered it over the flour bag. I waited in the hut till the rain stopped. Ma cursed Mama for sending a small child for such a job. Thereafter, Mama was not worried about her flour but her child. It was more than three hours after I had left home. Mama could not wait anymore and left to look for me. By then the rain had stopped and I was running towards home. Mama met me on the village side bank of the river.

She was shocked to see me fully wet and without a shirt. I had hidden the flour bag with the shirt at the rear of my small body. She wiped me with her sari and wished to see the flour to ascertain whether all of it had gone wet. She was surprised to see the full bag of flour devoid of even a drop of water. Water hadn't touched even a corner of the bag. She was in tears to see the common sense of her small child. She narrated the story to Ma. She too was very pleased to see me and hear the story. Ma could have her *roti* for a few weeks without any problem. Thereafter, Mama took care and always sent Parmeshra for the job with more amount of wheat, well in advance.

Ma's condition didn't improve, but deteriorated day by day. After a few weeks, she couldn't see properly in the night at times. One afternoon, without informing anyone, Ma left home surreptitiously and reached Babu's place to fight for the last time and get all her deposit back. Mama wasn't aware of Ma's plans. She abused Babu and his family members at the top of her voice and gathered many other people near Babu's house. It was a do-or-die situation for Ma and had reached a bit too far beyond anyone's control. Ma had decided to expose Babu thoroughly.

I had seen Ma walking towards Babu's house. I immediately informed Mama about Ma's plans. Mama was very worried and doggedly followed her. She had the sari on her face. One could only recognise Mama as I was with her. There was total chaos. Ma was nearly demented and had refused to return and threatened to kill herself on the doorstep of Babu until they returned all her money and gold ornaments. They got scared, as until then no one in the village was aware of the facts and motive of Babu. This episode was an eye-opener for everyone. Mama requested Ma to return home as she was not well. At last, seeing the situation, many elder people of the village supported Ma's stand and intervened in the matter. Though Babu didn't like it they offered to discuss the matter with him on Ma's behalf. A few days later, Babu's wife came to our house and returned a few gold ornaments and some money to Ma. Ma was not in a position to even judge or see whether it was all that she had handed over to them. Mama wasn't worried on this account and informed Ma loudly getting closer to her ear, as she couldn't hear properly. 'They have returned all the money and gold that you had kept with them.' She said.

By now Ma knew Babu and his wife very well and was sure that they wouldn't do so. She smiled with tears in both the corner of her eyes and said, 'Bahuria', as she referred to Mama, 'You are too decent a lady. May God give a Bahuria like you to everyone.' She understood that Mama didn't want her to lose her faith and worry unnecessarily.

Ma had very long hair and because of the summer she felt uncomfortable with the long hair falling to her knees. Ma requested Mama to trim it like a man's. Mama didn't agree to her proposal and requested her to bear it for some more time as she would be okay very shortly. Ma knew from her heart that she wasn't going to survive for a long time. Ma couldn't look after her long hair anymore and had developed nits and lice. She scratched her head vigorously.

Mama sent Parmeshra to call her brother, Naresh, who taught in a secondary school at one of the nearby city as a science teacher. He loved Mama and Ma very much. As soon as he heard of Ma, without wasting any time, he came to look into her condition. Initially, he thought of taking Ma to the city to consult a good doctor but seeing her condition, he knew it was not possible to take her to the city. By now she was completely bedridden. He made a profile of all the information from Ma, wrote her medical history and returned to the city. He consulted a doctor in the city. Initially, the doctor wasn't ready to prescribe any medicine but on his insistence, he prescribed some medicine to Ma, based on the medical history and his verbal explanations. He rushed to the village to hand over all the medicines and looked after Ma for a few days. Ma showed signs of improvement, and could even get up to eat or drink but couldn't walk or sit for long.

Father and Nirupama were also called to have a look at Ma, as thereafter they might not be able to see her anymore, as Ma wouldn't live long. Father reached only after a fortnight, as did Nirupama. Ma's condition was no better. In fact, she was completely bedridden. There was no one to nurse Ma other than Mama. She even passed her stool and urine on the bed. Ma always said Mama, 'Bahuria, You are not an ordinary human being. You are an angel who does everything for me, even remove and wash my excreta.' Nirupama was her own child, but she hardly entered the fetid room. Whenever, once in a while she went to Ma, she covered her nose and mouth with a cloth to avoid the stench of urine and excreta in her room. Though Ma couldn't speak properly, she took umbrage at Nirupama's behaviour as she could see, feel and realise the difference between Mama and Nirupama. I could see the tears flowing from the corners of her eyes. At times, she caught hold of Mama's hand and cried for a long time. She wished to say many things but couldn't and spoke through her tears. She thoroughly regretted her sleazy behaviour to Mama. Father stayed for a few days, got fed up of the problems at home and left to join his office.

I sat near Ma everyday, for a long time and removed the flies that sat on her body. I had a hand-fan made of palm leaves that I used for removing the flies from her body. Nirupama hardly ever came near Ma and was busy visiting everyone's house in the village. Rest of the time, she spent going through the old wooden boxes of Ma to look for anything that could be of any use to her. In fact, once Nirupama requested and said, 'Bhabhi, remove the earring and necklace that Ma is wearing forthwith so that in case she dies, at least we would be able to use it.' Mama was very upset and snapped at Nirupama. God knows, whether Ma could hear her or not, as we had taken her to be a deaf woman, but I could see tears oozing out and flowing down from both the eyes. Ma's life decreased further seeing the perfidies of her own offspring. She had only one son and a daughter and she had struggled all her life to bring them up. Today, her own son was nowhere near to look after and nurse her. And her daughter was only interested in her ornaments or any property that she could lay her hands on. After a few days, she was completely bedridden and couldn't even move her body.

After a few days, even Nirupama left. In any case she didn't want to stay there, as she had to do something some time or the other for Ma. Mama shifted her bed in the same room where Ma stayed. I had no choice as I was very scared to sleep alone and couldn't leave Mama. Ma's room smelled of urine and stool. Though every morning Mama used to wash her thoroughly and even at times sponged her whole body with dettol, but once again, by evening the smell developed in her room. We had no choice as Mama had to get up many times in the night to give her water and at times fan her with the hand-fan. She also changed the mattresses made of old clothes, used under her, that used to be wet with her urine. Mama used to take all the used clothes of Ma everyday to the river and wash them with caustic soda powder. Kusmi did it for sometime, but subsequently refused, as she complained of vomiting sensation after seeing Ma's clothes. Our neighbours had a well but didn't allow washing these clothes there. We used the well for drinking water and regular baths. After washing the clothes in the river, she dried them in the sun putting them on the roof of the house, sprinkle powder over them to assuage the stinking smell of urine and replace them on Ma's bed. She hardly had time for herself. Whenever she moved out of the house, she promised me a candy and said, 'If you don't move out of Ma's room till I return you will get a candy.' This routine drudgery of Mama continued for almost a year and half but she never ever showed any inclination to stop. Kusmi mostly helped her in cleaning the clothes but even she refused to wash the clothes with offal and urine.

At times, even Mama used to be scared in the night, as our house was a newly constructed concrete house with the rear part having a thatched roof. It rained the whole night with the strong wind making alarming sounds in the air. We slept very early in the evening and never came out of the room till it was first light. In case we felt the need to go out to the toilet in the night or had loose motion, it was a Herculean task to come out of the house to go to the toilet. We had many palm trees ringed around our house. The whole night the leaves of the palm trees made various sounds that scared even Mama. Our house was outside the village and we had no other house nearby. One could see the cremation ground from the window of the house on full moon nights. We also suffered from the fear of Ma's death. Mama knew that Ma might die any time, and checked every hour in the night to ascertain whether she was alive or not.

One night, Ma was very critical and yelled very loudly for Mama. So far she had never been able to speak so loudly. Mama got up instantly. Ma was in a very critical condition. Mama gave her a little water to drink that came out from the sides of her mouth. She put the lantern up to see her face clearly. Her condition was critical, she was nearing her death. She asked me to call Parmeshra. It was early morning but still dark. I didn't dare to go out of the house. Mama herself ran towards Parmeshra's house, leaving me near Ma. I was very scared. Ma time and again looked at me and made a gesture with the eyes as if she wished to talk to me. Mama asked Parmeshra to call the Pundit of the village immediately. Mama brought some flowers and leaves of the tulsi tree with her while she returned to complete the rituals and the last wishes of Ma.

Mama took out the holy water of the Ganges and the leaves of tulsi plant and put it in a small pot. She asked me to offer Ma the holy water and the tulsi leaves. She also brought the calf that we had in the house and made Ma touch the tail of the calf.

It's a myth in the village, amongst the Hindus, that after one's death one had to cross a river named the Vaitarni to reach heaven. That was only possible once a young calf was earmarked for this purpose and spared for life long. It was possible only when the calf's tail was touched by the dying soul, while his or her soul left the body.

Mama made Ma touch the tail of the calf. Ma had caught hold of me with one of her hands around my back on to my tummy. Ma held me with both her hands and cried for a few seconds. I couldn't understand what was happening and was utterly confused. I did all what she ordered. I once again poured the holy water in Ma's mouth, Mama asked me to put it five times and put a diya of pure ghee near the head of Ma's bed. The calf was brought out, the diya glowed near the side of Ma's bed. Mama came out and informed Parmeshra, Ma is dead, she is no more.' I cried for Ma. We had lost a human being who stayed with us in this house, which otherwise was not liveable. It was very difficult to stay in that house. Many villagers, relatives and the pundits arrived after Ma had left forever. Ma had left, her body was put on the floor. Everyone cried for Ma once she had left. When she lived and suffered not even her own offspring came to nurse her. All this had a great impact on my heart. What was this world all about? Why are human beings so materialistic? Why could they only see their benefit in everything? A person who had abused Ma a few months ago, now talked big of Ma, after her departure, about her deeds. Even Babu arrived and consoled Mama. My puppy genuinely looked concerned and time and again tried to get across the human crowd gathered on the veranda. One of the people kicked her and she ran back and sat near her house sadly. She tried many times to locate Mama and me.

A few of the young boys were immediately rushed to inform all our relatives including father. Everyone waited for father to arrive before cremating Ma. Mama had wiped her whole body before anyone could arrive. That ensured that Ma's body didn't smell, otherwise even after her death the villagers would have made many stories to talk about Ma's death. Ma looked very different from what she was. Her hair had also been trimmed a few days back on her request. One chapter was over. Parmeshra was orphaned. He loved Ma the most, even more than me. I had hardly stayed with Ma but Parmeshra had grown before her. He had shared all her happiness and sorrows of her life. In fact, Ma arranged his marriage with Kusmi. Ma had taken care of all the formalities of their marriage including the expenses.

I was an innocent witness with no prejudice to judge the pretended and real tears on the dead body of Ma. Babu too spoke very greatly of Ma and cried on her body. His wife embraced Mama and cried loudly, showing solidarity to Mama. They also wished to express to the villagers that it was they who were the really near and dear to Ma. Mama had no reason to cry. She knew well how Ma had suffered quietly for a long time. It was good she had got rid of the excruciating misery and sufferings. Even I felt the same! But we had a personal loss. There was no one to listen to our talk in the night. Whenever I got bored of Mama, I went and sat with Ma. She took out money from her charkha and handed it over to me to get a candy. There was no more fear of Ma. Mama was also very worried for our crop and the cultivation. The whole burden had shifted on to her shoulders.

There were other categories of people not allowed to touch her body, mourning for their well-wisher outside the house. The Dusadhs, Chamars, Muslims, the Raiyats, Mushars and Doms, everyone had coalesced around to cry for Ma. I could see the genuine tears in most of the eyes of that crowd. As and when the Brahmin crowds, left they ran to have a glimpse of their real Ma. Many of the lower caste ladies had borrowed from Ma quietly for the wedding of their children and during pregnancy of their loved ones. Ma always helped them. Kusmi too came wailing to see her Ma. She had even brought her baby with her. That was the gift of Ma to Kusmi. Ma had asked Kusmi to name her child as Ramvilas. Earlier, Kusmi had objections to give her child a rustic name, but after her death she cried before her body and said, 'Ma look, even your Ramvilas has come to meet you. Please bless him Ma, he is your child only.' It was eye opener for the spectators to see Kusmi's love for her.

Another touching moment, was for Lucky the watchman, who had lost his hookah or bidi partner. They had been sharing the night hookah or bidi for more than two decades. Both his hands were paralysed but he could survive just because Ma had helped him to reach the city and consult a good doctor. He could barely move his hands but he reached near the dead body of Ma and cried like a baby. His tears conveyed his love for Ma. His tears dropped on the body of Ma. He too had lost his mother. I remember Ma telling us the story of Lucky. 'Beta, he was a real courageous man in the village. He had a muscular body and was very strong person of the village. He was assigned the task of the village watchman by the government on the recommendation of your grandfather.' My grandfather was a teacher and the most respectable person of the village. Whenever a Patwari, Tahsildar or any government official visited the village they contacted grandfather and took his help. He was the sole person in the entire village who could read and write English also.

Lucky had offered to come for Ma's funeral but was not allowed, as he was not keeping well and wouldn't have been able to walk the long distance that we had to cover on foot till the crematorium ground on the bank of the Ganges.

Yusuf, the *raiyat*, had come to pay his last homage to Ma with his whole family, including his wife and small child Ajra. Ajra had grown a little bigger than I saw her last time. Mama had requested Kusmi to ensure that they get a place to stay and food. My puppy was not seen after she was hit and intimidated by some young boys. Every morning, it used to caper around the veranda and came up to ask for food. Today she didn't turn up. Perhaps she could smell the problem. Even the goat and its small baby were not seen. None of the cows were milked in the house. Matra had come and taken the animals away with him. Nothing was moving as per routine. Mama was all alone to arrange for Ma's funeral. She had paid some money to Parmeshra to ensure that whatever was required for the funeral was brought in time. Mama had just been paying money to people after taking out from the corner of the saris where she had tied some cash. The pundit was paid for the things required for rituals of the cremation. Father was supposed to arrive by evening directly to the crematorium at the bank of the Ganges. I too was asked by Mama to proceed with them in case father could not turn up. The cremation ghat, on the bank of the Ganges, was more than ten miles away from our village. We had no choice other than moving on foot. Mama was very worried for me and had requested Parmeshra to take care of me exclusively as none of us would be able to return before midnight.

Many people had gathered. There was total confusion and I took a lot of time to locate Mama, while the body of Ma was lifted chanting *Ram Naam Satya Hai...* Everyone was in tears. Mama's tears had dried. She was left with no tears to cry. She had enough of it. Mama too was looking for me. I was moving with the pundit and on his instruction lifting a fire urn, containing the cakes made of cowdung. I was asked by the pundit to chant five times loudly; *Ram Naam Satya Hai...*

Our cows gave milk for us to drink and even cakes of its dung that would be used to burn Ma. May be one day Mama and even me.

The pundit moved ahead beckoning everyone to follow him. Mama came running to tell me something but could not talk to me. The pundit stopped, prohibited and said, 'No one should now give a call from the back or disturb him, he should not return towards the house with the fire bowl.' I was holding the rope of the fire bowl, and Mama kept murmuring something at my back. Perhaps she had brought something to give me that I could eat. It was almost afternoon and her child had not been able to eat anything, not even drink a glass of milk or water. Parmeshra was given another set of a torn half Dhoti for me to use in case it was needed after cremation. She gave Parmeshra the beat-rice mixed with sugar wrapped in a torn piece of her old sari. Parmeshra came near me and said, '*Chotanbabu*, I have got something for you to eat. Don't you worry, whenever you feel like eating let me know, I will speak to the pundit'. He kept murmuring and walking behind me. I was very scared and took the Pundit's warning very seriously and didn't turn my neck at all and kept walking straight as if I was tied with a log. I wished to look at Mama but I didn't take a chance. *As something might happen to her as well*, I thought.

Ma's body was kept outside the village in a mango grove, to chalk out the route to be taken to the cremation ghat on the bank of the Ganges. We had to cover the whole route on foot. There was no other mode of transportation other than a bullock-cart, and its use was not feasible in the case of carrying a dead body. Moreover, the track meant for the bullock-cart took a longer route than the route that could be negotiated on foot. Everyone decided to eat something and get freshened up before getting started for the arduous journey of carrying the dead body on the shoulder.

Babu was one of the assiduous members of the cremating team. I was the lone child and a silent spectator of the elder's talks and deeds. I too was given beat-rice and sugar with water sprinkled over it to eat. Each one of us went to the river and had a wash. All of us set out for the cremation ground. On the way, everyone kept changing their place to share the load of the dead body on their shoulders. We reached the cremation ground, on the shore of the Ganges, only in the evening. It was decided to hurry up the rituals before dark. The pundit swung into action and took charge of the rituals. I was given a bath. Ma's body was given her last bath with the water of the Ganges, while the pundit chanted the mantras and shlokas. Her body was put on the wood pyre made by the *Doms* at the ghat. They took away the new clothes from her body and a new set of clothes were put on her body. Mama had ensured that the earrings and the nose rings were not removed. The Doms at the ghat removed them too. I felt like crying openly but due to the fear of Babu and other elders, could not cry openly. She was mine and Parmeshra's ma only. How do they decide what should be done to Ma? I kept talking to myself.

There was one more body brought for cremation. It was also of an old woman. Babu called the *Dom* to find out about the caste of the dead person whose body was brought. *Dom* very openly said, '*Are Sahib, body ka koi Jaat nahi hota hai,* (there are no caste of dead ones) why at all do you wish to know the caste of the dead? Since you have asked, actually she is from a Chamar family.' Babu was upset. He spoke to a couple of other elders and decided to tip the *Doms*. Babu tipped the *Dom* with some money to ensure that the other body was taken reasonably away from the body of Ma before the other pyre was made. The *Dom* once again tried to make him understand that at this place it was only a body, not of any caste but Babu was not ready to listen to his argument. How does it matter whether the body that had to be cremated was a Brahmin or of Chamars! Though it was utter folly, but on the insistence of Babu, the *Dom* convinced them to arrange the pyre approximately thirty-forty feet away from Ma's pyre. They had a different system of cremation and it was lit before Ma's pyre. Perhaps she was fortunate enough to have her son to carry her load on to his shoulders and even light the pyre with his hands. But Ma was not so lucky. Her son had not been able to reach in time. The typical smell of burning of a body moved the atmosphere, as they had not put any perfume or piece of sandalwood along with the body. The wind blew in our direction and we could smell the burning flesh. I was damned scared to see the burning pyre, her head and feet could be seen while the pyre burnt. Would Ma also be burned like the other body? I was in panic and my heart and mind had gone beyond control to see a human body burning right before my eyes. I didn't know what was happening to me. But I was not available on this globe mentally or physically. I was very perturbed to see it burning and felt like saving her and taking her out of the burning fire. I was going through hell.

I sat in the lap of Parmeshra and cried loudly. No one could understand the pain I was going through. Father had not yet reached. Everyone finally decided to light the pyre before sunset. It was rather late. Father could not make it for the funeral. The pundit asked me to complete the rituals that father was supposed to perform. Ma was an unlucky woman. Her last rites could not be done by her own and only son. I cried while they covered the face of Ma and started putting the wooden logs over her. My heart was sinking. How would Ma tolerate so much of load on her body! I took the pitcher of water and poured the water around the funeral pyre. A twig of mango tree, dipped in ghee, was given to me to take to the burning fire in the pot, I had carried all through my journey to the ghat. I lit the twig on the fire and moved around the pyre to light it. The pundit almost carried me on his lap. I was nervous and scared, I was not too sure how and what was done to the humans after they were dead. All I was told by my mother was that they become a star in the sky. But I didn't know that they become the stars only after they are burned with the ghee and wooden logs. I cried, sitting in Parmeshra's lap in one corner, while Ma's pyre burnt. It made a typical sound while it burnt. It was about to be dark. Birds were rushing towards their nests to meet their loved ones whereas I burnt my Ma, my saviour. The sun was about to set; its light scattered all around the clouds. It was also saying goodbye to us for the day, but it would come back tomorrow once again to give us light, heat and drive our life further but Ma would not come back ever. She would go to the sky and take a shape like my grandfather had taken. She would be a brighter star because she would be nearer to us for sometime; afterwards the shine would fade away. People would forget her after sometime, like we had forgotten our grandpa.

Everyone was tired. My feet were swollen I had never walked so much before, that too barefoot. Though we always remained barefoot in the village, we had never walked so much at one stretch. It was all over. Only a few people took care of Ma's body while it burnt. Rest of us all moved to take baths and get ready for the return journey. It took three hours. Most of them reproached father for not been able to attend the funeral.

By then, the other pyre had burnt and was reduced to ashes, things were over and they had left. Even Ma's pyre was coming to an end. There was nothing left of her. It was all burning wood with circling fire rotating over the wood, nothing else. The pundit and other elders collected some ash remains of the funeral pyre. It was collected and put into one of the small pitchers covered with a clay saucer, what we called as *Asthi Kalas.*

It was all over before father arrived. He touched Babu's feet and cried. Babu embraced. He was totally oblivious of the things that Ma, Mama and I had gone through at the hands of Babu. I was the sole innocent witness of the pain and agony Ma had gone through before she died. Probably, I had seen Ma's woe, closer than what mother had seen. Once father finished with everyone he saw me in the dark, sitting near Parmeshra. Parmeshra too moved towards father, holding my hands. Parmeshra cried on seeing father. He always addressed him as Chotababu. He hugged Parmeshra and cried. I touched his feet and greeted him. Probably, he didn't see me doing so. One of the villagers brought his attention towards me and said, 'He has done a commendable job and not only walked to the cremation ground but also performed all the rites that you were supposed to do.'

I was not supposed to wear anything other than the dhoti to cover the lower part of my body and a half sheet to cover my top. It was time for father to cover up for his mistakes. He was feeling guilty for not being able to make it to the funeral. He didn't want people to talk about it anymore in the village. We all left the cremation ghat and reached the nearest roadside hotel for dinner. We were about twenty-five people and everyone had the meal of their choice. Father spent lavishly for their meal. I was not enjoying things as I was depressed from the core of my heart.

Mama and I were the witness to the fact that father didn't bother about Ma's illness. He had no time to show Ma to a good doctor. The least that he could have done was to take Ma to the city where he worked and had shown Ma to one of the good doctors. He never did that. All he did was to send some money every month to Mama to show Ma to a doctor. It was not enough. Mama, being a lady, couldn't do the things that a male member of the house could do. Father had no spare time for us. He wanted to hide his illicit personal affairs with the Bengali female from the villagers, though it was known to most of the people. They took advantage of his lack of interest in the family affairs. Mama had no resources to take Ma to the city and show her to a doctor. Still, she had tried to arrange through her brother, Naresh, who taught at the secondary school but it was too late for Ma.

Everyone had their meal and it was time to return to the village. It was difficult to walk back in the night. I could barely walk and somehow managed to hobble my way back to the village. I kept following Parmeshra like a lamb that follows its mother.

One of the villagers was talking to Parmeshra and laughed very sarcastically. I focused my ear onto their conversations. '*Arre* Parmeshra, your Chotababu is having a gala time. He has two wives, one official and another unofficial. His unofficial one is going to give birth to his child,' he continued.

Parmeshra was angry and said, 'You are talking rubbish. I don't trust you, sahib'.

'*Arre Bhai*, when the child will be born, then only you will trust me, I know you will not, otherwise. But the whole village is aware of his relation with that lady steno working in his office. They even stay together.'

'Does *Malkin* knows about it?' Parmeshra inquired.

'*Arre Bachche*, you are going to have a brother or sister very soon.' he said pointing towards me. Parmeshra was upset. He interrupted and said,

'How could you be so impertinent? Control yourself. Don't talk such a thing to a child.' I could not get the meaning of what he was referring to. But I had not been able to forget the talk and wished to discuss it with Mama.

It was difficult walking back in the muddy track to the village. Many a times we walked over mud. The night was noisy with the frogs and tadpoles making noises as did the locusts. One could hear the hullabaloo of villagers trying to frighten us away and warning us not to enter their village thinking that we were dacoits. People were scared to see so many torches that many of the elders carried in their hands and used them at times to locate the track and embankments. Many of the villagers gathered bricks and stones from the roofs, collecting it in their *gamcha*. That was the only weapon we had to fight in the village against dacoits. The people were worried and alerted in the villages that we passed through. They were satisfied only after meeting and knowing the reasons of our travel in the night.

We reached the village very early in the morning. I was completely exhausted after the tedious long walk back to the village. My legs were swollen. Mama was very scared of father as he always humiliated her and never treated her as a human. In fact, in most of the functions or gatherings he insulted her openly before everyone.

I could see Mama's face. She hugged me and asked me to go to sleep. She gave me a bath before entering the house. She offered a glass of milk with turmeric. I was very tired but didn't want to sleep alone in any of the rooms and moved behind Mama. She understood what I wanted. It was still dark and I didn't have the courage to sleep in the room alone. Mama briefed me to sleep quietly as the elders may discuss the plans for the *Bhoj* while they had their refreshments. 'All the villagers who had accompanied the dead body would have all their meals at our place till the ritual of thirteenth day was over,' she said. 'We also would have to arrange for *Bhoj* for three days. Father would be busy and he may lose his temper on you if you disturb. You go and sleep.'

It was a ritual followed in the villages, wherein after the death of any members of the family a *Bhoj* was organised. In the *Bhoj*, not only the people from our own village had to be invited, but from the neighbouring villages too. The prestige of a family was directly proportional to the number of people invited for the *Bhoj* and the kind of food offered.

Father was a prodigal showman and was not as pragmatic as Mama. I went to sleep, sitting on the floor of the corridor, near Mama where she sat to hear the discussions of the elders, planning for the *Bhoj*.

I woke on hearing a noise. Father was scolding Mama. I closed my eyes pretending to sleep with the fear. 'I will kill you if you ever utter any word against Babu,' he said. She replied politely, 'Ma is dead just because of him, do you know. He should not interfere in our life. That is all I want.' Mama lamented. Father was piqued and hit her. I could hear the noise of his hand falling on her face. She continued sitting near me. Father kept shouting and threatening her but she didn't open her mouth. After sometime, he left the house. Subsequently, Mama had put me on the bed in one of the rooms.

Mama cried lying on the bed where she had put me. I got up and asked her not to cry. She thought I was not aware of the things that happened in the house a few minutes before. She was helpless. She did not know how to keep father happy. Right from day one, the day we had shifted to the village, I had never seen father treating her well. He always humiliated her. She was the most decent lady and mother. What were the reasons for such treatment to Mama? It was pathetic. We never had any happiness once we heard the news of his arrival. We knew he was a guest in the house who would like things to be done the way he wished us to do. He always brought groceries with him, including toffees for me. That was all we knew. He never ever took me in his lap or spoke to Mama and me with love and affection. He was crazy. We were of no importance to him. He treated us worse than a stranger. It was difficult to deal with him. At times, I wondered how Mama could spend ten years of life with a person who never bothered about her and didn't even like her.

I wished to discuss with Mama that I had heard a man talking to Parmeshra, but seeing her condition I didn't find it proper to discuss it at that moment. I was told by one of the boys at the village, elder to me that a baby comes out of the tummy of his mother. I touched Mama's tummy, many a time to find out if there was a baby. Though Mama had told me that she had brought me from God. 'I had gone for puja to a temple and had beseeched God to give a good baby like you. I closed my eyes and he put you on to my lap.' She informed me. But the day Kusmi delivered and brought a baby, I had heard Ma discussing the things with Mama, that had also given me an idea that a baby came out of the tummy of the mother. But I was not clear at the first instance, as to how did they get in. I kept thinking and was happy to hear that I would have a brother or sister in our house to play around. I was happy and sad as well, as that fellow would spoil the bed and do *Phoo* on it.

It was afternoon. Father had gone to sleep. Mama and I talked lying on the bed. I asked her about the baby that she had in her tummy. She denied having any baby and once again confused me and said, 'As I had brought you from the temple, God gives babies to everyone at the temple.'

I once again asked, 'How did Kusmi get a baby?'

She could make out something was wrong. Why was I asking such questions to her? She asked me, 'What has happened? Why are you asking about baby? Tell me.' She wished to know.

I replied, 'A man was telling Parmeshra that I will have a brother or sister very soon.'

She could smell a rat. But she tried to ignore, pretending as if she knew nothing, to avoid such discussions with me. She asked me to forget it, 'They were joking with you.' She said.

She massaged my feet with mustard oil. I felt very relieved. Though mother knew the problem very well, she didn't want me to know all these things and get worried. I could see her face. She looked very worried and restless. Perhaps she wished to know or reconfirm from Parmeshra what was the conversation he had on this with the villagers.

In the evening, once again there was a large number of elders gathered to discuss the plans of *Bhoj* that father was contemplating to organise. Mama had informed father not to spend more, as our house was under construction and still lots of things were required to be done, before it was completed. It needed a lot of money to complete the construction. He was not ready to listen to this at all, and was worried of his status in the society. He was determined to do the *Bhoj* in a grand way, whereas Mama had different ideas in her mind for the *Bhoj*.

She had also told him point blank, 'As long as Ma was alive you were not bothered to look after her health or show her to a doctor. If this much of money would have been spent on her illness perhaps she would have been alive today.'

These bitter truths hurt him the most and he lost his temper and whacked her on her face. I could hear the sound of his hands falling on to mother's face. I was shaken. I cursed father hiding behind the sacks of paddy taken out for sale to the village Bania. I could see the mark of his fingers on her face. She had covered her face to hide her agony from the visitors. She gave up.

She was not interested to give him any advice anymore. Moreover, the story of the arrival of a new baby had put her in deep trouble. She didn't want to talk to Parmeshra on these issues. She feared that he might inform father about it. She was totally broken. She could make out that this pussyfooting was not going to work anymore. There was no one to support her.

At last, she thought of catching the bull by the horns and once again started the conversation with father. Primarily, she wished to know whether that Bengali lady, Paromita was really pregnant and was carrying his child. She didn't have guts to ask him straightaway and kept talking unnecessary things with him. She changed the topic and said, 'People talk very ill of you in the village, even the lower castes.'

He asked, 'What!'

Mama replied, 'You will not be able to hear the truth.'

He lost his temper and asked her to be open and not to twist the topic.

She asked, 'Is Paromita, that concubine, pregnant?'

He was totally piqued and slapped her on her face and said, 'How dare you?'

She had expected that and had decided to know the facts and his views on this. Mama very clearly and firmly told him, 'The whole village has been talking about it, how many mouths would you shut? Don't you cohabit with that concubine? If not, how come she is pregnant? I know she is a woman of easy virtue.'

He got the message. He didn't reply and moved out. She too got her answer. It was a known fact, and even he knew that it was not going to remain a secret anymore as two of the villagers worked in the same city as father worked.

Guests started trickling into the house. Nirupama arrived with her children and husband. She was only interested in Ma's gold ornaments. Earlier also, she had asked Mama to hand her over some of the gold ornaments of Ma. Probably, she wasn't aware that Ma had kept all her ornaments at Babu's place. In fact, they were not aware of the incident that took place between Ma and Babu. Mama or the villagers did not even tell father. It was a difficult situation for her. She knew, Nirupama would approach father for the share in the gold ornaments.

After Ma's death, even Mama's family members arrived to join us in the village and pay their homage to Ma. Her brother, the teacher Naresh, had also joined us on her funeral at the ghat and was aware of the whole story of our family. He was informed by one of the villagers about Paromita and her relation with father. He was looking for an opportunity to discuss the new development openly with father and mother, separately. Most of the time I spent with him. Being a teacher, he knew the psychological effects of the mental trauma that I had gone through as a child.

I always moved around with him. I had shown him the bird's nests that were made in the piled hay, in one corner of the house. Many birds had taken shelter in the holes of our concrete house. I showed him a nightingale, that had laid eggs, in one of the nests made in the hole of the concrete wall. We spent most of the time together. He understood me well and paid attention to my feelings. He told me many stories of my granny and Nanaji. He too was a teacher. He was not alive and I hardly remembered anything of him.

Everyday, we went for a walk on the banks of the river with the puppy. It was no longer a puppy but a grown up bitch. I hadn't named her as I was not aware that she could be given a name too.

Many of my cousins had arrived with their parents. I was not aware of my relations with them but played and enjoyed with them. Mama had no time to look after me or to know about me. I had got lost in the crowd in the house. Some of the relatives spoke to me with love and some hated me. Everyone arriving had a similar drama to perform. Just before entering the house, they wailed loudly till mother or father could see them wailing. Thereafter, it used to be a normal affair. Parmeshra remained busy in arranging the material for *Bhoj*. I had a fixed routine of going with the pundit everyday for some rituals or the other under a mango tree in the mango grove.

I was not allowed to put on normal clothes and sleep on the bed for thirteen days till all the rituals of Ma's death were over, because I had performed the last rites of Ma. But Mama at times didn't like her child sleeping on the floor and put me on the bed. This was vehemently objected by Nirupama. She made a lot of fuss for allowing me to sleep on the bed with her children. Mama was very upset. Some of the older ladies and relatives objected to Nirupma's idea. But once again, it was her house before, than Mama's or mine.

Mama knew she was not going to succeed in this and dropped the idea of having any argument with any of the relatives visiting us. The atmosphere at the house was typical. No one had any feeling for Ma's death. Everyone was interested to ensure that their child got the best of food to eat and a place to sleep. None of the ladies wished to work or help Mama in any of the household work other than a couple of the older lot. Most of the ladies remained busy gossiping or visiting other houses in the villages.

It was time for everyone's head was to be tonsured. I was the first one to get my head tonsured by the local barber, who had helped us in all the rituals of Ma's death. The barber at the village played a very important role in the rituals of death. I looked very different from before. While bathing, the water dropped on to the body and gave me a different feeling. I was not allowed to eat until and unless the rituals were completed for the day. Everyday, the pundit took me to the riverbank to perform some ritual.

Pundit said, 'The coming three days would be crucial for you as we are going to organise the real rituals for the death of Ma. They would be for a longer period.'

I was totally under the command of Naresh and the pundit. Naresh ensured that I was comfortable and gave me something to eat, at times, though the pundit didn't allow me. It was a totally different atmosphere at the house. It was a celebration rather than mourning after the death of Ma. People discussed of the forthcoming *Bhoj* openly and instructed father to ensure that the quality of the food on all the three days were as discussed.

The three days' *Bhoj* was enjoyed by everyone. Many people from other villages came on bullock-carts to have the feast and enjoy. Many of them probably didn't even know Ma.

In fact, in the village, people waited for some elder to die, so that they could have a good feast for three days. I recall one of the older person aged about eighty-five, who was always teased by the herd of impudent whelp, 'Baba, when would you die? You have lived enough; now we want to have a feast.' they said laughing.

He used to be damn cheesed off and react, 'I have had the feast of all your grandfathers' deaths, I will have the feast of your fathers' deaths and even yours, before I die.' Every imp guffawed at his reply and clapped. There was no respect for the elderly lot in the village. Children had learned this kind of talk from the elders. It was pathetic.

Somehow the tension of *Bhoj* came to an end and it was all over. Father had to sell off all the grain that we had in the house and had also borrowed from other colleagues at the office, promising them to return the borrowed amount after taking loans from his Provident fund.

Most of the guests had left, other than the real close ones of Mama or father. Naresh was given the task of summarising the expenses that was incurred for the three days of *Bhoj*. It was much beyond the expectation of father. He had yet to pay the bills of the provisions that were brought from the nearby smaller town. This was the reason, Mama had advised him not to spend unnecessarily as we would be broke for years together and would not be able to even complete the construction of the house, for a long time. It would take years to overcome or recuperate the full loan taken by father for the purpose of *Bhoj*.

Mama was asked to take out all the gold that Ma had, so that they could be sold and some of the loan amount could be returned. She was nervous; she didn't know how to explain the truth. She fumbled and said, 'Ma had kept all her ornaments with Babu and his wife. We tried to explain to you many times, but you neither had the time nor trust on us.'

He didn't believe Mama and lost his temper on her for twisting the whole thing and hiding Ma's ornaments. He was piqued and was about to raise his hands on her. 'I don't know how to deal with you. You are not a human being but a greedy bitch.' he murmured. 'I give you five minutes to take out all the ornaments of Ma that you have hidden, and even yours. If you don't, even God would not save you,' he continued grinding his teeth. He was about to catch Mama's long hair but Naresh intervened.

Naresh was aware of the whole story and tried to convince father. He took him aside and briefed him on the whole incident. He regretted his decisions but it was a bit too late for things to be retrieved.

Nirupama created a lot of hue and cry when she was denied Ma's gold ornaments. Both the husband and wife had a tiff with father and blamed him for lying and supporting Mama.

I was utterly confused as a child, to see the behaviour of elders. Was anyone really concerned or worried on the death of Ma? No one was affected by Ma's death other than Mama and me. She had been a shield for both of us. She protected us from many of the problems arising in the village. Once Nirupama could make out there were nothing that she could get from Ma's property, she decided to leave. Father provided her with cash and clothes for her children and husband, once again after borrowing, before they left.

Father was a frustrated man, as he had to look after a pregnant urban lady at the place of work, and the amount of money that he had borrowed was not easy to return overnight. Mama was very worried as she knew that once father left, all the vendors would harass her for the borrowed money. He too left, promising her to send some money to be paid to some of the vendors immediately. It was only Naresh who could understand her plight. Mama openly discussed about Paromita with Naresh. He had advised her to go to court, in case father married that lady, but she was totally against any such action. Naresh offered some money to her to be used in case of emergency, as we hardly had any grain in the house to survive the whole year. He too left after a few days. During this time we had come a little closer. He had become very friendly with me. I missed him when he left and cried for him. We had gone to see him off till the outer canal of the village. He was a nice human being, but he too faced the similar problems as any other teacher faced in the village. He too had a very large family. It was difficult for him to cope with the expenses of his own offsprings. He liked Mama very much, but was helpless. He couldn't have done more than what he did for her.

It was once again Mama and me with our puppy. After the death of Ma, the house had become even more scary. Mama was a strong lady but she too was shaken after the death of Ma and we didn't feel like staying in the house. It was all over. Ma had left us. There was no more weaving of charkha in the afternoons. There were no afternoon chats as well with Ma. Mama was totally alone and had no one to talk to or share her feelings. She was depressed. She didn't sleep properly in the nights. Our main door used to be locked right after dusk or last light and was opened at first light only. The whole night I used to hold Mama's sari and put my face between the cleavage of her *Pupu* or tummy. I never left the corner of her sari. I followed her like a shadow, everywhere, after it was dark. Ma's death was a loss to us. Our life had changed entirely.

As usual, Lucky, the watchman, arrived every night but didn't have his partner to talk to; he coughed and gave a call every night to ensure that everything was all right. He left only after Mama responded to his coughing. Lucky always had a bidi kept by her in one of the holes on the wall of the cowshed. After Ma's death she had ensured that Lucky didn't feel left out and didn't stop coming to our house in the night. She didn't want him to discontinue coming to our house in the night, for reasons of safety. As that gave her a lot of confidence, she had exclusively kept the bidi and matches for Lucky to relax in the veranda and smoke peacefully. Lucky had his bidi every night, but missed his partner and her hookah. Even after a few months of her death, Lucky cried for Ma at times. He was not too sure of Mama's thinking and feelings for him and had inhibitions in asking anything from her. He liked to have a hot cup of tea with a lot of sugar but could not ask her. He could demand from Ma anytime he felt like. Every evening he joined Ma to have a cup of special tea with extra sugar. Even Ma liked to have tea with extra spoons of sugar. One night Mama asked Lucky to come and have a cup of tea as and when he felt like having. Lucky could not use his hands for lifting anything but somehow he could manage to drink, eat and smoke.

On one of the afternoons, Mama wished to clean the room where Ma lived all her life till she died. She opened all her boxes and personal belongings that she stored in a tin box that she called 'Calcutta box' – a tin box given to her by one of her relatives who worked at Calcutta. She had many older things stored over a period of seventy years. Mama showed me the rag of a silk sari that she wore on her wedding. She had worn that sari for the last time before her husband had died, on the eve of *Butsavitri* – a festival when all the ladies worship the banyan tree and put thread all around the tree for the longer life of their husbands. That was the day she had put on that sari for the last time. She remembered how Ma had informed her about the silk sari of her wedding. She had once informed her and said, 'Bahuria', as Ma referred her, 'This silk sari my mother had kept for a long time before I was married and came to this house.'

I opened her charkha and found many candies wrapped in cloth and paper. This was the place she stored the candies and even gave me some at times, in the afternoons. She was a diabetic and was totally unaware of the damage those candies containing sugar would do to her. Mama had tried her best to make her understand that it was as harmful as poison for her, but she never took it seriously. She had many silver coins, with an inscription of Viceroy or Lord Mountbatten, stored in a *pouti* – a small pot made of a special type of grass, by the ladies in the villages. Ma was a master in making the *pouti*. It was an art that she had inherited, being passed down from one generation to another, but was gradually getting eroded. Even Mama could not make the *pouti* like Ma. She had kept a small gold locket in a red thread to be given to me, but due to the strained relations between her and Mama she hadn't given it to her only grandchild, that's me.

To clean the articles of Ma and remember her everyday had become a routine, and a great way to pass time for Mama and I. The only one photograph we had of Ma, was the one taken by one of the photographers while Ma and I had gone to a fair during Dushera, in a nearby village. That was also taken on my instance; otherwise Ma was not interested.

Ma had left not knowing that we missed her everyday and we loved her more. Even the puppy missed her as whenever she climbed on to the veranda she looked towards Ma's room. Whenever she tried to climb the veranda Ma scared her with her stick or made a noise to scare her. There were no more restrictions, no more construction of the house, she could come and sit near the beam as and when she felt like. There were no more the games of *Ghoda-Ghoda* by Kusmi and Azim, no more freeing of calves by Ma. One of the calves was no longer tied as it was freed after it was taken for 'Vaitarni Daan' of Ma. It remained in the house and sat with its mother but was never tied. It was freed. Its mother was not milked anymore. The calf used to be confused as it was not tied and until and unless Mama touched him pretending to open his rope, it didn't go near its mother, as the old habits die hard. Even the cow mooed loudly with pain in her nipples. Her udders used to be heavy, full of milk and she mooed till Matra milked her and removed some milk. Matra carried that milk to his house.

Everything had changed after Ma's death. All of us were affected including the trees and the animals. Everyone waited for Ma's arrival, which was not possible. We missed Ma till we forgot her completely and she became one of the farthest stars very dimly visible in the sky.

Chapter IV

LIFE AFTER MA

Our house itself had seemingly become orphaned after Ma's death. It was no more the same as it used to be with Ma being there. Every morning, Mama had to get up very early to ensure that the cows were given their last feed before milking and left the house with Matra for the whole day. In any case, one of the cows was not to be milked and whenever Matra wished to have milk he could milk her. I had to take the cows to a place across the river, from where Matra took over for grazing, before the cows returned in the evening. Our cows were never milked in the evening, as we had sufficient milk in the morning itself. The calves were allowed to be with their respective mothers the whole day. They were tied separately only in the evening. They made a lot of noise in the morning to reach their respective mothers but were released only when Matra arrived. They recognised Matra very well and as soon as he arrived they became very restless. Even their mothers made a lot of noise. Matra feared Ma and arrived early and in time everyday. There was hardly any day when Matra arrived late, as long as Ma lived. I had had to call him or look for him very rarely or once in a blue moon.

After Ma's death, Matra arrived late almost everyday and our house used to be the last one for milking and releasing the animals for the day. Even the calves could not be unleashed, as it was possible only after milking the cows. Everyday Mama had to request Matra to come a little early but it had no effect on him. She could make out the difference between her command and Ma's.

It was not the case for Kusmi or Parmeshra. They arrived everyday on time. Kusmi busied herself, leaving Ramvilas on the veranda. He had grown up and could climb or go down the steps of veranda very well.

Time and again Kusmi asked her, 'When would the construction work start?'

Mama had no answer to that and said, 'God knows, but certainly not before completion of one year from the day of Ma's death.'

She got the message. Kusmi was not bothered for the construction of the house but she was bothered about the prestige of the family and also the happiness that would return once the construction work started. She would be able to boast amongst her peers and others about us, the family she worked for. Our social status directly reflected on them and was related to their status in the village, especially amongst the lower castes.

We resumed our afternoon sessions of clearing Ma's boxes. There were many things that we discovered and came to know about Ma's generous nature. There were many *Rokka* – the papers of pledge of land – and other things that were found in Ma's box. People had not paid back the full amount of money, yet she had allowed them possession of the land. Though Parmeshra used to be against it, Ma never ever did any injustice to anyone. Kusmi was asked to throw all the junk that came out of Ma's steel trunks.

Kusmi resumed the afternoon chat sessions with her. In the meanwhile, Yusuf arrived to discuss the plans for the agricultural crops that was to be planned for the year. Yusuf greeted her, '*Assalamalikum*!' Mama, was embarrassed. She folded her hands and replied his greetings. 'Namaste!'

She had very little idea about the type of land and the crop she should go for. She sent Kusmi to call for Parmeshra. Yusuf was asked by her to sit on the cot. But Yusuf refused and sat on the floor. He knew Ma would not have even offered him to sit on the cot. Even if by mistake he had sat on the cot, Ma would have let him had it. Mama along with Yusuf and Parmeshra discussed the kind of paddy that was to be sowed for the coming year with the amount of manure to be used in the fields. Parmeshra advised her correctly so did Yusuf. He had no other land to cultivate other than ours and was very open and honest with Ma. He had apprehensions that she might like to change the *raiyat*. Yusuf was very worried and wished to know her mind. She categorically stated, 'You can be rest assured, I would not change the *raiyat* as long as you treat and cultivate these lands as if they were yours.'

Yusuf was more than happy and replied, '*Malkin*, I am very poor and have three small children.'

She once again said, 'You will only discuss the problems either with Parmeshra or me.' She also handed him our share for the cost of ploughing the fields. Mama offered him food before he left totally satisfied. He had brought a sack full of vegetables that Mama and I wouldn't have been able to finish for weeks together.

Every night, was a nightmare for us. I cursed God for making night. Why had he made nights? Mama and I used to be in deep trouble, we didn't come out of the house even for *Phoo*.

After the summer vacation, our primary school at the village reopened and both the teachers requested parents to send their children to the school from the very next day. We had to carry our own sack to the school, to be used as a sitting mat. We carried our books in the bag made of old clothes. All the Brahmin children sat in the front row, whereas the lower caste, very few of whom attended the school, sat at the end of the class. Many girls also attended the school with us. None of the students wore any footwear. We all attended the school barefoot. Moreover, we had no dress code. We didn't know that there were schools that had dress code or school uniforms. I had done my class two from one of the municipal schools, at one of the nearby towns where father worked. That school at least had benches for the children to sit but at the school in the village, we had to sit on the floor on the sack that we carried from home. Those who didn't bring sack, sat on the floor. We mopped the floor with cowdung every Saturday as our extra curricular activities. It used to be neat enough to sit on. I was obviously a bright student and was liked by the teacher. We had only two rooms in the school and the students from class three, four and five shared the classroom. One of the teachers stayed in the village itself and the other one came from his house at the nearby village. The teacher who stayed in the village, was liked by the villagers and offered food, free of cost turn by turn, as he taught the children after school hours. We hardly had anything to study in the school and generally played or made noise, while the teachers remained busy discussing about the village politics, crops or the cows or buffaloes which were pregnant at their home and were about to calve. They discussed how to take more milk out of them.

I sat right in the front row of the class, near the place where the teacher sat on a wooden chair. The children had repaired it several times. While teaching, I found one of the teachers peeping out of the school through a small window quite often. We couldn't understand the logic of his peeping out time and again. One day, once he left the class I along with another boy, Vimal peeped out of hole to find out what he was up to. We could not ascertain anything, as nothing was visible, other than the ladies taking their bath on the banks of the river close to a well. The ladies in the village had a specific place to bathe and none of the male members other than children were allowed to that well, especially in the morning hours when the well used to be over crowded with young women and girls. It continued. The teacher very religiously came to teach us during those hours; taught little as he peeped out of the broken shutters of the window and the holes of the walls. We tried our best to solve the mystery of his peeping but failed as there were nothing other than girls and ladies taking semi-nude baths, most of them topless. As far as we were concerned, it was just a *Pupu* that we saw everyday. We could see the ladies taking bath or changing. I slept with Mama and even touched her *Pupu* at times. It remained in our mind for a long time as to why the teacher always remained punctual for the class only at the time when the ladies took their bath and thereafter he was not interested anymore to even listen to us. A few children did mention that he might be looking at the *Pupu* of the ladies taking bath topless, but it was beyond our imagination as the *Pupu* was nothing very secret or unusual for us. We, right from our childhood, were quite used to seeing the *Pupu*, defecating bottoms and hear the wheezing sound of urinating of girls and women sitting in a circle and having a chat while defecating.

One day, the teacher even tried to gesticulate to one of the ladies crossing from the narrow lane behind the school wall leading to the river. It was hardly at any distance. One could see the ladies and even hear their conversation clearly. Later, we discovered that the teacher was caught in the night with one of the lower caste females in the schoolroom playing *Shadi-Shadi*. We too played the game of *Shadi-Shadi* with our classmates in the school. We at times replayed the things seen in the marriages taking place in the village, and touched our head with the head of the girl we liked. It was the game of *Shadi-Shadi* for us. We had lots of time to spend in the daytime and had no equipment or sports gear to play any games. After the school hours, we always played some improvised game in the evenings.

Mama remained worried for my education. She had very high expectations from me. She didn't like the village school and she was planning to request father to send me to any of the boarding schools, especially to a *sainik* school. The environment at the village was not conducive to studies and Mama tried her best to keep me out of it. Hardly any parents were serious about the education of their children, and had no choice other than sending their children to the schools at the village. Mama was very worried for my education, more so because I was her only child. She wanted me to join the Armed Forces and become a Colonel. Mama wrote many letters to father to get me admitted to any of the schools in the nearby town, as the school at the village didn't impart good education. Moreover, he himself worked in a town and could have easily arranged and afforded a good school. Father was not interested either in Mama or me. He didn't want to keep us in the town with him as that would have curtailed his freedom with Paromita. Everytime she wrote letters to him, she didn't forget to mention about my education; mainly emphasising on shifting me from the village atmosphere so that I could be given better education. Father never bothered to reply to the letters that Mama wrote.

Mama was in trouble and fed up, as right after the departure of father, some of the vendors approached her to repay the loan taken by father after Ma's death. She had to face embarrassment. They were not interested to listen to the excuses and wanted their dues. It had gone beyond control and she finally decided to sell whatever little gold she had, to repay the loans taken by father after Ma's death. She took Parmeshra and me with her and approached a Marwari *Bania* to pay cash in lieu of gold. I could see she was not happy and was in tears to part with the pure gold coins given to her by her parents in her marriage. Parmeshra also requested her not to take such a step and wait for another six months for the new crop to come, but she couldn't take it anymore. Every week, one or another vendor approached her and spoke very rudely. We came back after getting some money in lieu of gold. Mama sent Parmeshra to return the main part of the loan that could not be avoided anymore. She came back and did not eat at night. She cried holding me and asked me to promise her that I would become a big officer and fulfil her desire. I could see the storm in her heart. She was not much worried about father's extramarital affairs with Paromita. But she was worried for the property that we had in the village and my future. She was worried that even Paromita's children would claim their share in our ancestors' agricultural land and other property in the village.

After school hours, Mama never allowed me to go out of the house and play with other children of the village. We spent most of the time together doing something in the house. She taught me whatever little she could. She also read the stories of the Panchtantra that I enjoyed.

That year the monsoon broke a little early and it rained very heavily. The strong winds blew the whole night and scared us further. One night, one snake entered the house and unlike Ma, Mama was very scared. She went to the terrace and yelled for Parmeshra. I always followed her like a shadow. By the time Parmeshra arrived the snake had slithered away and was not seen. He waited for a while and said, '*Malkin*, it must have gone out. You wouldn't have been able to see. In case it comes out or is seen again, please call for me, I would come running.'

She allowed him to go. After some time, once again it was seen. Both of us climbed on the cot and didn't get down out of fear. It was totally dark and one could hardly see anything in the light of the lantern. She got down from the cot and lifted a stick to scare it out of the house. Perhaps Mama was not aware or she could not see that it was a cobra. No sooner had she lifted the stick and brought it down towards it, it opened its fangs. She was damn scared and yelled, 'Chotu, don't get down from the cot and freeze. It's death. If it touches anyone of us we are sure to die.'

It was a big and dangerous one. Mama panicked. I could barely see it in the moving light of the lantern that Mama was holding. She opened the outer door and waited for it to move out. Mama didn't have the courage anymore to go behind it or touch its tail with the stick. She kept making noise with the stick by tapping it on the ground. It was not at all scared or bothered by our presence. This continued for a long time, as she tried her best to guide it towards the main door but failed and that fellow entered into a hole on the wall of the house. She was very worried and took me on to her lap. She did not allow me to come down at all on the floor. She locked the main door and we went to the bed. She remained worried and ensured that the lantern glowed for the whole night right near our bed. Mama couldn't sleep and kept getting up, time and again, with the slightest noise to check on the floor of the room. It was very hot in the room, we were sweating but didn't have the guts to open the door and sleep in the corridor of the house. Next morning, Parmeshra was told about the suspected place where it had entered. Parmeshra tried to dig and see, but couldn't find it. It remained in our mind for a long time and we were very scared to move around even in the house, after it was dark.

It rained incessantly and continued for a few days. Parmeshra or Kusmi did not come. Mama had somehow managed to cook food on the cowdung cake. We were totally confined to the house. In the evening, Parmeshra came and said, *'Malkin, Malkin Gajab ho gaya.'* He was heaving. Mama got very scared. '*Malkin*, cholera has broken out in the village and three people from my caste have already died.' he continued. 'Please do not come out of the house at all.'

Earth moved beneath her feet. She was funked with fear. Parmeshra was asked by her to come inside but he denied and said, 'No *Malkin*, I can't come in, as I have just arrived after cremation of one of the females who died of cholera.

As soon as he uttered that, she moved me inside the room and asked me not to come out. She kept talking to Parmeshra. I could hear both of them talking. She inquired from him many details. He was drenched in the rain and was carrying a sack over his head to protect his head from getting wet. She asked him to leave. She locked the main door. Her feet were trembling. She became restless, closed all the doors and windows. She didn't want even the outside air to enter the house and touch her child. I was not allowed to go out of the house not even for toilet or morning rituals. She boiled water and kept it in one of the old aluminium pots for me.

Next morning, she opened the main door only when Matra had arrived to milk the cows. Rain had stopped. She quickly went out to feed the cows and asked Matra to go away and return only once the situation in the village improved. He too was very scared, as everyday one or two deaths occurred in the village. He too recounted some exaggerated stories to her that panicked her more. It was not only our village that was infected by this disease but couple of more villages were also infected and many deaths were reported. Matra asked her the ways and means to prevent the killer disease, as he was very worried for his child and wife. She had no answer and asked him not to eat anything till things improved. She didn't cook anything in the house. I was given the beat rice with curd to eat. She herself didn't eat anything. It was afternoon. We were busy talking with each other and playing inside the fortified house. We could hear the voice of some people talking and wailing followed by the call '*Ram Naam Satya Hai... Ram Naam Satya Hai...*' It was enough indication that once again someone had died and was being taken for cremation. The way to the cremation ground passed through the road before our house. She went up to the terrace, and was horrified to see that the person who died of cholera, was not of any lower caste but a Brahmin. She came running down and murmured, 'The curse of a natural calamity does not see the caste or creed. All are equal before it.' She became more nervous and wished to know about the identity of the person from the upper caste who had died. Things had gone beyond control. People had started leaving the village and moving to other villages to their relatives.

In the evening, Kusmi came to our house. She was panicky and knocked at the door shouting, '*Malkin, Malkin*, please open the door.'

Mama could make out it was Kusmi and opened the door. She tried to enter the house; Mama stopped her from entering and yelled, 'No! You first go and take a bath after leaving Ramvilas in the veranda before entering the house.' She did not allow her to come inside and was firm about it. Kusmi tried her best to convince Mama but it didn't work. She requested her to keep the small child at least, with her as many of the children suffered in her locality and died. She asked her to leave Ramvilas with her. '*Malkin, bahut log mar gaye,* even many elders had already died.' Kusmi cried before her. '*Malkin*, save my child from the catastrophe otherwise I too will kill myself.'

She returned after having a bath. Mama allowed her to stay in the veranda. She asked Kusmi to get Parmeshra as well, but he was busy carrying the dead ones to the cremation ground. The stories narrated by Kusmi were horrifying and I could see Mama shivering. 'Do not give normal water to Ramvilas.' Mama cautioned. She handed her over a bottle of boiled water and pot of curd and freshly cooked *Khichdi*.

I was not allowed at all to step out of the room and was told not to touch the puppy. She had a tough time. It rained continuously for days together and she could barely manage to stay dry and was not even able to get food. Whenever Mama opened the main door, she came running with the expectation of getting food but was disappointed. I requested her and said, 'Mama, please give her something to eat else she might die.'

She replied that it would not die but she would bring the disease in the house and both of us were sure to die then. I was not aware of the gravity of the situation and was confused as to what was happening in the village. The puppy was given something to eat through Kusmi. Mama did not allow her to come inside and she ate her food in the veranda. She too never moved out of the premises and howled with her head raised. Her howls added to our fear.

Mama was very upset and said, 'If things do not improve we too will move to one of the nearby villages to our relatives' house.'

It was said that the disease could even spread through the air from the dead body that they carried through the road passing in front of our house. She was not really aware that this disease didn't spread through air and was worried as the bodies were carried through the road adjacent to our house. Mama hardly had anything to eat throughout the day and starved. So did I. She didn't allow me to eat anything other than curd and boiled rice.

The whole village wore a deserted look. No one came out of the houses other than the male members engaged in cremation. Parmeshra was not seen at all. Only once he had come to see his family members in the night a few days back. Thereafter, none of us saw him. Kusmi was very worried and time and again requested Mama to allow her to go out and look for him. Mama denied permission to leave the house and warned, 'If at all you left the house, you won't be allowed to come back to the house'. She was damned scared and kept her child in her lap.

One of the villagers, who had gone to cremate the deceased, got infected and died himself after a few days. This created a furore in the village and thereafter, no one was ready to help anyone for cremation. Things were getting out of hand. An exodus started from the village. There was no one to help. No medical help or whatsoever was made available from the Government. In any case, none of the government agencies could have reached the village to help us, as there were no motorable roads. There were no culverts on the irrigation canals and rivers were full of water in the rainy season, and the villages remained cut off. It rained continuously, which added to the misery of the people both alive and dead. There was no firewood available for cremation. People started throwing the dead bodies, especially dead children into the flooded rivers. Many of the dead bodies were half burnt with the help of cowdung and were thrown into the river, as the cowdung cakes were drastically insufficient to burnt the dead bodies fully. Moreover, there was no shed at the crematorium and the villagers were forced to burn the bodies in the open, which was very difficult in the rainy season. They used insufficient cowdung cakes for the cremation of the body. It was a very pathetic condition. Many children died and were cremated by their family member themselves. No one else came forward to rescue others, as everyone remained confined to his or her problems. The lower caste suffered the most, many people died and were just thrown in the near by river that was flooded by the rainwater. There was no dry firewood readily available in the village. Whenever anyone died, the respective families cut the wood of the old, dead mango trees and used it. No one was ready to cremate the dead bodies. There were no resources available to the villagers.

One of the young girls of the lower caste, was thrown into the river along with a plank tied to the dead body. She was not cremated due to fear and lack of firewood. Her body was washed ashore, across the river to a nearby village. Two of the shepherds loitering with their cows could see the dead body. They were oblivious of the disease. The body was taken out of the river. Since she had died a few hours before, it was not at all mutilated or deformed. Finding her semi nude, both of them were said to have had sex with her dead body. Ultimately, the disease spread in their village also and many more people got infected with the disease. This was the story told to Kusmi by Parmeshra and, in turn, Kusmi to Mama. She was horrified to hear of such a filthy and squalid act by the young boys. Many more rumours spread in the village and the people panicked and started running away from the village. Some teachers and clerks, those who were contemplating to leave the village, told the villagers that anyone staying in the village would be wiped out and no one staying in the village would survive. That created a furore amongst the villagers and everyone decided to leave their home and move out of the village.

One night, I requested Mama to take me out for toilet. She was very worried. I had hardly anything to eat as far as she was concerned. I had loose motions and went out three to four times in the night. She was nervous and lost hope and thought that I too was infected by the deadly disease and wouldn't survive. She made syrup of salt and sugar and asked me to drink. I had it immediately. I was also given camphor or *kapur* with sugar to eat. I couldn't swallow and vomited. She panicked and was very nervous and lost all hope. It was midnight. She could not have asked for help, as there were none to come forward.

Kusmi was also worried and said, '*Malkin*, a child who had died a few days back in my locality, had similar symptoms before he died.' It was the ultimate and Mama was in tears. She held me in her lap and started crying.

'I had lot of beat rice with sugar as I was feeling very hungry and developed the loose motion.' I informed her.

She didn't believe me and kept crying moving her fingers on my forehead and hair.

We hardly had any exercise for the last ten days. We were totally confined to our home and were not allowed to go out of the house. Our digestive system had weakened due to lack of any physical activity. I was not aware of what was happening in the village neither was I told that there was a deadly disease that had spread over the village nor that many people had died. I too became a little nervous, and asked her the reasons for her crying. I got up and asked, 'Mama, will I die?'

She cried even louder and said, 'Please don't talk like that, nothing will happen to you. I will not allow you to die. God can't be so cruel to me.'

After the solution of sugar and salt that she had given me, I was feeling a little better. Moreover, I had couple of hours of proper sleep. Time and again, she kept her hands on my nose and checked whether I was breathing or not. The whole night she didn't sleep and time and again, she brought the lantern near my head and checked my shorts whether I had leaked in the shorts or not. It was terrible. I too at times felt that I would die very soon. Moreover, I had heard the conversation that she had with Kusmi regarding the symptoms that children had before they succumbed to the disease. Since I was awake for a long time in the night, as our sleep was disturbed by loose motions, I slept for a longer period in the morning. She tried to wake me up to ensure whether I was alive or dead. She was more than pleased to see that I was alive.

More than twenty-five people had died, including children within a week's time. Mama heaved a sigh of relief to see me alive and asked me not to eat anything till I was fully recovered. I was given rice water with salt to drink. She didn't allow Kusmi to give anything solid to her child, as well. All of us – my puppy, Ramvilas and I suffered, as we were not given 'stomach-full' food to eat due to fear of diarrhoea.

The rains had stopped and a bright sun shone in the sky. Mama found the courage to come out of the house to find out the real condition of the disease. It was the first time a bright sun shone in the sky and one could think of venturing out of the house. I was asked to stay at home. Even Kusmi had accompanied her. They could hardly find anyone out of their house and could not get any real information on the problems that people faced.

She told Kusmi, 'Go and find out the situation of the village and also call for Parmeshra if he is around.' She didn't allow Kusmi to take Ramvilas with her.

Kusmi was more than thrilled to venture out and look for Parmeshra. Ramvilas kept crying for Kusmi. She was back with Parmeshra and was happy to note that there were no deaths for the last two days, because most of the villagers barring a few had left the village. Mama was very happy to hear this. Since there were no deaths, it assuaged the fear in all of us. But half the villagers had left for other places to safeguard their children.

Parmeshra was not confident enough to take Kusmi and Ramvilas back home and said, '*Malkin*, please keep them with you for a few more days. As of now, nothing could be said about the condition of the disease.' Mama was happy as she herself didn't want to send Kusmi away. She wanted some one to fall back upon in case of emergency and also someone to share her views.

During that period, none of the other inhabitants of the other villages dared to enter or pass through our village, for fear of the disease had spread to the extent that people had stopped crossing through the *kuchha* road of the village. All the domestic animals of the villages were left at the mercy of God and loitered in the village.

The damage was done, people had lost their lives and everything was over. A team of two male nurses, what they called as compounders in the villages, visited to ascertain the number of deaths and its cause or the family that was infected first by the disease. Fear of death remained in everyone's mind for a long time. It took months together before life came to normal in the village. After this incident, people decided to go for a big *Havan* in the village. A *Yagya* was organised that continued for a few days and developed more self-confidence amongst the villagers and also assuaged their fear. Even the elders of the other villages participated in the *Havan* organised in the village. Things became normal, but many people including children had lost their lives.

Schools reopened and life became normal in the village. Everyone shared their feelings, fears and experiences of the time. It was hair-raising. I was permitted by Mama to attend the school of the village. We also resumed our evening games and other activities.

Matra resumed his routine work of milking the cows and taking them to the ground for grazing. Mama asked me to take the cows to the place where all the cows gathered and were taken over by Matra, for the grazing ground. I reached the place with our cows and found many of the lower caste children playing and joking around amongst themselves. Some of them were big and strong boys, who cracked sordid jokes about the upper caste children whenever they found us alone. One of the boys was doing something to one of the buffaloes and everyone around laughed. I couldn't understand the things they were up to and went closer to see for myself to know the reason for their laughter. I was a little scared as well, as Mama had warned me many a times not to mix with the lower caste imps and play with them. I went closer. One of them laughed at me and said, 'You too want to have fun.' Everyone laughed. I was utterly confused. I went closer and found that two of the boys had opened the upper layer of the *Phu* of the buffalo and had put their finger inside. One of them had even put his *Phu* inside the buffalo's *Phu*. I was aghast and shocked to see such a dirty act by the urchin lower caste boys.

I could not understand what kind of game it was, putting the erect *Phu* in the buffalo's *Phu*. I remained bemused and kept thinking about this. What was it, that everyone plays with *Phu* only? The boy's *Phu* was totally erect and straight. I knew even my *Phu* became erect but only in the night when I went to sleep and my bladder was full of urine. Otherwise, does this *Phu* get erected in normal cases also? All these questions kept bugging me. I had no one to share my doubts or clarify it. The only friend I had was my mother. I walked up to her and asked, 'Mama, how does this *Phu* get erect?

She was foxed and couldn't understand what I wished to know. I once again repeated my question. She tried her best to ignore it but I didn't allow her to. She got angry and said, 'Do not touch your *Phu*, otherwise it will vanish or I will take it out and throw it out for the crows to eat. Several times, I have warned you to eschew these lower caste urchin boys. God save you if next time, I find you playing or mixing with them.'

I asked politely, 'Then how will I urinate?

She laughed and changed the topic and avoided my questions. I could make out she didn't want to reply to them.

One day, while we were out playing, we found many of the children watching a cow tied to a rope and a bull copulating with her. I too joined them to see what was happening. The bull time and again tried to climb on her and even put his *Phu* into hers. I could make out there was something wrong with this *Phu* business. Everyone played with the *Phu* – even the cow and the bull. Of course, the cow herself could not play but the bull was kissing and licking her *Phu* and trying to touch her *Phu* with his.

What was this game? In the school I asked one of the boys quite elder to me and studying in the fifth standard to explain to me the things that was happening to that cow. He said something, which I couldn't follow. But I was learning various new things that was not known to me before and also making many new friends who would tell me cock-and-bull stories about the things happening all around. I was new to the village environment but they had been watching the bulls kissing or licking the cows' *Phu* or touching their *Phu* right from childhood. For them it was nothing abnormal, but I was not used to all this and was dying to know what was happening.

As time passed in the village, I was getting attuned to the rustic atmosphere and learning many things not required to be known by the children of my age. Mama was getting worried as I had learned many abusive words that village boys generally used. She was upset and once again requested father, through letters, to take me away to the city or put me in any of the boarding schools. Most of the children busied themselves in activities like riding buffaloes while they grazed, or going to the mango groves and playing some improvised games or walking to the reserve forest nearby and watching, teasing and throwing stones at the monkeys. Many times, we disturbed the hive of the wasp and while it followed us we ran to safety, laughing and giggling. I was not at all aware of other activities and was only now gradually getting attuned to them. Earlier I could never stay without Mama and didn't like playing with village boys.

On one occasion, while playing in the bamboo groves, we found many birds chirping in the grove. We rushed to find the reason and were astonished to see a big snake. One of the boys called it as 'Dhaman' rat snake. It was moving towards the bamboo grove and all the birds tried to scare it with their beaks. It got irritated at times and snapped back. We kept watching for some time. One of the boys threw a stone and the snake slithered down, like a slide, from the grove and moved like a bullet train on the ground. I was very scared and froze with fear. Some of the village boys followed it and forced it to retreat in one of the holes on the ground. It was quite big one and could not get in fully. One of the boys caught its tail and started pulling. They tried their best. They could not get it out and it caught one of the boy's hands with its tail. He got scared and left. Immediately it came out of the hole and rushed like a rocket and climbed on to a nearby palm tree. I was amazed to see the courage of the village boys and thoroughly impressed.

I was even scared of a rat in the house or a house lizard. I never spoke anything about this to Mama. Many times, a couple of my friends had advised me not to speak of such things to the elders and I stopped sharing anything with her. I enjoyed going out of the house more than before and spent most of the time playing with village children. Mother didn't like the idea of mixing too much with village children and asked me to come home directly after school. I had forgotten whatever little I knew and had lost total interest in studies. Like any other village child, I too enjoyed riding a buffalo and even took baths in the ponds along with the buffaloes and enjoyed jumping off their backs in the deep water. In the afternoons most of the buffaloes enjoyed their bath in the pond water. I too climbed and jumped off their back and enjoyed with the other children.

One day, while I gambolled around and was having a whale of a time in the pond with all the other children and buffaloes, Parmeshra saw me. I tried to hide behind a buffalo and went under water but since he loved me, he was pained to see me mixing with the village imps. He couldn't digest seeing me taking a bath with the buffaloes and learning all sorts of dirty things from the village children. He yelled for me and said, 'I have seen you. If you do not come out I will inform mother or bring her here.'

I came out and pleaded to him not to inform her about it. I was brought before mother. I refuted going inside the pond. My clothes were dry as we went into the water nude, removing and keeping all our clothes on a tree near the pond. She touched my *kamarband* – the sacred thread that everyone wore in their waist in the village, and sure enough, it was wet.

Parmeshra was pained and requested mother to write to father and shift me to one of the schools in the city. '*Malkin, ek to bacha hai, is ko sahib banana hai tabhi to Ramvilas ko kahi laga dega.*'

Mother was very upset and for the very first time, she hit me with a stick and cried for a long time. She could not hear to see her child go astray, down to the level of lower caste children. She was pained with my behaviour and activities at the village.

I had matured. I enjoyed many things with the children that Mama was not aware of. I even joined the village boys and girls and played a game of *Dekha-Dekhi*. It was a game that we played in isolation in the summer afternoons, when all the elders in the village went to sleep. A few like-minded children, a little elder to me, had introduced me to this game that we played every afternoon. We sat in a circle with a girl and boy alternately, and displayed our *Phu* to each other one by one. At times some of the boys got it erected and showed it to the girls. I did not at all enjoy this game initially and was very shy to even display my *Phu*, but gradually adapted to the game. Even the girls were not at all shy to display their *Phu*. It had become an afternoon ritual for us. Everyday, we gathered but changed the venue.

It was my turn to call them to my house in the afternoon. All of them arrived. Mama had gone to relax and was busy talking to Kusmi. We busied ourselves in the game of *Dekha-Dekhi*. Since there was pin drop silence and Mama could not hear any noise from anyone of us, she came to the room to find out what game we played. We were caught red-handed and admonished by her. All the children were sent away and I was taken to task. She admonished, 'If you display your *Phu* it would be taken away by the crows or the snakes.' I was very scared but enjoyed playing the game of *Dekha-Dekhi*. Mama scolded me and warned me with dire consequences if I ever played or ventured out with such dirty children.

I confessed and said, 'We play every afternoon with different girls and boys. It is a very common game amongst the children in the village. Even the girls never object to this game and the girls elder to us also at times join us.'

She knew that whatever little good things she had imparted and inculcated in me were getting diminished. She was seriously thinking of sending me away from the village.

I was growing and had become almost like a village child but was smarter than them in all respects. I knew better other than others what developed and generated in the village. Many times my puppy too accompanied me to the places I visited every evening with other boys in the village. She had grown big and could scare the smaller children with her bark.

One day, once again there was a Durbar near Babu's house. Many of the lower castes had gathered to complain and seek justice. Ladies and girls were not permitted to join this meeting. Many of the children too gathered to see the fun. Mama was not aware that I too had sneaked out of the house to join the fun organised at Babu's place. Proceedings started. One of the persons complained that a Brahmin married man had entered his house and forcibly had sex with his wife.

From the group of lower castes gathered, one of the young boys got up and said, *'Babu Sahib, ab bahut hi Chamchori bad gaya hai.'* What he meant was that *Chamchori* had drastically increased or proliferated in the lower caste and the culprits were mainly the upper caste boys or men.

What was this *Chamchori*, that was referred to time and again. It had gone over my head then, as I had not been able to understand. *Chamchori* was the word used by the lower caste or amongst the villagers for stealing of someone's pussy.

I couldn't understand the things happening and discussed there, but the lower castes could. For the first time, even Parmeshra was very furious and warned the upper caste with dire consequences, if caught on the spot entering their house for *Chamchori*. This was a clear indication to the upper caste as to how brazen they had become. This also manifested clearly that the supremacy of the upper castes was waning, as the lower castes raged against the feudal and tyrannical old system of the village. Many married upper castes were named by the lower caste, seen by the children or ladies doing *Chamchori* or even caught at times. The upper castes also blamed the ladies of the lower caste for wanting to have sex with them at times and inviting them in.

Proceedings continued but it was not of any interest to me. As soon as I reached home Mama wished to know the agenda of Durbar that was conducted at Babu's sit out. She asked me, 'What was the matter?'

I replied, 'It was a case of *Chamchori*.'

She was aghast to hear that word from my mouth. She inquired further, 'Do you know what is it?'

I said, 'There were a lot of hot discussions going on. I couldn't understand what had gone wrong.'

I also asked her to explain as to what it was. She asked me to go on to the terrace and pick up the bedsheet that was put out for drying. I could make out she didn't want to explain to me about the details of the *Chamchori*. After all, what it was? I wished to ask the village children about the details.

Mama yelled for Kusmi and asked for the details. She explained to her. I couldn't understand. All I could make out were the names of the upper caste males that she muttered were involved in *Chamchori*. Mama said, '*Ram Ram, ye Brahman longon ko kya ho gaya hai?* What has happened to the Brahmins? Why do they venture into hell? Their pseudo-faith and strong belief in casteism is thoroughly exposed and abundantly clear. On one hand they say the Chamarins or Musharins are untouchables and on the other, they don't hesitate to have sex with them.' she exclaimed.

I could make out it was something dirty but what was it? She even joked with Kusmi about Ramvilas and asked, '*Iska asli Baap kaun hai*?'

'*Malkin*', Kusmi said shyly.

Mama informed her that Ma had told her about the person who had fathered Ramvilas.

'What I would have done *Malkin*, he is very sexy and has a big one, he is better than Parmeshra any day.'

'*Besharam*,' Mama added, '*Touba kar*, you will go to hell.' Kusmi laughed and nodded her head.

What was the link between Ramvilas and the *Chamchori*! I was further confused. He was a baby, just three years of age. How could he be involved in a game of *Chamchori*. Or if it was a dirty matter, only an elder could play or do so.

'*Malkin*, cases of *Chamchori* have drastically increased in the village, as the young girls have grown big and are happy to discover sex and enjoy with the upper caste boys. Some of the girls are not even twelve and haven't got their *Mahina*, (as they referred to menstrual period in the village) still they get involved in this.' Kusmi said.

Everyone in the village discussed about the *Chamchori* even the girls at the school. I asked one of the girls to explain about the *Chamchori*. All of them giggled and said, 'You are still a kid and wouldn't understand.' All of them once again laughed and giggled, keeping their hands on their mouth.

I too wanted to grow. I wanted to prove to them that I was not a kid, and that they were so. I said with displeasure, 'Even you all are kids.'

All of them once again laughed. 'No I am not,' one of the girls said.

I didn't know what was the difference between them and me. They were little elder to me, may be by a few years. One of the girls asked me, 'Did your *Phu* get up?'

I replied, 'no.' Once again, all of them made fun of me and laughed. Some of the girls and the boys while playing *Dekha-Dekhi* taught me how to tickle the *Phu* and make it erect. I learned a new game from the children that they played everyday. I enjoyed playing that game some times in the group and at times even alone. I spent most of the time with the children in the village, especially the girls and enjoyed playing games of *Dekha-Dekhi* or tickled each other's *Phu*. In fact, most of the time the elder girls at the school took the lead for the afternoon games. Mama was not really aware of the kind of training that I had been getting in the village from the children.

We had a retired school principal who was constructing his house beside our house. He had also arranged for a well in his house that was quite near the boundary wall of our house and could be seen from the terrace of our house or from the courtyard. His house was about to be completed. His wife spent most of her time with Mama. She was very happy to note that she would have a nice neighbour. She had planned to get my tuition arranged with the retired teacher. She was very happy and treated them very nicely. Both of them had developed very good relations with her. Their house was completed and I started going for tuition to the retired old teacher. Mama was very happy and satisfied. I had become better than before in studies. Since I was in the fifth standard, he also taught me English and started with ABC... Mama was relieved and stopped worrying about my studies.

She had also returned all the loans taken by father during Ma's death, after the crops were sold. She could manage the crop very well with the help of Parmeshra and Yusuf. Earlier, we could not have pulses to eat in the house and could eat pulses only once a week or Mama prepared a little only for me. After the new crop, even Mama could eat pulses with rice or *roti*. She had a tough time after the death of Ma, as father had sold most of the grain available in the house. Moreover, he couldn't send any money to us, as he had to repay the loans taken from the provident fund and friends at his office. We were left at the mercy of God, but Mama's experiences and diligence came in handy and we could overcome the bad days within a year itself. All her ornaments were sold. But now she was not worried, she had been able to locate a teacher for her child who would fulfil her dream.

I had passed the fifth standard with good marks, though there was hardly any standard in the school. Everyone of us had passed, barring few of the lower caste children who hardly came to attend the classes. Even Ramvilas had joined the village school. Our school was only up to the primary section. I was a grown-up boy and was admitted to a school in the neighbouring village. Mama was worried, as I had to cross rivers and the irrigation canals to reach the school and didn't want me to go alone everyday. She requested a few other parents to send their children to the school. None of them wished to send their children due to the fear of drowning. I continued going to school. At times either Mama or Kusmi accompanied me to a certain distance or at times Parmeshra.

It was once again winter and we had heaps of hay all around to play hide and seek. Every evening all the children gathered and played hide and seek in the heap of paddy hay stacked before thrashing. It was all done manually in the village. We had no electricity in the village.

After the evening games of hide and seek were over, I reached home and was very happy to see a very stylish visitor in the house. She was Pratima, daughter of the retired teacher, our neighbours, who had come with her two daughters. The wife of the teacher had introduced them to Mama. Mama was aware of them but had not been able to meet them ever. She stayed in the city and her husband was a practicing doctor. He had to move to London for higher studies and sent his family to his in-laws' place. She was apprehensive as to how these children, not used to village life, would spend a year or so in the rustic atmosphere. She too, was worried for the education of her children for a year or so, as her husband was to return from London after completion of FRCS.

Both daughters of Pratima were a little older to me. They wore very attractive readymade clothes that no one could afford in the village. I felt shy to talk as I was not dressed well and as stylish as they were. They studied in a convent school in the city. They also had a lady teacher to teach them besides their grandfather the retired teacher.

Mama called me and said, 'Chotu, did you see, how smart they are? I want that you should also talk in their style.'

As they spoke in English, I wished I could. They always wore shoes while stepping out of their house, whereas I never had one. I was told not to come for tuition till they stayed in the village, as the old man, the teacher, remained busy teaching his granddaughters. They hardly associated with the village children. I could see them playing or listening to the radio from our rooftop. They also wore bodices under their outer clothes being a girl, whereas being a boy I did not. I had not seen any girl or lady wearing undergarments. None of the ladies or girls wore any bodice in the village. The male members in the village did wear underwears that were known as twelve bore *kuchha* or double barrel *kuchha*, stitched by the local tailor. It was known as twelve bore as it had two long legs opening like a double barrel gun. The design of the underwear were almost fixed and used to be lines in different colour. Children could not even think of wearing the under garments. May be there was no system or the people could not afford it. I had seen many girls and ladies taking nude baths in the river well. None of them wore anything like that. The ladies wore a petticoat whereas the girls wore salwar directly, with nothing under it.

Whenever Pratima's daughters came to the well to take a bath, I observed their undergarments. They wore tight ones with elastics on the top and designed with coloured flowers, some times a V-type or at times U-shapes. Their skin looked fairer when they removed everything and remained in the panties or undergarments. One of them was big and had *Pupu* also. The white lining on the top and the coloured panties on the lower part gave a very pretty look. Both of them had a very whitish complexion and it was great to observe them in the undergarments when they got wet. I could even see their lower part but hardly had any fascination to see their *Pupu* or the lower part without clothes. I was fascinated by their undergarments and the tight slacks that they wore. Whenever they put them for drying on the terrace, I showed them to Mama. It was something new for me as I had not seen any of the girls in the village or the ladies wearing such undergarments.

I coveted the sort of undergarment they wore and inquired from Mama whether the boys could wear them under the shorts. She replied, 'You are still small and we will get you one, once you grow.' I wished to grow faster to put on the undergarments but only the ready made ones, not the one that were stitched by the tailors at the village. It was not attractive at all.

One day, Pratima saw me looking at the girls while they took their baths. Both the girls were aware that I observed them everyday while they bathed. They had no objections and once I had requested them to show me the undergarment that they were wearing. One of them, had lifted her middy and had shown me the tight panty, showing the cleavage of their *Phu* very prominently. The girls had no objections to my presence, as most of the ladies and the girls at the villages took baths in the open and could not care less about being observed by a boy aged about nine or ten. At times I took a bath with the ladies and girls at the same well.

I was not at all interested to watch their *Pupu* or the lower parts, as Pratima perceived. Only the undergarments and their dress they wore fascinated me. They had many of them and changed everyday. Sometimes they used to be long and sometimes very short.

Pratima called my mother on to the terrace and complained, 'This boy looks at the girls when they take their bath everyday. I will be forced to complain to Babu if he doesn't listen.' She bickered with Mama.

Mama was shocked and became very upset. She didn't know what to reply and apologised to her immediately. She also assured her and said that I would not go to the terrace when both the girls took their bath. I was called and caned by her. She went inside and cried, holding me, murmuring, 'What will you become, a *Goonda*? I have a lot of hope and am living only for you.'

I promised her not to repeat it. I also said, 'Mama, I was looking at their undergarments not at their *Pupu* or *Phu*. She too didn't believe me and scolded me once again.

The elder girl, at times played with me and even liked my company but after this incident Pratima briefed them not to talk to a dirty child like me. While Pratima remained busy with her mother and father or went out to the village, both the girls came to our house and liked to play with me.

Every evening, we used to play hide and seek in the hay of the stacked paddy. They liked my company and always hid along with me. We always loved to hide together and held each other's hands. Something used to happen to me while we played together and we never confronted each other and remained in the same team. I felt very bad as they were no longer allowed to play with me. I missed them everyday and waited for them to come on the terrace. I had learned all the games that they could play, including skipping and related activities with the rope. I could do better and faster than the girls. They admired me for skipping so fast and better than them.

After Pratima's complaint, Mama had become very upset and once again tried for my education in the city. I was in sixth standard and had to go to the other village to attend school. There were very few children whose parents agreed to send them to the school located in the other village. Our school started at ten in the morning and finished at four in the evening. We had to walk five kilometres, one way to reach the school. I didn't want to attend school as by the time I came back, it used to be dark in the evening and could not meet or play with the girls. Many times, I threw my cloth bag full of books before her and refused to attend the school.

My complaint had reached Babu and it had become a matter of talk in the whole village. The village elders discussed the issue and called Mama and Pratima to ascertain the facts. I had not been able to understand the problems that they wished to discuss with her. She refused to join them with her child and cursed Babu for creating a humiliating situation for her. This was made a big issue in the village and it was even informed to my father by one of the villagers. Mama was broken on this issue and had also given up on my education. She had decided to discuss the issue of my schooling with father, but after Babu's complaint, Mama didn't have courage to do so.

It was almost a year of Ma's death and father had never visited us. Mama knew he would come, as he had to perform the rituals of Ma's death anniversary. He once again planned to have a *Bhoj* in the village for a day. It was the system prevailing in the village. He had not been able to repay the loans that he had taken after Ma's death for organising the *Bhoj*. Further borrowings, once again, would add to the existing loan tremendously.

This old tradition of *Bhoj* for everything in the village, had increased the burden of expenses on the upper caste and they generally remained in debt till death. The old traditions included extra expenses of *Bhoj* during marriage, for three days; after death, *Bhoj* for three days and for *Upnayan Sanskar* of the Brahmin children, the *Bhoj* for three days. All these added to the extra expenses of the upper caste. And the more one could spend, the more the family was respected. This false and hollow tradition took its toll on the financial condition of the Brahmin families. This deteriorated the financial condition of the upper caste families successively. On the other hand, the lower caste had no such hang ups and they could do any petty job and earn. Moreover, they had no such expenses. There had been progressing because of their hard work. The upper caste maintained that touching the plough would lead them to starvation and poverty. They were superstitious about touching the plough and working in the fields. The lower caste took advantage of this situation and stopped ploughing the fields of the upper caste. The upper caste suffered a big loss in the one and only source of agricultural income. Most of the upper caste families not having any earning member as a teacher or clerk, had a tough time for survival and had to compete with the lower caste. Then most of the upper caste having a fixed income out of their service, took a lead and destroyed the harmony of the village that harmed the upper caste more than the lower caste. The lower caste could do any petty work and made up their loss but the upper caste could not do without the lower caste and neither were they ready to plough their own fields.

Mama was worried about the expenses and the loan that would arise because of the *Bhoj* planned by father, on the occasion of Ma's first death anniversary. We learned that father was about to reach on the occasion of the death anniversary of Ma. She was very worried as the villagers might poison him against us. She had already organised the items needed for the rituals for Ma's death anniversary.

On his arrival, the very first thing father planned to do was to sort out the issue relating to the complaint made by Pratima to Babu and Mama's refusal to attend to his calls. He castigated Mama and ordered her to come to Babu's place. She squirmed in discomfort. Mama was very upset but had no choice. I was also dragged to Babu's place and both of us were asked to apologise to him. I could see Babu being very generous and asking father to forget about it. We returned home. Mama was humiliated and cried for hours together. I didn't want to face father as I was very scared of him. He pretended to be aggressive to hide his sins, of having a child from his lady colleague working in his office, without marriage.

Parmeshra could not take this humiliation and argued with father. He revealed the talk that took place in the village and said, 'Do you know what Babu and other people talk about you? Do you want to hear that?'

He had no answers and ignored the topic. He asked Parmeshra to organise things for the Bhoj in the coming week followed by a Puja.

Mama tried to broach the topic and initiate the talk of my education in any of the city schools but he was not ready to discuss anything about this. He said, 'He will look after the properties at the village and run a *tabela*. I don't want him to study and go out of the village to work.' I have another child who will do that and he would look after our property at the village,' he rebuffed.

Mama was piqued and refused to accept his diktat and replied harshly, 'I will show you that my child will bring more pride to the village and the country than your illegitimate children that you have at the city.' She was furious but diffident as well. I had never seen her losing her temper so badly. Father looked askance and tried to soothe Mama. She had refused to accept father's suggestion and the decisions taken for me. She had also told him that she didn't wish to take any financial help from him for my studies. Father was taken aback, as he could never envisage that Mama would be so curt to him. She had outrightly rejected the diktat of Babu and anyone else in the village as far as her child's future was concerned.

Pratima too, was feeling guilty for escalating such an inconsequential issue with the illiterate lot of the village, who all had made it a big issue for nothing. She was not very familiar with the village politics and mentioned casually about the things happened with Mama and me. That not only created problems for Mama and me but also for Pratima, as whenever her daughters came out of their house, many people taunted them for wearing undergarments and many ladies and young girls requested them to show them their undergarments. Moreover, Pratima was not aware that her complaint would be used by Babu for his personal vendetta.

Father had no time to understand and go into the details of the problems and reacted and reached conclusions hastily. He, in fact, didn't want to go against Babu, mainly because of his extramarital affair with the Bengali female. He wanted Babu to support him. In any case, there were none who could stop him or question him on this.

Bhoj was over and probably father had left us once and for all. He neither came to Mama nor me as he did previously. Every time before leaving the house, he used to talk to Mama and brief her on many things and take me in his lap and embrace me and even give some money in my hands. That ritual was also broken.

One day, Pratima came and apologised to Mama for the mistake that she had committed by going and discussing her personal issues with the illiterates of the village. She had inadvertently hurt our feelings. Mother was a decent lady and didn't say anything to her and even offered her a cup of tea. Pratima also offered me a tin of jam. We didn't know what it was. Mama couldn't read the English words written on its cover. She knew it was an effort to patch up by Pratima. Mama also knew in her heart that my intention was never to see the *Pupu* of the young girls. She knew I was fascinated by their undergarments but she couldn't have shared that with Pratima.

Mama requested Pratima to convince her father to teach me as well, but she didn't agree to that. She had no hopes for my education and tried her best to make me understand the value of education, but the environment at the village was not at all suited for education and no one could dream of miracles. With every passing day, I was getting trained in the dirty things from the village children. At times she accompanied me halfway to the school to ensure that I reached the school on time. But it was no good even at the school, as we had nothing to do other than playing with the children from various other villages and learn even dirtier things, as that school had older boys. Mother had no hopes.

One day, we heard that one of the lower caste girls was influenced by a ghost and a soul had entered and taken control of her body. All the children decided to have a look at her. She was tied to a bamboo fixed to the ground, and was time and again whipped by a holy stick given by the Tantrik. She was in a pathetic state and looked dangerous, as she could not have taken a bath and changed her clothes for days together. Mama was not aware that I had gone to that place along with other children. It was dark. I didn't return home. She summoned Parmeshra and asked him to look for me. He came to the place and took me home. She caned me for a long time and cried with frustration. I knew she was depressed due to the behaviour of father and at times took her frustration out on me. She wished to take revenge on father by imbibing good things in me but it was just not possible in the atmosphere of our village. That frustrated her the most and time and again she lost her cool on me. She had no one to vent her frustration on.

The situation in the village was precarious and was fraught with risk of a full-fledged caste war. It was getting worse due to the outrageous behaviour of the Brahmin youths with the ladies and girls of the lower caste. Frustration amongst the lower caste youth of the village was rising. Parmeshra took the lead and accosted Babu, as he knew that even Kusmi had to go through this so-called, *Chamchori* many times. The situation was gradually turning against the upper caste and the lower castes were uniting to take action against the upper caste youth venturing into *Chamchori*.

One of the young girls was forced to have sex with a group of upper caste boys in front of her mother. The lower caste had an acrimonious meeting with Babu wherein they objected to it and reported against the incident. Babu assured them that he would take up the matter in the next meeting. The mother of the girl was not satisfied with his answer and cursed him on his face, in front of many of the elders of the village. One of the elders lost his temper and abused her and justified the act of the upper caste boys.' '*Ae randy!* You too had slept with me several times, *tera kutch ghata? Nahi na!* Then why are you making so much of fuss?' he replied gutturally. They could sense the tacit support to the upper caste and decided to exhibit their strength. This enraged the feeling and hurt the sentiments of the lower class. The girl's mother was also told how they had sex with her when she was young and in her prime. They even pointed out that her children were actually the product of the upper caste and they had rights on them. Her sentiments were deeply hurt. She winced and went back wailing to her *Tola*. Her cry touched the heart of many of the upper castes and some of them openly supported and condemned the act by the upper caste boys. It was a very difficult situation for all.

Parmeshra took the lead as he hated Babu from the core of his heart. He called for a meeting of all the lower caste elders and decided to react to this, but he could not augment the full support of the people and things didn't materialise. Babu had come to know that Parmeshra had taken the lead and tried to instigate the other lower caste families to react to the occasion. His effort certainly emboldened them and they perhaps paid a little heed to it. Earlier, such issues were not given importance and they quietly tolerated the excesses.

Parmeshra was called by Babu and warned, 'You restrain yourself from such acts otherwise we would be forced to throw your family out of the village.' He was shaken. Though he stayed on our land but he knew the cunning ways of Babu. He discussed the matter with Mama. She too advised him not to indulge in such things unnecessarily that might escalate into big problems in the village and may even cost someone's life. Parmeshra was very excited but she pacified him and asked him to concentrate on the coming crops with Yusuf.

My puppy had not been seen for a few days, Mama requested Parmeshra to look for her. Later, we discovered that she was busy loafing around with her friends. Most of the time she was not visible and only arrived in the evenings. We had not been able to feed her on time and she moved out to look for food and had got used to loitering like other street dogs. Mama ensured that she was given food. In time she had become part of the family and Mama always fed her before having her food. She was no more an untouchable for us. Mama had removed her from the list of untouchables. In fact, after the death of Ma we had no list of untouchables. That was also a matter of concern by the upper caste of the village, as to why we did not strictly followed the system that prevailed in the Brahmin families in the village.

My puppy was very close to Mama, as she fed her everyday. Whenever Mama moved out of the house, she was sure to accompany her. Mama too liked her behaviour. She was a very docile and obedient bitch. One day, Mama could see that she was growing sideways and informed me that she would bring many puppies in the house. I was damn thrilled. Mama was worried as she might soil the place and that many dogs would be in and around our house. She requested Parmeshra to make a small house for her near the cowshed so that she could manage to deliver at a secluded place without much of hassle.

I resumed my school with a couple of other children and Mama continued her effort for my school admission at any of the nearby towns. Mama even tried for my school admission through Naresh, who was teaching at one of the schools at the city. He avoided the problems stating, 'Right now let him continue, as at the lower level it doesn't matter much, after seventh standard he could be shifted to a city school.' Mama was not able to do anything. She had explored all the possibilities and achieved nothing. She had given up. She tried to guide and motivate me to work to the best of my capabilities at school.

The teacher at the school, hardly taught anything and mostly deputed the lower caste children to do their personal work while the upper caste children played most of the time, after prayer. There were very few teachers who had to look after all the classes. It was not possible for them to look after all the classes and they ensured that the students remained busy in something or the other. At the school, many of the lower caste children didn't like the attitude of the upper caste children towards them and even abused them at times. Muslims were the worst affected. The other children teased and addressed them as *Katuwa*. I was not able to understand but I too addressed those children as *Katuwa* without knowing the consequences of it. One day, I even asked my mother the meaning of the *Katuwa* children that studied at our school. She herself was not aware of it and advised me to not to tease any children and concentrate on studies. Even the lower caste children called the Muslim boys as *Katuwa*. One of the boys complained about it to the Urdu teacher and it was brought to the notice of the headmaster. Some of the boys were severely punished. I could make out that mother was right, it must be a very dirty word. That's why those boys were punished. I decided not to repeat those words ever. One of the Muslim boys liked me and even offered me monkey nuts everyday. He had become my good friend. He too attended the school from one of the neighbouring villages like me and travelled by bike. At times he gave me a lift till one of the irrigation canals, though it was not in the route to his village.

One day, while coming back from school, I found many children running towards one of the bullock-cart tracks that led across the river. I too joined them instead of going home. There was a 'badly stuck' jeep in the river sand. Its base had almost touched the sand of the river. They tried their best to pull it out but the more they tried the deeper it went into the sand. Almost every child from our village and many from other villages had arrived to see the fun. I, at an early stage of life had stayed at a small city and at least seen motor cars and buses, but it was like a lifetime experience for the children of the village. I too hadn't seen a jeep or any other motor vehicle, for the last four to five years or right from the day I had come to the village. Many of the elders too, had arrived to watch the fun. They tried their best to drag it out of the sand but could not succeed. At last, they brought a couple of oxen and tied them to it with a rope. While pulling, the vehicle lurched and tilted in another direction. They gave up the idea for the day, as it was getting dark and they took shelter in the Sarpanch's house for the night.

The mission of its arrival was the canvassing for forthcoming elections. I was not able to understand what was an election. But I was sure of one thing, that it was the time when they paid two rupees to each member to vote for the specific person. Everyone was excited to get two rupees each and some of the families even managed to get ten rupees during each election.

I reached home. It was dark and Mama was not there. She had left to look for me leaving Kusmi and Ramvilas at the house. He was a big boy and now could run with me. After half an hour or so, Mama returned fuming. She lost her temper and scolded me for being late. I informed her that I had been watching the stuck jeep in the sand of the river. She was very sad and said, 'Son, have not you seen a jeep in the city?'

I replied, 'Mama, I don't remember.'

She hugged me in her arms. She could make out that it was something new for the village children. I informed her that it had come for election purpose. I also asked her whose jeep it could be? She answered, 'Government!'

'What and who is this Government?' I could not understand what was this Government. She tried her best to explain to me about the government but I failed to understand. I kept thinking that whoever this Government must be, one thing was clear. It must be very rich. The aircraft that flew over the village was of the Government, the trains, buses – you name a thing, it was of the Government. I had heard many elders, at times talk openly and criticise the Government for laying the air route over the village and not being able to make a motorable road to the village. I had in my mind that this Government was a very rich person and must be enjoying his life.

The only time we could see some motor vehicles in the village, was at the time of elections or any social problems like a fight between Hindu-Muslims or upper caste versus lower caste. The last time, as Ma had informed us, many people were killed during the fight between Hindus and Muslims. The fight was over the crop of the Muslims that was eaten by the buffaloes of the Hindu lower caste, mainly the Yadavs. Many of them were injured and had suffered loss of limbs. That was the last time villagers had seen a motor vehicle of the cops that arrived in the village. Even the elders of the village had rushed to see a motor vehicle arriving in the village.

During the elections, a voting booth used to be established at the village school and the votes used to be cast by a few upper caste youths on behalf of the lower caste. The lower castes were not allowed to come anywhere near the voting booth. Some of the lower caste tried to cast their votes but were threatened by the upper caste. The upper caste youth collected the money from the party for the number of votes being cast in the village. But gradually, the scenario had changed and the lower castes were gearing up to cast their votes and fight for their rights. This time was envisaged, as two of the lower caste candidates were also standing for election. Those candidates wished to visit the houses of the lower caste and discuss the political scenario in the country. The upper castes didn't want any lower caste candidates to visit the village, as that might bring an awakening amongst the people of lower caste and it would be difficult to repress and cast their votes in the forthcoming elections. Things hotted up. Parmeshra was excited to discuss their problems with the lower caste candidates contesting the elections.

The lower caste had organised a meeting to support and cast their votes to the lower caste candidates. Tremendous change had taken place over a period of time in the village. Awakening of the lower caste was rapidly, on the rise due to the speeches of the lower caste national level leaders delivered in the public meetings organised in the lower caste-dominated villages. These leaders spoke in a derogatory manner about the upper caste and instigated or enticed the lower caste openly to annihilate the upper caste. They spat venom and injected and embedded it into the mind of the lower caste. They virtually, launched a movement against the upper caste by travelling to all the villages dominated by them. It was no more an easy task for the upper caste to repress the lower caste or keep them under control. They were getting fidgety about it due to the apprehension of revolt against them by the lower caste in all respects.

The basic reasons of awakening amongst the lower caste, was the lack of means of earning their livelihood in the village and the exodus to a larger city like Calcutta. Some of the lower caste did casual work in the cities and were better aware of things than the people staying at the village. Awakening among them was increasing. They played a major role and polarised the lower caste against the upper caste. As the elections were nearing, the tension was increasing in the village. Babu tried to intimidate the lower caste by calling a meeting, but that didn't make much of a change in their attitude. In fact, some of the lower caste had already joined the Naxalites operating in neighbouring states, like West Bengal and had prepared themselves to fight to the finish with the upper caste. For them, it was a battle of survival and there was no looking back.

There was a marriage arranged for the daughter of one of the upper castes in the village. Preparations for the marriage were almost over, people were dancing and enjoying in the courtyard. It was evening time. Suddenly, we heard a bomb blast in the village. Mama and I were damned scared and locked ourselves in the house. But Pratima had two young daughters and didn't want to take any chances. She came to the terrace and crossed over to our place. I, along with Mama, Pratima and her daughters went to the roof, then on to the lintel of the unfinished part at the rear of the house, and from there down to the ground, locking the houses from inside. All of them shivered. So did I. We ran towards the village but none of the houses were open and we didn't know what to do. Everyone had locked their houses and didn't open their doors at all. We were returning to our houses where we met Parmeshra who had come to take us.

He informed, '*Malkin*, don't you worry, as it is a deliberate effort of the lower caste to show their strength to the upper caste.'

They also had specific targets in the village. All of us sat outside the house shivering. We didn't allow Parmeshra to move out of that place till the dacoits left shouting slogans against the upper caste.

It was an eye opener for the upper caste in the village. Some of the youth, targeted the lower caste girls once again and one of the girls openly came forward to claim and speak out the name of the upper caste youth who had fathered the child. She openly informed that she carried the child of Babu's grandson. Though he didn't accept that he had impregnated her, but it was clear from his face and choked feeble voice before the elders. The lower castes were very upset about this and openly threatened to take action against him.

One morning, while Babu was on his way back, after morning rituals from the riverside, he was attacked by the lower caste youth. He was injured severely but somehow survived. He remained in bed for months together before he could become normal.

It was a big blow for the upper caste and they planned to unite themselves and also arrange for illegal firearms for their safety. It was a question of survival and dominance for the upper caste. Elections were over. Though the lower caste had tried their best they couldn't manage much and once again the MLA of the upper caste was elected from our area. But it had done an irreparable damage to the relations between the upper and lower castes and peace and harmony of the society in the village. These problems were not confined only to our village but had spread to almost all the villages. Even the Muslims raised their voice against the Hindus, mainly the upper caste. Since the enemy was common for these communities, the Muslims and the lower caste joined hands to fight the mighty upper castes. This combination of lower caste and Muslims created a formidable opposition for the upper caste.

The lower caste and Muslims mainly survived on the agricultural income out of the land holding of the upper caste. But they had learned to survive by doing minor petty jobs in cities like Calcutta and even Delhi. They had a second income for sustenance and also got financial assistance from the Naxalite groups. They refused to work in the fields of the upper caste. In case some of the upper caste made alternate arrangements to cultivate on their own, it was destroyed by the lower castes just before it was ready for harvesting.

The caste system of a small village had taken a big form and had changed the political scenario, not only of the village or state but also the country. The situation in the village had changed completely. None of the lower caste trusted the upper caste anymore. This division amongst the people on a caste basis had done no good to anyone; it was a no-win situation. Refusal of lower caste to work on the land of upper caste had immensely affected the agricultural production of the village. At the same time, the lower caste had to face great difficulties to earn their livelihood and had to depend on casual work in government projects, like construction of road, culverts or bridges. It was also not possible to get these easily. The lower castes were affected tremendously and lost their day-to-day fixed income. This was the main fixed income that they had from the land of the upper caste. Some of them had not stopped working on to the lands of the upper caste they liked. Parmeshra was one who never stopped working for us. In fact, he had more knowledge of the crops or the lands than Mama or father.

The gap which had developed between the upper and the lower caste was not so easy to be bridged in the village atmosphere. The literacy rate of the villagers amongst the upper caste was very low, what to talk of the lower caste. Even Yusuf was scared to bring his wife and children to our house as he had apprehensions about the villagers, mainly the upper castes.

Mama made it very clear to him and said, 'It is our responsibility to ensure that no harm is done to you or your family members. I will brief Parmeshra to ensure your safety. It would totally be our responsibility.'

It was easy to say but very difficult to do. Yusuf had developed a fear in his mind and didn't like to venture out and risk the lives of his family members.

The social structure of the village was totally destroyed. The respect earned by the forefathers of the upper castes with their good deeds, was waning and withering away due to the atrocities of the upper caste Brahmins and others over the lower castes. The cultural programmes organised after the main festival of the Hindus, were a risky affair and no one wished to participate due to the risk and fear of mob attack. Every year, the cultural programmes were organised and people of all caste and creed participated wholeheartedly and enjoyed themselves. Even the Muslims participated and contributed by singing some *Ghazals* or *Quawallies*. That was the only entertainment the people of the village had. Many moderate people from various strata and caste, tried their best to smoothen the situation in the village but it had reached beyond redemption. I remember, Ma used to be the biggest contributor for the cultural functions and the Dushera Puja celebrations, but that was a thing of past. Both the castes in the village were out to harm each other and planned strategies to bring down the other instead of negotiating with one another and solving the problems amicably. It had reached a stalemate. There were no hopes of getting it resolved through negotiations.

Things had gone to a level that the lower caste were looking for an opportunity to misbehave or even have sex with the upper caste ladies or girls. Though they knew it was not so easy, but the intentions were manifest and abundantly clear and they openly talked of producing Dusadhs or Chamars in upper caste families. This was the repercussion of the talks of the upper caste elders and sharing of information, with one another that how many lower caste females they had laid and how many children they had fathered from the lower caste females. This had become a status symbol for the upper caste and they openly boasted of having had sex with the lower caste females. The older lot were the real culprits, who had not only fathered many children of the lower caste females, but also took this as their rights and exploited it to the extremes. The young generation had to suffer for the wrongdoings of their forefathers. They had fathered many of our cousins from the lower caste women. The young generation of the lower caste had the same bloodline as ours and rightly, they raised their voice for their rights. They had the same intelligence level as any other upper caste children, as they were fathered by the same people as we were. And once they asked for their rights we felt strongly about it.

The young generation amongst the lower caste, were a formidable challenge to the upper caste as they had exposure of the cities and developed analytical skills. One of the foremost things, was the angst and hatred that they carried from childhood for the upper caste people. They had not been able to forget the atrocities forged on their parents by the upper castes, right before their eyes. Since I had not been able to forget the atrocities the lower caste had to go through in the village, obviously they wouldn't have forgotten either. The memories of their childhood wounds, given by the upper caste, remained fresh in their mind as ever. They had the commitment to root out this old system and diminish the dominance of the upper caste gradually and eliminate it completely. There was no going back for them. It was now or never. They didn't want to leave things half-way. The punishment for the complete revolt or showing displeasure to the upper caste was the same. They were also precisely aware that they would be able to survive without the support of upper caste, but the upper caste would not survive without their help. They were the hands of the upper caste. Over a period of time, the upper castes had cut their own hands that worked for them. The upper caste had completely ruined the hands that worked and fed them. Since it was created by ourselves, then why crib? It was a very volatile and precarious situation in the village.

Gradually, the lower castes moved out of the lands of the upper caste and made their hamlets on the government lands or the village tracks marked for the development of the roads or the government land reserved for grazing. The basic fears that the older generation of the lower caste had, was that the land on which they were residing and made their houses on would be taken away. Most of the houses of the lower castes were made on to the lands of the upper castes. That was the fear that had always haunted the elders of the lower castes. The younger lot had eliminated the basic fear from the minds of their elders, so that they could gather their support as well.

Parmeshra even asked Mama if she wished him to vacate the land given to his forefathers by our ancestors. Mama was very upset on hearing this and asked him to prepare the papers to transfer that part of the land to him. He got the message and apologised to Mama. He also was in tears and promised her not to repeat his actions ever. Ramvilas was a big boy and could understand most things. He, at times, moved to the field with Parmeshra and was getting attuned to the culture of our house. He too had strong feelings and hatred for the upper caste and at times he too spoke against Babu openly. The hatred for the upper caste had percolated down to the lowest level amongst the lower caste. They had more feelings than the elder lot and didn't have an iota of respect for the upper caste.

Our relation with our neighbours had improved. At times the retired teacher called me for tuitions. That gave tremendous amount of satisfaction to Mama and she forgot the past totally. Whenever she cooked something new, she ensured that she gave some to Pratima for her children. At times even her daughters came to our house and played with me. I had a lot of toys given by Ma from the village fair and I also had a bitch, my puppy that was about to bring many other puppies. They liked my bitch and played with her. Whenever we played with the puppy, she lay on the ground putting her legs up in the air.

Many times I could locate the ticks on her face, neck or the ears. I picked them out with my fingers and didn't get scared in front of the girls. Both the girls used to scream with fear to see me removing the ticks that looked like bubble gum. They had named the big grey ticks, stuck on the body of my puppy, with a lot of blood inside, as bubble gum ticks. The older girl liked me and loved to play with my puppy and me.

Gradually, I had taught them the game of *Dekha-Dekhi* and both the sisters also enjoyed playing that game with me in the afternoons. They liked the game more than I did.

One afternoon, when they arrived, the younger one and I played the game whereas the older one didn't wish to play. We tried our best to know the reasons and convinced her to play with us, but she didn't agree. All she said was, 'I can't play this game for four days. This would be applicable every month and during those days I wouldn't be able to join you for this game,' she lamented. Both of us were foxed to know this new thing but couldn't understand the mystery of those four days. We played this game and even the older one joined in other than the four days in a month. We generally played this game either in my house or at their house. I didn't want to go to the school, as I loved playing the afternoon games with them rather than go to school for nothing. They too used to be restless and took the lead in the game. I had grown bigger and felt something different whenever I played the game with the girls. At times my *Phu* even got erect. They admired and touched my *Phu* at times.

One day, I discovered that the older girl had developed hair near her *Phu*. Both of us asked her about it. She said, 'Everyone has hair near their *Phu*.'

'I don't,' I said.

She replied, 'Even you will have once you grow a little bigger.'

Many times I looked at my *Phu*, to see if I had any hair but there were none. It means I had not yet grown enough.

Whenever Mama removed my shorts thereafter, I used to be nervous. That had never happened to me before. Many times I refused to have a bath in front of my mother. One day, Mama removed my shorts before giving me a bath and could see my *Phu* erect. I cried and put on my shorts with anger. I felt shy of removing my shorts in front of so many ladies and girls at the village well. Mama knew I was growing up. I tried my best to avoid taking a bath with her near the village well, but I had no choice. Everyday, she dragged me to the well with her. Young girls looked at my *Phu* and I felt shy of removing my shorts. Even I could see the *Pupu* of many girls bathing. I could not openly tell my mother that I was growing and had a different feeling whenever I saw young girls removing their clothes and taking a nude bath. Many other boys also took their bath with me. Did they feel the same? I wished to know. Some of them were elder to me. At times, I could see their *Phu* also erect while their elder sister or mother bathed them.

It was time for me to study in the seventh standard as I had passed the sixth standard. None of the upper caste children failed in the school. If at all they failed, it was easily managed by their parents to pass them and promote them to the next standard. I was in seventh in the same school.

Pratima's husband was about to come back from UK. She gave this good news to Mama. 'I have had enough of this village life,' she said.

Mama was happy to note that they would be able to put their children in the convent school once again, whereas her child would remain in the village school. That worried her the most. After a few weeks, Pratima took the girls to the city. I was very sad, I didn't feel like staying in the village. I had lost my friends whom I liked the most and had come very close to them. I felt like running away from the village and reach any of the cities and study in a good school. The girls' father was a doctor and had a lot of money. Pratima had informed her that they would purchase a car, once her husband arrived back from London. I could not have imagined anything like that. I felt very small in front of them. I refused to attend to the school at the village and cried everyday and requested Mama to send me to a school at the city.

I too wished to put on a school uniform as both sisters had shown me their school uniforms. They had a tie and belt as well. That gave a very impressive look. They spoke in English with their mother. They had school shoes, black leather and white ones in canvas, besides the shoes that they wore in the house or while they moved out of the house at the village. They had radios in their house. They could listen to All India Radio, Vivid Bharati, Binaca *Geet Mala*, Radio Ceylon, BBC. Every morning, we could hear the signature tune of All India Radio. At times, we also heard

Bhule Bisre Geet from the Sri Lanka Broadcasting. The girls talked of movies actresses and actors, comedians, villains et al., whereas I knew nothing of that sort and could only visualise about the puppet shows, village fairs, and snake and monkey charmers, dramas and, of course, the *Nautanki* that elders talked about quite often in the village. They had torches and searchlights in their house. They could see the monitor lizards and the snakes before they entered their house. We always moved out with the lantern in our hands. Many times Mama had narrowly missed stepping over a snake. Once she had put her foot onto a cobra but just managed to move her feet before it could bite her. I had promised her to get many of the torches and searchlights once I became a Colonel in the Army.

I had become violent. Seemingly oblivious to my chats with the girls, Mama was talking in a trembling voice. She had failed to understand the reasons for such thoughts. I plonked all my books down on the floor and refused to attend to such a filthy school at the village where children didn't even put on slippers. Very few of the teachers wore slippers or sandals made of plastics, stitched and repaired many times at several places. I used a sack to protect myself from rain, while coming back from school, whereas they used imported tiny umbrellas. We sat on the floor at our schools. We also had to carry our own sacks. They had the sleek school boxes made of steel or aluminium with a locking device to carry their books, whereas I used a bag made of old trousers of my father, stitched by Mama or by a tailor at the village market. They carried water bottles to the schools whereas we drank water from any of the ditches on the way to the school. I was bewildered to know that they carried water to school. What kind of place was that, which didn't even have water for the children and they had to carry it from their home! We were at least well off on this count. We had plenty of water all around. In fact, in the rainy seasons, the Ganges arrived right at our doorsteps. They had buttons and zippers on their frocks or slacks, whereas we had rope made of the same clothes that of the shorts made by the tailors. We used soot or twigs to brush our teeth, whereas they used Binaca toothpaste with toothbrush.

Many times, both the girls made fun of me while I hitched my knickers up time and again. At times my *Phu* was visible, as these shorts never had any buttons. We had no knowledge of putting on undies. The very first time I had seen those two girls wearing colourful panties, I too wished to put on readymade clothes and school dress and go to a school at the city. I prattled on about my studies, school and my future. 'Don't you want to make me a military officer?' I asked Mama. The girls informed me that to become a military officer, one had to go to a *sainik* or a military school. What were these schools? I could only imagine. Even Mama was probably not aware of it. Mother tried her best to convince me but I didn't budge. She offered to give me fried grams and sugar everyday for the tiffin for school but I rejected the offer.

I moved out of the house and spent the whole day with my pregnant puppy, in the mango groves talking to her. She was my best friend. She understood my feelings from the core of her heart. She licked my cheeks and put her paws into my hands, to give her consent, whenever I asked her any question. I knew I would miss them both very much, if at all Mama sent me to any of the schools at the city.

We had many schools coming up in the nearby tribal-dominated villages with boarding facilities, but those schools were meant only for the tribal Christians or anyone who adopted Christianity. That was not acceptable to the Brahmins and even the lower caste of the villages.

There was only one Santhal family in the village. His name was Sofla, and he too had left and migrated to a tribal-dominated village, where missionaries had opened a boarding school and a hospital. As long as they stayed in the village, his wife visited our house to hand over the beat rice and collected, double the quantity of paddy. Her husband gathered snakeskins and sold them to concerned people operating in the cities. He was an expert in skinning off the rat snakes and other amphibian snakes available near the ponds. He was experienced at locating the holes, where snakes could be available and after digging its hole, caught it alive at the throat, pressed its tail under his feet and skinned it off from the only hole that it has at the rear of the body. He threw the live body after skinning it off. The snakes died a terrible death as they were skinned off live. They crumbled and died a pathetic death after several minutes.

It was nothing new for the children who had been seeing him right from their birth, but it was a great experience for any child or elder who had a chance to see the whole process for the first time. Once, both the daughters of Pratima had seen the whole process of skinning of snakes along with me. They were shaken on seeing the process. It was not as easy as it looked. Sofla took precisely three to four minutes to skin off a snake after he discovered its hole. It involved great risk and at times the snakes, generally found near the ponds or the bank of river, bit him. He used to roll the skins very tidily on to the wooden *patti* that he carried with him. Sofla's family was the only tribal family in the village. These tribal communities ate almost every moving creature other than perhaps vultures or crows. One couldn't find a squirrel or any other reptile in tribal-dominated areas.

The tribal ladies at the village had a typical posture of urinating, as they never sat to do so. They always lifted their garment at the lower part, quite similar to a lungi and urinated standing like a man. It was something new for Pratima's daughters and me. Once I had moved near to a tribal girl while she was on the job and laughed loudly, finding it very funny. I also advised her to sit and urinate. She felt very embarrassed and complained to Mama, along with other tribal ladies. Even Mama couldn't control her laughter. Mama made me understand and said, 'That is the system that has prevailed amongst the Santhal (a tribe) girls and the ladies at the village. It is not funny, and you must refrain from such a thing.' She added angrily, 'What is your problem?'

I nagged Mama frequently about my admission in city schools. I had no interest in studies, and I didn't wish to continue at the village school. Most of the time I spent whiling away with the village children outside the house. Mama was very worried and lost her temper. I too reacted at times.

One day, Mama promised me and said, 'I will send you to the town school after you pass your seventh standard and move on to the eighth.' I was very pleased and resumed my school at the village, seemingly oblivious of the predicament that I had to encounter if at all I was to move to a city school. I informed all my friends and behaved differently, as I was one of the candidates who would be going to study outside the village. I felt myself to be very different from the other children. I controlled my tongue and chose words cautiously and avoided abusive language that I had learned from the village boys. My mind worked overtime and remained engaged in visualising *sainik* and military schools. I dreamed of my uniform. Many days passed dreaming about the better things in life.

In the afternoons, Mama told me the stories of the Gorkha soldiers that had camped in her village for a few weeks, when she was a child. They had camped to reorganise themselves before moving to Burma along with the tribal soldiers. Even today, I vividly remember many of the stories told to me by her, about the sacrifices of the soldiers and the officers of Indian soil during the British days and subsequent wars with Pakistan and China. I too dreamt of being a part of those stories that people fondly remembered and passed down generation to generation.

I had not been able to forget the times I had spent with Pratima's daughters. I had learned many good things from them. Once they touched Mama's tummy where she tied her sari knot and asked her, 'What are these scars you have on your tummy?' Mother replied, 'A monkey had scratched my tummy.' Pratima spurted into laughter. It was nice meeting and playing with them. I hadn't forgotten the games that we played with the stones with the girls and boys of the village and picked up the game of skipping. They had given me ideas of the outside world that existed beyond the boundaries of the dirty petty politics of caste, religion and properties at the village. I wanted to do something better and different like both the girls. I wished to talk, dress, and study differently. I waited very anxiously for my seventh standard to finish and move out to the city. Mama was sick and tired of my excitement of moving out to the city and of the questions I asked her everyday relating to my admission at the schools in the town and the school dress. Mama was very worried. She had thought I would not take this seriously and she would manage by telling me a cock-and-bull story. But, by now, she could make out I was serious about it and was not going to forget Mama's promise to me.

Chapter V

FATHER

One day, the headmaster of our school was passing through the road that led to the neighbouring village. Mama requested him to have a cup of tea and guide her about the schools at the nearby town, where I could be admitted after I passed out of the seventh standard. He gave concrete information about one of the schools at the nearby small town. She was happy but didn't know how to plan for the cash that she would need every month. My term in the class was coming to an end. I was passed by the headmaster, as my behaviour at the school was comparatively better than any other boy of the school, though I was very poor at studies and the standard of the school was much below the required level.

Mama contacted a teacher of the village, who taught in one of the primary schools at the same town where she had planned to get me admitted. He had recently joined the school as a primary teacher and hardly had any experience of teaching. Even he was not really aware of the admission procedures and the documents required for admission. He didn't do his homework at all and asked Mama to send me with him to the city in the coming month. I was damn thrilled as I dreamt of the trains, buses, cars, a different lifestyle and readymade clothes, and a school dress.

On the other hand, I was getting worried about my puppy and her puppies, which she was about to give birth to. I had never slept alone. When we arrived at the village, I shared my bed with Ma and after Ma's death, I had no choice and had to sleep with Mama. I was ambivalent and had many apprehensions and fear in my mind but decided to fight against all odds and do everything to fulfil Mama's dream. I had seen Mama suffer at the hands of father and Ma as well. She could never enjoy life. Her life was like that of Sita of the Ramayana, whereby half the life she spent in a jungle and the other half without a husband. It was a similar case with Mama. I didn't want to add to her misery and suffering. I had decided to compromise on all the problems and suffering to do something in life.

It was time to move to the town with the teacher. Mama didn't sleep the whole night, neither did I. We were fully aware of each other's feelings but didn't wish to share them fearing that it might make us weak. Mama put all my clothes in a bag, made of father's old thick trousers, recently and exclusively made for me and asked Parmeshra to carry the rice, pulses, grams, beat rice till the bus stand, from where I could board the bus for the town. I walked with Mama. She came to see me off till the irrigation canal, on the outskirts of the village. It was the first time I was moving away from her. I could see the tears flowing out of the corners of her eyes. She didn't want me to know. She, in any case, had covered her face with the sari. None of the Brahmin ladies were allowed to walk in the village without covering their faces. Mama took advantage of that and kept weeping throughout her journey till the canal. The canal was full of water and Parmeshra helped me in crossing it. Mama kept standing on the other side of the canal till I was visible. I too cried. My heart sank. I kept looking back and waving my hand at her. I knew how miserable she must be feeling without her only child. Everything else at home was meaningless for her. My puppy tried her best to cross the canal and follow me, but Parmeshra ensured that she didn't. I had briefed Mama to take care of my puppy and the puppies that she would bring. She had promised me to look after her. Mama had given me ten rupees for expenses and had promised to send another twenty next month. The teacher was perhaps given the money for the admission, books and notebooks.

I was walking eagerly with Parmeshra, following him like a baby lamb, thinking of my mother. I didn't know how my legs moved forward. Mama had given me her slippers brought for her by father two years back. They were a little big for me and I could not keep pace with the teacher and Parmeshra. I removed them and put them in my cloth bag and moved on. Though the town was not very far from the village, but the vehicle followed a longer route and took three hours to cover the *kuchha* dusty road of forty kilometres. One could easily cover the distance on foot or on a mule or horse in five hours. Anyone who died was taken to that town, as it was located on the bank of River Ganges. Even Ma was cremated on the bank of the Ganges at the outskirt of that town. We reached the bus stop; Parmeshra was tired as he had carried rice and other food items weighing not less than forty kilos. The bus had developed some snag and was being repaired. In the meantime, the teacher planned to have something to eat. He brought some vegetable made of gram with chilli powder and mixed it with the beat rice given to us by Mama. I didn't enjoy eating and kept looking at the bundle of cloth, that Mama had neatly packed last night with all the eatables. She had used Ma's old sari. I was missing everyone at the village, including my puppy. I didn't talk at all, not even to Parmeshra. He could make out that I was depressed.

It was time for him to bid us bye and move back to the village, as Mama must have been waiting for his return to take the feedback on me. He advised, 'Chotu, study properly and do well in life. Your mother has a lot of hopes from you.' He turned to move back. I caught his *dhoti* and cried loudly, I couldn't control my feelings anymore. He hugged me and said, 'It is for your own good. Don't you have to become a *bada* sahib?' He once again requested the teacher to look after me and left.

I kept looking at him till he disappeared from my sight. The teacher took the tickets for both of us. The bus started taking me further away from my mother and my puppy. For the very first time, I had come out of the house all alone. The teacher kept chewing *pan* with tobacco at every stop, wherever the bus stopped for more than ten minutes. I sat near the window and everytime he spat, a few drops of saliva dropped on my thigh, which I wiped it with the corner of the shirt.

We reached the town in the afternoon. We took a rickshaw and moved to a place very near to the Ganges. I was reminded of Ma's funeral. It was on the banks of the same river. The teacher asked the rickshaw to halt. I unloaded all the stuff that we had brought from the village. He showed me a room with tiles on the top and a jute mat on the floor. It had no windows and lights. There were a couple of other children staying in the other rooms. Everyone had to cook his food. That night the teacher and I were offered food by one of the boys. I spread the bedsheet on to the jute mat and slept. It was totally dark. I didn't even have a lantern. I didn't sleep for a long time and kept thinking of Mama. I cried. Things were not as rosy as I had thought them to be. I was tired of crying. My tears had dried, leaving a stain on my cheeks. In the morning, the teacher woke me up to go for the morning rituals to the shore of the Ganges. I found most of the children easing themselves. I could make out it was no better than the village. The basic difference was that we went to a smaller river at the village and here we had a larger river. I was asked by the teacher to get ready so that I could be admitted in the school.

We rushed to the school. The teacher filled the form as directed by the school staff. I was thrilled, as the school looked very impressive. The principal had a nice office with a plastic globe on the table, and the photographs of the former presidents and prime ministers on the walls. I was not in proper clothes as they were all packed in a cloth bag. I couldn't keep my clothes tidy and all of them had crumpled in the bag. It was quite conspicuous in the bright daylight. Though it was washed in the best soap cake available with Mama and was spotless, it was had totally creased. I was nervous to see the principal's office and the staff room. A bell rang and many children rushed to their respective classes. I was advised by the teacher to reply all the questions asked by the principal properly and boldly. I shivered with fear.

A thought came to my mind, that if the principal failed me and admission was denied, I would have to return to the village and Mama would feel very bad about the whole affair. Moreover, she had spent a lot of money for my admission, including our travel expenses.

I was wearing my mother's slippers. They were old and a little big for me and made a funny *chat, chat*... sound while I walked like duck. I was standing in the corner of the office when the principal arrived. The teacher also rose from his chair and wished him. I didn't know how to greet him and touched his feet as I always did to my father or mother. This was the system that prevailed in the village to greet the elders. He sat on his chair and called me near him. As I walked, the slippers made that *chat, chat*... noise. I tried my best to avoid the noise but couldn't help it. He looked at my feet and the teacher. He had a look at all the papers kept on his table along with the forms that were duly filled by the teacher. He could make out that I had come from a village school. He asked a couple of questions that I replied to. He also asked me to name the photographs that he had displayed behind his chair over his head. I could name some of them. The teacher gave me a dirty look. The principal also asked about my father, who worked at Pakur Collectorate. The principal could not understand the logic of sending a child for education at a school where neither of his parents stayed. He could smell a rat. There was something wrong. He called me near him and once again looked at my feet and asked, 'Son, whose slippers are these?'

I replied innocently with some degree of consternation, 'My mother's.'

He got the answer to all his doubts and called his clerk and ordered him to complete the formalities for the admission. I had tears in my eyes that I wiped with the corner of my shirt.

He looked at my face and asked me, 'What do you wish to become?'

I replied, 'A Colonel.'

He laughed loudly. I wondered, what was wrong. Was there something very big that I said? I was confused as to why he laughed at all. He asked the teacher to get my uniforms. I could attend the school without uniforms till they were ready. I could see the teacher's face. His colour changed as he knew Mama wouldn't be able to afford the cost of the uniform immediately. Everything was completed. My dream was going to be true. Our school uniform was not as impressive as that of a convent school; it was khaki knickers and a white shirt with an open collar, black leather shoes with white socks.

We came back to our room. The teacher kept murmuring and cursing Mama, as he was not paid that kind of money that was required to be spent for the uniforms. On the way, we had brought one stove, which was operated by wood sawdust and the wood waste. A real challenge for me! I had never ever cooked anything and neither did I know how to ignite and use the wood sawdust stove. The teacher called two of the boys and ordered them to help me understand and learn the use of the stove and cooking. We hardly had anything to cook. All we had to cook was rice and dal.

I was excited and took out my brand new stove and managed to compress the sawdust till its neck and burn the firewood inside the hole in the centre. I managed to cook my food for the day and realised it was not a simple task as we thought it to be. I had brought a new lantern for my use and opened my book, notebooks, pen, pencils and placed it all on a wooden plank that I collected from one of the boys.

Initially, it was miserable but after a few days, I got used to the atmosphere. I had bought a school uniform as Mama had arranged for the money. I joined school and started my studies but couldn't cope up with the pace of the studies in the class as, firstly, I had joined the school a few months late and secondly, my base was weak. The school at the village had not been able to impart proper education. I could hardly understand mathematics, English and science. I was very worried and shaken on realising this. I spoke to one of the boys, older to me, who was in tenth standard to guide me at times. I knew it was not so easy. I had also brought a beginner's alphabet book and waded into my studies of English from the grassroots. A for apple, B for Ball...

Every month, Mama sent me some rice, dal and twenty rupees either through Parmeshra or the teacher. I was not allowed to go back to the village before the school had vacations. For the first time, I learned to write letters. I wrote to mother and father. This was the first time I had written a letter to father. I was not fully aware of his office address. Whatever little Mama had told me, based on that, I posted a letter to him. I was very happy and waited for the replies of my letters. Every evening, I visited the cottage of the landlady to find out about my letters. Children generally received their money orders or letters here. I was excited that someone should write to me so that I too could boast of my letter. I kept waiting for the letters that never arrived. I forgot about it and decided not to write any letter ever in life. One day, almost after a month, I received a letter from Mama and was thrilled to receive it. I showed it to everyone. This trend continued. I wrote to her every week and received a letter or two every month.

I missed her very much. It was very difficult to cook everyday, as I had to collect sawdust from the sawmill that was far away from our place and also required money for it. Most of the time, instead of cooking rice or *dal*, I used to get sweet potatoes from the nearby vegetable market and ate them for dinner after boiling. It used to be cheaper for me instead of cooking a complete meal. That affected my health very badly and I was not keeping well. Many times I cooked *roti* but had no money to go for vegetables or condiments that was required for the vegetables. I couldn't even buy sugar and, at times, I bought jaggery from the roadside vendor. That was of poor quality and unhygienic as well. Many flies sat and fed on the uncovered jaggery bricks sold on the roadside. I generally had my roti with salt and mustard oil instead of ghee. I had made a friend, Prakash. He was from a Marwari family and was quite rich. At times he wished to visit my place of stay. I always avoided that due to the inferiority complex that had formed over a period of time.

One day, after school broke at half day, Prakash accompanied me to my place of stay. I had not been able to cook anything in the morning and was hungry.. He too wished to have something. I was very shy to show him the *roti* that I had cooked the previous night and kept rolled in a cloth. He could see the bundle and asked me to share it with him. I informed him that it was not for him and said, 'Prakash you wouldn't be able to eat the food we eat.' He insisted. I took out the *roti*, applied mustard oil and salt over it and handed it over to him. I had finished a couple of them before he could have had any. I was very hungry. He could not eat even one and left it. He was very upset to know the kind of food I had everyday. He could make out that I couldn't afford to even eat good food and was living on a shoestring budget. He always sympathised with me and shared his tiffin with me in the break at school. I never carried any tiffins. Most of the time Prakash carried some coins with him and used to enjoy *Gol Gappe* or *Jhal Muri* during the break. At times, he even offered some to me. I had got a good friend. He stood first in the class and put on the best of uniforms. He was very good at studies as well, and had a tuition teacher to teach him regularly at his residence. His shoes were always polished and shone, whereas I could only wash my leather shoes with water and dry it in the sun every Sunday, making it harder and more uncomfortable.

I never had a soft drink in my life. One day, Prakash asked me to accompany him to a hotel where one could get Coca Cola and Fanta. In those days it was available. Perhaps, later on, it was banned by the Indian Government. I was scared to even enter the hotel and was not aware of the cost of the bottles. He offered me to choose any of the brands that I liked. I had chosen an orange coloured one. It looked very attractive. I was very grateful to my friend for offering me the soft drink. I reached my room and informed all the boys staying in the neighbourhood. I also showed them my orange palm and tongue to make them believe that I indeed had a soft drink. Some of them even asked me how it had tasted. I told them in detail about my experience of having a soft drink.

I took Prakash's help as he had a tuition teacher who came to his house to teach him. I used to ask him the problems, which I couldn't understand in the class, and solved them all with his help. He never made fun of me and supported my feelings. I was quite open with him, as I had nothing really to boast or hide from him. He had come to know the truth about me.

It was examination time. I was very scared and didn't know what to do. I hardly knew anything about English and was sure to fail. I had somehow managed to complete mathematics and all the other subjects but I was totally at sea in English. I could barely read or write English. Rightly so, I failed in English in the half-yearly test of the eighth standard. There was no one who could help me out in this. I was very worried and wished to share my problems with my Mama but I didn't, as she would have felt very bad. I spoke to Prakash and requested him to help me out. He handed over a couple of books and lined notebooks to me. I practiced the letters, words and sentences of English. I toiled to improve my writing and ensure that I learned the name of the animals, birds and other things in English. I read everyday and learnt by heart all the words and the problems that we had in our English textbooks for standard eight. I was very nervous as the final exams were approaching. I had not been on leave for a long time and had decided to meet Mama only after the final exams.

Our final examination was held as scheduled and I did fairly well. I knew I would pass in English as well, and had done better in all other subjects. It was time to visit the village. All the other children were geared up to leave for their respective homes. I too arranged all my clothes and got ready to leave for my village. Prakash had gifted me a couple of kites with thread, as I could not afford the thread. I was very thrilled and approached the teacher to take me home with him. It was quite sometime since I had been able to meet Mama. We arrived late in the evening. Mama was very sad to see my condition. I had gone very weak and my skin had tanned. She hugged me and cried for sometime. I had brought one small torch for her so that she could use it in the night. She was very pleased and asked me, 'How did you manage to save a few rupees for the torch?' I avoided the topic, as that would have put her off. She could use it in the night. I was very happy as she had to move around with a lantern in hand. Now she could use the torch and had no problem even during rains and strong winds. She couldn't move with the lantern outside during those times as it used to be put off by strong winds or the glass broke due to sprinkling of rainwater over it.

Mama wanted to feed me for the next one year so that I didn't have to cook and eat during my stay at the town. Her love and affection was unmatched. There was nothing to match the love of any mother for her children and she was something extraordinary. My puppy had given birth to many puppies and some of them were scared of me. They didn't come near me like their mother. She was very happy so see me and spent most of her time with me. She had changed helluva lot. Her udders sagged under her belly, and she looked totally different from before. I could inspect all her puppies. Some of them looked very sickly, skinny and starved. They tugged at the udders of their mother. She moved time and again as she perhaps didn't like it and seemed fed up and irritated by their tugging.

One afternoon, I could see my puppy vomiting near her puppies and rushed to find the reasons. She had spewed raw meat for her puppies. I understood the logic and observed them quietly. All the puppies kept licking her mouth as she vomited the raw meat. Probably, she was unable to feed her puppies out of the food given to her by Mama, and she fed on carcasses to make up for the deficiency of food. I was surprised to see the sacrifice of a mother for her offspring. Even the animals loved their offsprings so much and fought against all odds to bring up their children. God had given animals the ability to feel and care for their offspring. My puppy had been able to manage the food for her babies. I didn't mention this to Mama, otherwise she would have not only thrown my puppy out, but also all her babies far away from the house. I didn't tell anything to Mama and also ensured that she didn't see her feeding meat to the puppies.

It was time to return. My holidays were over. I behaved differently from the other children of the village, and confined myself either to kite flying or other games in the house itself with Mama or other children. I was also gradually becoming aware that the game of *Dekha-Dekhi* was not a good one and was a risky game. Many of the village boys still continued the game, but I kept out of it as I felt shy and a different fear had grown from within. I even had developed soft pubic hair near my P*h*u and felt ashamed to display it in a group, as we did earlier. Mama was more confident and trusted me more than before. I reached town. As usual, Mama had come to see me off with Parmeshra but this time there was no teacher to accompany me. I had mentioned to Mama that I could travel alone and she was quite confident of me.

Prakash informed me that I had passed in all the subjects, including English. I was thrilled and immediately wrote a letter to my mother informing her of my result. Even though father had not replied to my last letter, I wrote to him once again about my results with the proper address. Mama had given me couple of covers inscribed with father's official postal address. I was feeling on top of the world as I was promoted to standard nine. We had to join school and prepare the uniforms, new books and take care of our personal appearance.

I always had a haircut from the barber, who sat under the banyan tree on the crossroad, near our place of stay. We sat on the brick that he had for his customer in front of a small mirror, to see the face after a haircut. He charged us twenty-five paise for a normal haircut, and thirty for the special. This time, I too had a special haircut, and paid him thirty paise. The difference was that after the haircut, he applied and rubbed alum with water and massaged the head for a while and also covered it with another cloth. The regular cloth that he used was perhaps washed once every year. He knew us well as we all had our haircut from him. I finished my special haircut, completed the formalities of looking in the small mirror and left.

Mama had given me sufficient money to get all the books, notebooks, pencils, erasers, etc. I used my shoes very sparingly and only for the schools; rest of the time I remained barefoot to ensure and preserve the life of the shoes for a longer period. I, along with Prakash, brought all the books according to the book list issued by the school and covered them with old newspapers.

Our school started. Mama was very pleased to receive my letter and wished for my bright future. As usual, I never got any reply to my letters from my father. I had discussed with mother about the first letter that I had sent to father. She had ignored the topic and said, 'You must have written the wrong address.' I too thought that it might be true. I discussed with one of the other children, whose father worked at the same town as mine. He testified and said that the address written by me was correct. Moreover, this time I had posted the cover on which Mama wrote the address herself.

One afternoon, we had a lot of time and decided to visit the banks of the Ganges with Prakash. Every morning, we had our 'ease out' there and there were nothing exciting about it. I informed him about Ma's cremation at the crematorium on the bank of the Ganges. He showed me the place that was not very far from our place of stay, but I was not aware of it. One could see the fires of the funeral pyre in the nights burning like a glowworm. I thought that it was the place where we had cremated Ma. Prakash, being a local, was aware of the one and only crematorium famous in our area amongst the Hindus in and around that town. It was known as Barari-Ghat crematorium, Bhagalpur. I, along with Prakash, walked over to that place. I remembered the place where Ma's body was given a bath before cremation and burned. I narrated to him the full story. He was horrified and didn't believe that I had lit the fire to her pyre and carried out all the rituals of Ma's funeral, as father had not been able to make it for the funeral. He was very scared to even stay there but I was not, as I had gone through the rituals of the dead body and lit the fire to Ma's pyre with my own hands.

Thereafter, whenever I had time I went there and spent a few minutes and spoke to Ma in isolation. Many times, I went into deep thoughts of Ma and felt her presence. I hadn't been able to reconcile to the fact that Ma's body was burnt and she would never come back. My heart cried many times for her and called to her with a firm belief that she would return. I deceived myself many times with the illusion that she would come back. Mama and I were isolated in the whole world and we had no one to fall back on or talk to or share our feelings. Even Mama was feeling helpless and cut off from the mainstream. I knew Ma was not there, but I associated with the place as I had last seen Ma there. Now I was confirmed that it was the same crematorium that was visible in the night from our place. One could see the glow of the pyre even late at night, like the glowworms in the banks of the river. At times, I watched the burning pyre till late evenings from our place of stay, sitting on a heap of mud on the banks of the river. I always remembered Ma and regularly visited the place.

Many of the boys were scared of me as I regularly visited the crematorium. They thought that perhaps, I followed the dead bodies of the rich, to pick up the coins that they throw on the way along sugar balls and fried paddy, while carrying the dead. They even thought that I ate the food or sweets or leftovers of the rituals on the crematorium ground. None of them spoke to me and they made a big story out of it. They branded me as a greedy ruffian and discarded me from their group. None of them wished to know about me or care for my broken heart. The hatred and gossip had even reached the school, where many children teased me as an urchin and son of an urchin. Prakash was the only person, who knew of those facts of my life and never bothered about any such talk and continued visiting me in my room. He tried to stop some of the boys not to indulge in teasing and hurt my feelings but it was of no avail. It continued unbridled and increased day by day. That made me totally insular and further isolated. I complained to Ma of my plight and cried several times sitting at the banks of the river. It gave me enormous amount of satisfaction and assuaged the pain of the teasing, tremendously.

Holi was approaching as one could see scarlet flowers and new leaves on every tree around our place of stay. Gulmohar and palash were the most attractive ones of the lot. Palash flowers were dark red all over and none of the leaves could be seen from our rooms or a distance. I had my own place under a palash tree, from where I could see the smoke billowing out from the funeral pyre that was burnt on the banks of the river, in the afternoons or mornings. Very few humans in life had the chance to become fire and smoke at the bank of the Ganges. That gave salvation from the rotation of taking rebirth eighty-five thousand times in the form of different creatures other than human. A human birth is only given to a soul once he goes through the ordeal of total circle of eighty-five thousand births.

My palash tree had beautiful scarlet flowers and was very thick. It obstructed my view of the crematorium ground. It was the sign of happiness and prosperity. How could it allow one to see the sorrowful sight of a crematorium? I chose a date tree that had no affect of spring and stood firm, without many leaves. Moreover, every morning the *Pashi* came to draw out the *Nira* juice from its top and remove its skin to extract the maximum flow of *Nira*. There was no happiness in its life, as all the food that it produced was drawn out by the *Pashi*. Every morning many crows and wasps fed them the earthen pot hanging on the date tree, before the *Pashi* off-loaded the collection of the previous night. Its life was no better than mine, and we shared each other's pain and agony without talking about it. Whenever I touched it, I felt the pain that it was going through. It did say many things but I was not in a position to help and it quietly suffered, while I watched it suffer silently.

I always sat under the date tree and looked in the direction of the place that provided the entire human kind with salvation. All the children were busy defoliating the trees and collecting the reddish scarlet flowers of gulmohar and Palash, to dry, grind and make colour out of it that would be used in the festival of colour, Holi. I felt it was a sheer waste of effort and destruction of trees to defoliate them of the beautiful flowers. The children broke the branches and twigs of the trees and carried them to their rooms. Most of the trees were broken and their beauty was totally destroyed by the residents of those areas. Children were also excited to collect the colour and purchase the pumps made of brass and other metals, according to their capacity to afford. Some of them purchased the plastic bottles with nipples, used for spraying colour over near and dear ones. I too had, bought one bottle with a nice plastic cap with a 'crow beak' nozzle. Everyone was in the Holi mood. Our school was about to be closed for a few days on the eve of Holi. I had planned to spend Holi at Prakash's house, as both of us knew it was difficult to enjoy the colour or Holi at the place where I stayed, for I was shunned by most of the boys. They had taken me to be one of the lower caste, who fed themselves on the leftovers of the crematorium rituals.

It was our last day of school before Holi. Most of the boys spoiled each other's shirt by sprinkling ink from their inkpen and some of them also used colour in their inkpens. All was set to shift in the evening itself to Prakash's house. I was in the Sanskrit class when the principal arrived at our class. The teacher from my village accompanied him. He had helped Mama and me in my admission. I could make out he had come for me. The principal spoke something to the class teacher and the class teacher asked me to leave with them. I came out with the teacher from my village. 'Your mother has arrived to meet you.' He said. I was exulted and jumped with joy. First of all Holi, and secondly, Mama would be with me. I thanked God for his generosity. It was a great day for me. I planned many things on the way as I never liked that teacher and was not very close to him. I kept planning the things that I would do with her. I had decided to take her to Prakash's house and show her that I had a good friend who always helped me for everything. I was about to reach my room and ran forward to meet my mother to show her my uniform, washed by the expensive soap and the toothbrush that I had recently brought with the help of Prakash and the monkey brand tooth powder, the best quality available in our town.

I was surprised to see not only Mama but also many other people of the village. Mama was in white sari. She had no vermilion on her head. Her eyes were swollen. Her lips were dry and her face had a sickly pallor. She looked at me despondently. What was this? Why had Mama put on the clothes of Ma? I couldn't understand the things happening out there. I reached Mama and caught her hands. Her eyes were wet and teardrops streamed over her cheeks. She embraced me in her arms and said, 'Your father is dead.'

He was still so young. How could he die? I didn't believe it. I had not seen him for almost two years and vaguely remembered his face, while he was thrashing Mama in the night while I hid behind her sari. That night was the last I had seen him when he had come to arrange for Ma's death anniversary.

Mama was a shattered woman though she had hardly lived the life of a married woman. I was not fully aware of the facts of their life before my birth but I had been watching their relationship very closely for the last few years. I was fully deprived of the love of my father. Though Mama had narrated it to me several times, that every morning if father left for the office before I was awake, I cried for him for hours together. I slept with him and touched and checked his presence time and again on the bed in the nights. Whenever someone knocked at the door, I yelled, 'Pa', as I called my father. If mother delayed opening the door, I reached near the door and cried for it to open fast. I loved him but he had moved far away from us. He visited us once a year or at times only at the time of a crisis, sorted it out and left. Gradually, his arrival was synonymous to our suffering. Whenever he visited us, he whacked mother, thrashed me and spent his time like a guest and left. He was not bothered about the agricultural income that came from our land. He could earn a little extra money besides his salary, as he was in a government office like Paromita. She too earned and they had a comfortable life. Father hardly sent money to Mama.

I refused to accept that a young person could also die. I had seen people dying but most of them were the older lot. How come a young person like my father died! He was burly, strong and could lift me on to his shoulder with one hand. He could hit Mama so badly; she could never escape his anger. I refused to believe and said, 'Mama, don't you worry, he hasn't and can't die. They all are lying. He is at Pakur, I have written to him, he will come to see my result.'

Mama cried loudly and embraced me. I was utterly confused and couldn't understand how could father die. He was not seen. I tried my best to pacify her but she wasn't convinced. I could make out something was wrong, else Mama wouldn't put on the clothes that Ma used to wear. I was more worried for Mama's dress code than the death of father. Some people looked at me suspiciously. I didn't know what they had in their mind. The pundit called me and asked me to show my teeth to him. I opened my mouth and showed my teeth. He nodded his head in conformity. I couldn't understand what these elders were up to. One of the elders asked me to keep quiet and not to cry as I was the reason for my father's death. I was shocked. How could I kill my father! The pundit had confirmed that I had an extra tooth in the mouth that was the representation of being an unfortunate child for his father and mother, but especially the father. Mama was not aware what they were up to.

I cried, 'I have not killed my father.' I walked up to her and wailed loudly, 'Mama, I haven't killed Pa. They say I have an extra tooth in my mouth and that has killed father.'

Mama was furious with the pundit and asked him to leave forthwith and also requested two of the villagers not to touch the dead body of father. When she talked of the dead body, I ran to find it inside my room and the teacher's room. It was not seen anywhere. Where was it? I asked Mama to show me father's dead body. She herself was perplexed and broken. She had no strength to talk or cry anymore. Her eyes were not coping with the outflow of tears.

In the meantime, many people arrived whom we had never seen before. I wasn't sure of their identity as they were not from our village and even spoke our language, a little differently, in a Bengali accent. They were the family members of Paromita. Mama was not aware of this, as she had neither seen Paromita, nor her children or anyone of her family members. They informed us that the dead body had just arrived and was kept under the banyan tree on the crossroad. I could make out it was the same place where we got our haircut every month. It was the junction from where one of the roads led to the Barari-Ghat crematorium.

I left Mama and ran towards the banyan tree. It was not very far from my room. On arrival, I found one of the trucks parked under the tree. There were a few people gathered around the vehicle. I tried to peep into the truck but couldn't see anything. I was crying profusely. I tried to climb over the rear opening of the lorry but couldn't as it was too high for me. The height of the lorry was too high for me and I was unable to scale it. One of the persons standing near the lorry was observing me carefully. He asked me the reason for crying and my relation with the dead body. He didn't know about me. I said, 'I want to see the dead body of my father to ascertain whether he is really dead or alive.' He was touched to hear me. He stopped me from seeing the body and advised me to return to my room. I wailed loudly and came back to my room. 'Mama, the body is lying in a lorry under the banyan tree on the crossroad,' I said. Mama called one of the villagers and Parmeshra and asked them to take care of me as I was going out of my mind. Along with Parmeshra, I reached the lorry and went up to have a look at the body. It was properly tied with a rope. Parmeshra was in two minds and couldn't decide whether to uncover the face of the body or not. He advised me to wait till Babu and all the other elders from the village arrived. I was restless and wished to have a look at his face. It was a long time since I had been able to meet him or see him. The day he had left us last, I was fast asleep and even otherwise, I had been too scared to meet him as he had fought with Mama over Paromita.

It was afternoon and as usual, rituals for the cremation of the Hindus were to start before sunset. Everyone arrived at the cross-junction. The driver of the lorry was getting impatient and time and again was trying to find out from Parmeshra about the time of cremation and balance of money that was due to him. Mama came to the crossroad. The body was unloaded from the truck and kept on one side of the road. All the passers by had a look at the fun that was going on under the banyan tree. Even the barber who gave us a haircut recognised me and asked Parmeshra about the relation that I had with the dead person. He too sympathised with me and prayed to God to give us strength to survive without anyone's hand on our head.

Mama had stopped crying and she was worried for the money that was needed for the cremation and the related expenses. She called Parmeshra and asked, 'How much money is left with you?'

He whispered, 'Not enough to take care of all the expenses relating to cremation and other formalities.'

Mama was relieved to see Naresh, her brother, and briefed him to take care of the expenses on a returnable basis or in lieu of which she could pledge a few acres of land to him, once the rituals were over. He assured her not to bother and took the lead. I was given a bath at the nearby hand pump and was made to put on the same outfit that I had put on the very first time while on the way to cremate Ma. It was the second time I was undergoing these rituals and was generally aware of things. The first time I had not been worried, as I was not mature enough to understand the repercussions and the after-effect of death. Moreover, Ma was an elderly lady and I had in my mind that all the elders had to die sooner or later. But I was not aware that even a young person of father's age could also die.

I still had in my mind that there had some error in identifying the person and father couldn't be dead. God couldn't be so cruel to us. Mama had reached the place from where his funeral procession was to be prepared and taken for cremation. She was in a state of shock but she had no choice and had to make all the arrangements for the funeral.

She briefed me and said, '*Beta*, forget about what has happened! Now, be brave and complete the formalities.' She added plaintively, 'You are his actual child and only you would be able to provide salvation to his soul.'

I couldn't follow what she meant when she mentioned that I was his actual child. Are there any fictitious children also? Many questions came to my mind but it was not the time to be bogged down with such thoughts. I asked Naresh, 'Why did mother speak like that?'

He didn't want to speak the truth and said, 'Because you are the only child and the funeral rituals of a father have to be completed by his son, only then a Hindu soul gets salvation from the Chakra of rebirth.'

I was not able to understand the things. I lacked clarity, before I remembered the lady who was crying inside the driver's compartment of the truck. She had two small children with her. Who was she? Was she Paromita with her children? One of them was a boy. Was that the reason everyone had to think about the rights, as to who would perform the rituals of father's death? As far as they were concerned, he was also their father and Paromita's husband. Why were they deprived of their rights? Why couldn't she cry openly as Mama could? Perhaps she was treated by the society as a concubine because she was not married before society. And in the Hindu and conservative society of the village, a lady of such status had virtually no place.

There were many of his colleagues who had arrived from his office and many relatives of Paromita. Had Ma been alive today, what would have been her reactions? Many thoughts kept bugging me but I was only worried for

Mama and her dress code that she would have to follow in the village. Would she also be branded as a witch like Ma was? I was moved by the mere thought itself. I had seen Ma suffer at the hands of the villagers. The villagers had inflicted many atrocities on her when she was branded as a witch and had finally succumbed to the humiliation and trauma. Would Mama too have a similar fate like every other widow in the village? I was not able to reconcile with such thoughts and shivered. Once again, the children would call me the son of sorcerer because Mama is a widow. I was very upset and couldn't control my emotions.

The pundit had arrived with all his 'jingbang'. I was called to complete the rituals before the body could be moved. I had forgotten that I had wanted to at least have a look of his face to recall him. I sat on the ground to complete the rituals with the pundit. I could see Prakash, who had a bag in his hand. Perhaps he had come to take me to his house for Holi, as we had planned earlier. He was aghast and frozen to see me sitting with a pundit in the dress of a *Karta*, who performs the rituals of the dead relatives. My dress was sufficient enough to convey to him the facts and the tears of my eyes conveyed the rest. I wished to hug and cry on his shoulders. Mama could understand as tears rolled down my thighs and knees, after I saw Prakash. She went to Prakash and said something. He was stunned to meet Mama. She was the most decent lady, mother and human being I ever met in life. How and why had God punished us? My tears refused to stop flowing and defied my orders. The more I tried to control my emotions, the more emotional I became. Mama was in pain to see me in that dress.

I finished the rituals and everyone geared up to put the body on to the bamboo stretcher, meant for carrying the dead ones on the shoulders, by the Hindus. His face was uncovered. Mama could not see his face. It was full of blood clots on the nose and ears. She collapsed on seeing his face with blood clots all over it. She was made to sit on the concrete step under the banyan tree and given a glass of water. I panicked. One of the ladies cleaned his face and wailed. Nirupama was about to arrive. Babu requested the pundit to wait for sometime till Nirupama arrived and had a look at the dead body of her brother. I got up and wished to speak to Prakash. Mama requested me to not to touch him, as he would have to take a bath. I openly requested Prakash not to touch me and cried before him. He showed me the watercolours and plastic pumps that he had brought for me to enjoy Holi. I showed them to Mama and introduced Prakash to her. She was aware of him, as I had mentioned to her a number of times, when I had gone to the village after the result of eighth standard. She gave a despairing look and whispered, 'It is not in our fortune to enjoy or celebrate anything in life.' She thought I wouldn't be able to hear her as she had whispered very softly.

It was getting late. Nirupama didn't arrive. Mother was not allowed to move any further from that place towards the crematorium. The driver of the truck came running to Naresh for the balance amount that was due to him. He was having some conversation with the driver, while the body was lifted and the air was filled with the cry of *Ram Naam Satya Hai... Ram Naam Satya Hai...* It was repeated many times and the body was taken on the shoulders. Once again, I was not allowed to look back while carrying the fire in the terracotta pot, filled with cowdung cake, and the twig having its tip covered with a cloth dipped in ghee. Prakash stood at the same place. I had broken the rituals of not looking back and looked at Prakash and Mama with the corner of my eyes. This was the second time she had seen me moving out with the fire in hand for a very cruel purpose. I cried all the way.

Will I be allowed to write the name of my father in the school forms? What will I reply when they ask me about my father? There were many questions that bugged me. There were very few people left to care for Mama and me, perhaps only Parmeshra, whom we could trust more than our own relatives.

It was only a few minutes walk to the crematorium. We reached. I knew the next ritual that was to be performed. His body was taken to the river for a bath. I too participated this time. The last time I was considered a small child who might get scared on seeing the dead body of an old lady.

The pundit asked everyone to put some colour over the body to complete the rituals of playing Holi. It was pathetic. What kind of Holi was this? No one had any sympathy for Mama or me. People were more worried about completing the formalities as quickly as they could and move back.

Parmeshra had lost his master. He had seen father from his childhood. Both of them had grown up almost together. They had very friendly relations with each other. I had seen the blank look in his eyes. Perhaps, after Mama and me, he was the only human that was directly affected from his death.

I was the child that had the rare experience of playing Holi with the dead body of his father. The *dom* at the ghat had not been able to recognise me but I had been able to recollect him as he had a tiff with Babu for burning a lower caste body near Ma's body. I was asked by the pundit to hold the pot of the *Asthi Kalas,* holding the remains of father's body.

It was all over. We were back in my room. It was dark. Mama had gone to sleep. I had already had a bath at the ghat on the banks of the Ganges before reaching the room. Rest of the villagers were taken to the hotel for a meal by Naresh and seen off. I sat near Mama and kept my hands over her head. It was burning. She had not had anything to eat and drink for a long time. It was my room. I knew where the lantern was kept and where the stove with wood sawdust lay. I had many things to share with her but it was all over. There was nothing to share or enjoy in life. I had decided to keep my mother happy and didn't want anything to happen to her that might affect her health. I went out and brought a little curd from the street shop under the banyan tree. The remains of the broken earthen pot and flowers still remained on the road. I felt nervous once again after seeing the broken earthen pot that I had thrown with water before proceeding for crematorium. I hurriedly picked up curd for twenty-five paise and returned to my room.

Mama was still fast asleep. Naresh had not returned yet. I requested Mama to get up, and offered her a glass of water. She was in pain. Her mind didn't work. I brought the lantern near her and sat on the mat. I was feeling cold and had covered my body with the half-white dhoti that I was supposed to wear. I had grown up. I couldn't have worn the cloth I had put on after Ma's death. Mama hadn't seen the earthen pot containing the *Asthi Kalas* of my father's remains. That perhaps would have made her more upset. I had hidden it with the mango leaves brought for the puja and other rituals. Mama got up and washed her face. I requested her to have something to eat. She once again cried embracing me. I had decided not to lose heart, as Mama would become totally nervous. She was the last source of light and hope in my life. I didn't want to lose her. I had to a certain extent reconciled to the death of my father but I was more worried about Mama. I didn't want to do anything that even inadvertently hurt her or made her feel upset. She was surprised to see my maturity.

In the meantime, Naresh arrived. He too had brought curd and bananas for Mama and me to eat. Mama hardly had anything, I had whatever I could and sat near her. Naresh had another gentleman with him. He had accompanied the dead body of my father from the place of work to Bhagalpur, where he was to be cremated. They had decided to move his body to Bhaglapur, as taking the body to the village would have taken a lot of time and would have been very difficult to manage, as it was not even motorable. He was called inside. He too sat in the room on the floor. We were totally clueless about the reasons of father's death. No one had time to think on those lines at that point of time. Now everyone was curious to know the details of his death.

Paromita and her family members were aware of the problems and reasons of father's accident that led to his death. The man was Mr Bhattacharjee, the elder brother of Paromita. He was in tears and unable to express his feeling and loss after the death of my father.

Mr Bhattacharjee too was a shattered man and didn't know what to say to Mama. It was rather difficult to digest such a thing in a conservative society like ours, where one could never think of getting married to a married man. He informed us the details of the father's accident.

He had come out of the office late, whereas Paromita had left the office early to cook food and prepare the children for a night show movie. The theatre was quite close to their place of stay. Father was in a hurry and he was cycling home from the office. He was hit by the steel chain hanging loose at the tail of a lorry, used for fastening the rear planks needed to support the goods loaded onto it. The chain hit him at the rear of the head. He collapsed on the spot after falling off the bike. Since it was night, he was spotted late and taken to the hospital. Everyone knew him as he worked for the collectorate. They didn't have a proper hospital to treat brain injury. Paromita tried her best to shift him to Calcutta to a better hospital as the doctor at Pakur had given up. He succumbed to the injury while they were about to board a train for Calcutta at Pakur railway station.

Paromita had managed to get a lorry with the help of the local administration and moved father's body directly to Bhagalpur for cremation instead of taking it to the village. The clerk from our village who worked at the same office informed Mother. He rushed to get mother to Bhagalpur. I, in any case, studied at Bhagalpur.

It was end of another chapter. Mother was widowed at a very young age. She had taken a challenge to show my father that she could make me a big army officer without his help. Her aim was defeated. She had no motive to drive her to action. Father was the only son of his parents and he had also lost his father at a very young age. Ma had brought him up and provided him the best of things that she could in the village scenario.

It was a great loss for the two families. Paromita was even younger than mother and had two children to support. Her brother had clarified that in all his office documents, father had changed the name to Paromita and all the benefits of the government would go to her. As per the records held by the office, she was reflected as the real wife of my father. Naresh was very upset, as being a teacher, he was very well acquainted with the rules and regulations of the Hindu Marriage Act. Mama was shocked, as she could make out that I was deprived of all the rights that I had on my father. Naresh threatened Mr Bhattacharjee that he would go to court for the rights of his sister, but Mama was against it. She had no one to support and neither had any income. All she had in life was a child and she wished to make him a colonel.

Mother was very worried, as we had no other source of income other than the agricultural income. Even that income was half as we could not do farming ourselves and had to depend on either Parmeshra or Yusuf. Once we allotted our land on *Batai*, we were getting only the half of the agricultural produce of our land. That was not sufficient for the whole year, as some part of that income was once again reinvested for agricultural purpose like purchase of seeds, fertilisers, and labour. It was not enough to survive unless one had some extra income.

Whenever I went to the village market to get vegetable or any other item, firstly, I had to sell off some rice or paddy to the *bania* of the village to get some cash. Only after getting the cash we could go to the village market to get something. Mama could envisage that it would be very difficult for her to fulfil my requirements and her dream without any external monetary help. Mama had to sell kilos of rice or paddy to send me twenty to thirty rupees for my requirements in town. The Brahmin families were not allowed to sell milk or any dairy product like curd or ghee. Moreover, most of the villagers had their own cows or buffaloes and there was no market for any milk products. Even though one thought of selling the milk, it wouldn't be taken by anyone until and unless one decided to dispose it off free of cost. Many of the lower caste at times requested Mama to help them out with milk, whenever they had a newcomer in their house in the form of a small baby or for pregnant women. They generally took goat milk for their infants. That was in abundance in the village.

Mama was not even aware of the repercussions of leaving all the benefits to Paromita and her children after the death of father. She didn't know that she was entitled to family pension, and neither did Mr Bhattacharjee inform us that mother or the actual widow of a government employee was entitled to family pension, if an employee died in harness. I was too small to understand all this. Paromita, being herself in the office, was precisely aware of all the benefits that one was entitled to after the death of an employee. Even the Government group insurance schemes were transferred in her name and the money would go only to her. The only option Mama had was to fight for her rights or be at the mercy of Paromita, if she felt like giving or sharing the money that was to be released by the government. Mama was too scared to go to the court or file any complaint with the district administration.

We had no money to have *Bhoj* or cater to the distribution of copper and brass pots, that was in vogue at the village, after the deaths of near and dear ones. It was difficult for her to repay the expenses incurred for the funeral. Some part of the transportation charges of the lorry carrying the body was paid by the district administration and Naresh paid the rest on arrival at Bhagalpur.

Paromita's family took advantage of father. They used him. Paromita, being an educated lady, knew the problems related to bigamy as per the Hindu Marriage Act and she had ensured that all of father's official documents were changed in her name over a period of time. We were not too sure whether father had any bank account or any fixed deposit in our name or anyone else's name other than Paromita and her children.

Mama had decided to pledge some part of the land to Naresh instead of giving it to anyone else at the village or to the village *bania*. Naresh was not interested in it, as people in the society would have cursed him for having taken the land of his real sister on pledge in lieu of the money that was spent for the funeral and related expenses of his sister's husband. At the same time, it was very difficult for him to take the load of all the expenses required for the *Bhoj* or donation to pundit and poor in kind, like mixed metal pots, cows, etc.

A grand *Bhoj* with donation had become mandatory, as it would have been a great disrespect to a man who had done so much for his mother when she had died. Father had arranged for three day's *Bhoj* and donations to the pundit and other poor of the village. If nothing was done after father's death, the villagers would have cursed mother for being a woman with no feeling for her husband. Mama was unable to decide as to how to plan for the *Bhoj* and other things, though there was nothing left for us as far as society or village or respect of the family was concerned. Our existence was gradually getting eroded. Villagers were no more interested in our family, mainly because my father was the sole earning member and his earning hereafter had stopped. We would have been of no good to any of the villagers. Father had helped many people in the village for the marriage of their daughters or during crisis. Today, none of the villagers stood by us other than Parmeshra. He could hardly do anything for us monetarily. He himself was dependent on us for his livelihood.

It was afternoon, when Nirupama and her family arrived. I knew she was a great actress and always thought of her own benefits. I had seen enough of her after Ma's death. Both of them had small hearts and were very self-centred. I was reminded of the days when Nirupama was due for her first delivery. The doctors at Deoghar referred her to Calcutta. Father had sold all the grains available in the house and Mama stood by him and had gone out of way to save the life of Nirupama and her first child. Whatever Mama had saved from the house expenses she had given to father to save Nirupama's life. Those were the happy days of her life when Mama stayed with father and we had a very happy time, before he was transferred to Pakur and met Paromita. After he left for Pakur, we were sent to the village. Though Mama never demanded nor had she expected anything of Nirupama and her husband, she was waiting to see their concern for the deceased and his family.

No sooner did she enter the room, Nirupama wailed and hugged Mama. I too had tears in my eyes to see real tears in her eyes. Her husband kept talking to Naresh to know the full details. Even he was concerned about the post-death benefits that a widow was entitled to. He himself worked at the Collectorate at Deoghar, as a clerk and was well versed with the rules and regulations. He too offered to meet the collector at Pakur and explain to him the truth to help mother and me. I knew it was spontaneous but after sometime, none of them would be interested anymore in our affairs. Naresh took the lead and pacified Nirupama to face the facts of life. She even cursed Paromita and her children for such an incident and the death of father. She cursed her with hell and used abusive language for her but Mama never did so. Mama was a polished and decent lady. She knew there was no point cursing anyone as everything was over and it couldn't be undone.

Mama's dreams were shattered. She could envisage the future. There were none that would really help her out in such a situation and she would have to help herself. Naresh had explained to them. Nirupama's husband was fully aware of the situation so was Nirupama for the financial aspects of our life. He promised to Naresh to help him out with whatever little he could. Mama was not aware of the talks that Naresh had with Nirupama and her husband.

It was decided to move to the village with the *Asthi Kalas* from the funeral pyre of father. I locked my room. Most of the boys, who took me to be a greedy child having the leftover of the rituals of the funeral pyre of people at the crematorium, were gradually aware of the facts of my life and perhaps wished to apologise to me. That was quite obvious from their eyes and face. I was in the same dress as that of a *Karta*. All the boys cursed each other for spreading rumours about me, that I was a lower caste who fed on the leftovers of the rituals of dead ones. Now they knew why I loved to visit the crematorium at times and spent time on the banks of the Ganges sitting all alone. The teacher from my village who stayed at the same place explained everything to them. Many of them went near Mama and touched her feet. I had not told anything to Mama regarding my plight and misunderstanding of the children staying in and around my room. The teacher told them about the death of my grandmother at a very tender age and that it had shaken my confidence and had left its scar on my life permanently.

I was holding the *Asthi Kalas* of my father when Prakash arrived to meet us. He had been waiting for mother and me for a long time. He wished to meet us alone. I carried the pot and moved with him. He also called Mama. I was surprised to see Prakash's parents. He was a businessman and owned a few garment shops at Khalifabag Chowk Market in Bhagalpur. He asked Mama not to bother about the expenses for the *Bhoj* and other related rituals, as he would bear them. Prakash was aware of my daily routine of having a meagre meal of sweet potatoes for dinner and roti with salt and mustard oil for lunch. He was fully aware of our financial status and had explained to his father to extend a little help, whatever he could, to our family. Mama thanked them profoundly and cried for a while but refused to accept the cash that they wished to hand to her. They could understand her sentiments and didn't wish to hurt her feelings. Prakash handed me the cash quietly and we moved on. I promised to return from the village after a month or so. He loved me even though I had nothing to offer him. But God knows why he liked me the most in the class and we shared the same bench throughout our class everyday.

It was the day of Holi. People were celebrating with fanfare. Because of us, even Prakash and his family had spoiled their day and the festival. Prakash kept looking at me while Mama and I mounted a chain-pulling rickshaw to reach the bus depot to proceed to the village. Being oblivious of our plight, on the way, one of the children ran and sprinkled colour on my *dhoti* and on my body. Few drops of colour went over the pot of the *Asthi Kalas*. Mama could see one of the elders scolding the child. They could make out from the dress itself what had happened. But a child was not aware of our plight and had shared his joy with another child. Mama could see my face after the colour was sprinkled over me. She knew I enjoyed playing Holi and every Holi she and Ma used to put colour on me, the first thing early in the morning. If at all they were late, I used to pour colour of my own. She could see me laughing after seeing the children playing on to the street with colour. Everyone enjoyed the festival on the street and applied colours on one another. Mama could make out I was getting deeply involved in the celebration of Holi, on the street and might drop the *Asthi Kalas*. 'Hold the pot properly. It will break.' she cautioned. Naresh had followed us and had almost reached the bus stand walking before us. He too had colour all over his body.

There were very few passengers travelling that day. Everyone looked at us with empathy but didn't wish to talk. As soon as we entered the bus, the helper advised one of the families to move back and offered us the front seat. The helper of the bus tried his best to attract the attention of the passengers by shouting the destination of the bus. But in vain, as very few people had to travel on the day of the festival. Finally it left for its destination with few of us. It was difficult to pass the time and we wished to go into isolation. There was chaos on the street. People enjoyed with colour, mud, and cowdung mixed with water. Some of the children even threw colours and the mud at the running bus and laughed.

I remembered the time when we had come to the village and celebrated our first Holi with Ma. It was a grand affair and celebrated with much mirth. Ma had arranged for twenty kilos of milk sherbet with *Bhang* leaves to be served to the villagers. She had ordered Parmeshra to arrange for two of the *Nautanki* boys dressed up in girls' attires, to dance throughout the day before our house. All the ladies, children and men joined them to have sherbet and dance. Even Mama had danced with the ladies, singing the local traditional *Thumri* that used to be sung in the Holi at the tune of dhol and harmonica. She sang very well. Since we had a Gramophone in our house, she remembered the full *Thumri, Anchara Chodo Kanahi, Garei Main Dungi, Ab Na Darungi, Main Jaan Gayi Chaturai, Mujhe Gale Lagaye Jora Jori.* She had looked very pretty with red and pink colour on her white shiny cheeks. She was very pretty with sharp features and long hair touching her knees.

My *dhoti* was removed by one of the very old *Bhabhis* and she had coloured my *Phu* in pink. I had complained to Ma and Mama. They laughed while I snuggled. They made me understand that she was my *Bhabhi* in relation. It was to be done to the youngest *Devar.* Every lady loved me and played Holi with me. I was given a lot of importance in the village, mainly because I was the grandson of Ma. Besides, we were newcomers and had just joined the village. It was our happiest and the best day that we spent at the village with Ma.

I clearly remembered the first Holi when, the very first thing that Mama had done after getting up, was make me put on clothes brought by Ma. I looked like Krishna in the *Pitambari dhoti* and the silk kurta with *gamcha* tied on to the waist. Ma and Mama had coloured my cheeks. I too had coloured Ma's white sari and wiped my soiled hand with colour on Ma's sari, that had left my finger prints on the back of her sari. Mama had come laughing to show that to Ma, as Ma hadn't been able aware of the mischief that I had done quietly. After seeing the colour at the back of her sari, Ma had run behind me to catch me and put me into the bucket of the colour prepared by her for the elders of the village. *Will those days ever return?* I thought. I had seen Mama happy a few times in life and one of them was the first Holi that we had spent in the village with Ma.

Mother was fast asleep and her head lolled around the rear support of her seat and shoulder, so also were Nirupama and her husband. The bus kept moving at a snail's pace, making helluva noise, more than its actual speed. Naresh was awake but I was not in the mood of talking to him, as there was nothing to talk between us. I could see the marks of tears on Mama's cheeks and saliva drooling out of the corner of her lips. She was fast asleep. I wiped it with the corner of my dhoti. Her siesta was broken and she wiped her face with her sari. I was deeply worried and concerned about the rest of her life. It was difficult for her to stay in the village as I had seen Ma and many other widows suffer at the hands of the villagers, pushing them to death and having a hell of a life. The widows had a very tough time at the village and got no respect at all. They were looked down upon and were not invited for any auspicious occasion or puja ceremony. Moreover, they were also blamed for the death of their husbands.

The situation in the village was deteriorating day by day. The cohesion, harmony and feeling had lessened. Casteism, in any case, had increased very much. There were no feelings amongst the villagers.

We reached the village late in the afternoon. We were very tired, as I had to walk with the *Asthi Kalas,* holding it with both the hands for two to three miles. The pundit placed it at the same place where we had established the *Asthi Kalas* of Ma, after the rituals. A diya of desi ghee was put near it to glow. I had to sleep in the same room till it was either disposed in the river of our village or taken to Benaras. That was yet to be decided and totally depended on the financial support that we may get from other relatives and what we could manage. The whole village had poured to our house as soon as we arrived home. Many people cried and many of them admired Mama and me. We had no enmity with anyone in the village, as we were the most docile family out of the Brahmin lot. I could see even Yusuf sitting on the ground far away from the village crowd, with his wife and children. He knew he was an untouchable and couldn't have taken a chance. Ajra was his eldest child and she too had grown like me. Everyone tried to speak to Mama but there was nothing to say. No one could have shared our sorrow. It was futile talking about anything to the people. I walked out and sat on the ground with Yusuf. He was restless and said, '*Malik*, don't sit on the ground. I would get a sack or *pida* (a wooden plank with small leg used for sit out in the village for lunch or dinner).' I stopped him. His wife cried on seeing me. Their children were really not aware of what had happened. Ajra knew us and vaguely remembered me. Yusuf asked his children to do namaste to me. I was confused. Am I so big that now children should do namaste to me? I cried before Yusuf and requested him to look after our property and us. We were orphaned. He could feel my pain and sentiments. Even Ajra and her mother started crying. She wiped my tears and assured all possible help that they could extend to us. Yusuf knew Ma, mother and me like Parmeshra. Even Ramvilas was a big boy. He came and sat near me. Yusuf asked him to get a *pida* for me. He went inside and got one. We continued our conversation. Ramvilas vowed to do his best for mother and me. He had grown taller than me and had developed a muscular body, mainly because he did a lot of hard work with Parmeshra in the fields.

Parmeshra approached us and requested me to eat something and relax for a while. He had also brought a glass of lemon juice for me. He took Yusuf with him to his house and I requested him to help us out till the *Bhoj* was over. He assured me and said, '*Malik*, you don't have to say this. It goes without saying. We will do our best. You don't have to worry at all.' He also showed some money that he had brought with him. Parmeshra later informed us that he had sold two of his cows after hearing the news of father's death. It touched my heart. I asked Parmeshra not to accept that money and return it to him. He had also informed mother about this. She was touched to know the feelings and concern of Yusuf. She called Yusuf and asked him not to spend any of his money for anything relating to *Bhoj* or any other rituals.

In the evening, Babu arrived and asked us about our plans for the *Bhoj*. Mama didn't speak at all and mainly Naresh talked to him. He insisted on knowing the views of mother. She whispered from the cover of the white sari that whatever Naresh and he decided was okay with her. Naresh was aware of her plans and financial conditions.

Bhoj was organised on a limited scale. None of the villagers talked or genuinely enjoyed as father had died at a very young age. The formalities of *Bhoj* were over. It was time for everyone to depart. I had handed over the money given to me by Prakash. It was of great help for the expenses for the *Bhoj* and we didn't have to take any loan from the *bania*. Mama had sold all the extra grain that we had in the house. Naresh had also left. He was to join his school at the town after submerging the *Asthi Kalas* of father at Benaras. He was accompanied by one of the villagers to complete the rituals. I was not allowed, as I was too small to accompany them. Mama would not have allowed me to go; hence I didn't talk about it at all. Moreover, it was not a jolly trip that one would love to join the elders. Mama was surprised at my decision. It would have also increased the unwanted expenses. Naresh insisted and requested Mama to let me submerge the *Asthi Kalas* of my father, as the real son has the first and foremost right to accomplish the last rituals of submerging the *Asthi Kalas*. Mama knew I was mentally upset and might have problems without her and she decided against it.

It was once again Mama and me with many of the puppies in the house. None of them were visible as many people visited our house and they were scared. My puppy was not scared and always accompanied Mama and me wherever we moved in the village. All her puppies had grown up and couldn't be recognised. Some of them had grown quite big and obviously didn't recognise me. Whenever I returned home in the late evening, all of them ran and yapped at me but my puppy saved me. They behaved differently with Mama. My puppy was very docile and loyal to me. At times, along with her puppies even my baby goat sucked her nipple but she never objected to it. I could understand her feelings by looking at her face. So did she. Whenever I remained upset or sad, I sat on the fence at the rear of the house. She, my puppy, climbed on to the wall and sat near me. She used to put her front leg on my thighs and made the typical 'Ku-Ku...' sound, as if asking me to stop worrying and thinking about the past. She never moved out of the house, as long as I didn't move out of the house with her. She understood my feelings and me more than Mama and Ma. She probably was aware of what had happened to us. She knew that Ma had expired and was not seen anymore. She even complained to me as to why I had moved to the town and was not seen for a long time. She didn't want me to move to the city but stay at the village itself.

Mama was looking for me. She was aware that I wouldn't go to anyone in the village and must be sitting on the fence wall at the rear of the house. She came from the rear and put her hands over my shoulders. She knew I was in deep thought, looking at the red sun beginning to set, like our fate. The sun would rise once again for everyone but the sun of our life was set forever. I had a long *choti* (hair left at the centre of the head while the rest of the hairs was tonsured). This was the second time I had to shave off my head due to the death in the family. My *choti* was a bit too long and Mama tied it, making a knot out of it. I didn't want to leave her at the village and wished that she could move to the town and stay with me. She was totally broken. There was nobody to look after her in the house. If something went wrong in the night, she wouldn't get any help from anyone. Our neighbours were elderly people and they required help themselves.

Chapter VI
MAMA

I put up a proposal to her and said, 'Mama, we have nothing left in the village. Why don't you come and stay with me at the town?'

She refused, as there were no one to look after our property in the village. I could make out what was in her mind. She also wished to know more about Prakash and the amount of money that he had handed over to me as donation for the cremation of father. 'They are very nice people. How do you know them?' she asked curiously.

I told her the details of our friendship. It was mainly based on sympathy.

'How should we return their money?' she asked dolefully.

I too wished to do that but firstly, we were not in a position to return it immediately. Secondly, I didn't know what they had in their mind. I wanted to ascertain from Prakash before taking any such decisions. 'Let me speak to Prakash before arriving at any conclusion,' I replied.

It was time to return to the town. Mama requested me in the night to go back and resume my studies. I slept with her. It was too scary to sleep alone in the house. Mama called Parmeshra and requested him to accompany me to the town. Parmeshra wished to expose Ramvilas to the city life and requested her if he could send Ramvilas with all the grains that was required to be taken, as we had no money. Somehow Mama could cater for the monthly school fees and other little expenses.

It was a good proposal. I, along with Ramvilas left for the town. Mama had come to see us off till the canal and Parmeshra came till the bus stand. It was the very first trip of Ramvilas to any town. He was very excited to see vehicles and hoardings on the sides of the roads. We arrived at my room in the evening and unpacked the grains that we had carried all the way from the village. Ramvilas helped me in getting the food ready, that we ate together, and slept in the same room on the floor. Mama had washed my uniforms with the special washing soap at the well, instead of at the river with caustic soda powder. I got ready to go to school, whereas Ramvilas wished to stay for another day and move around in the town to see the Clock Tower, Meena Bazar and other places. He also wished to have a dip in the holy river of the Ganges to get rid of the sins earned by him.

I reached the school with the long *choti* tied in a knot at the centre of my head. Many children laughed and giggled at me and gave a strange look. Prakash was aware of the tragic incident and had informed some of the children in my class. That was a great relief and they didn't tease me much. Many of the boys some times pulled the knot of my *choti*, opening it fully. It was damn irritating and disgusting but I couldn't help it. I had to bear the burden of their teasing till my *choti* got merged with other hair on the head. Some of the teachers, oblivious to the facts of my life, inquired the reason for shaving off my head. I was unable to concentrate on anything, as the sight of the crematorium and the face of my father that I had seen before starting the funeral procession, full of blood dripping out of his nose and ears, kept haunting me time and again. I had nothing to prove to anyone as there was no motivating factor to drive our lives at all. My life was totally without any mission.

Ramvilas had left and returned to the village. I had accompanied him till the bus stand to ensure that he boarded the correct bus as he was totally illiterate and couldn't read and write. I missed him during the night; he too was genuinely concerned for Mama and me.

He was a very outspoken boy and always cursed the upper caste openly before me. Babu was his first target. He took keen interest, to ensure that the upper caste lost their hold on the older generation of the lower caste and the young girls of the lower caste were educated so as not to succumb to the pressure of the upper caste and oblige them by having sex with them. He was like a leader and could speak very well with anyone. While at Bhagalpur, in his two days of stay, he had tried to look for a job if he could. He was a very well built and enterprising fellow. He was not at all scared of the younger generation of the upper castes, not even a person like Babu. He was certainly a potential threat for the upper caste in the village. He was the sole person amongst the lower caste, who was admired for his pragmatic and sagacious approach and oratory. He spat venom against the upper caste openly, without any fear. His main aim in life was to exterminate the fear and dominance of the upper caste and also to weed out the sexual harassment or *Chamchori* among the ladies or girls of the lower castes. He was perceived and seen by the lower caste as a person who would bring a radical social and political reform in the village, that would safeguard their modesty and interest. He was not concerned by the ramifications, as he was fundamentally baffled by the story of the *Chamchori* of his mother, Kusmi, that had perhaps resulted in his birth. That was the main reason he supported the lower castes and raised his voice against upper caste dominance.

I started my routine life at the town and borrowed all the notebooks of Prakash, to copy the lessons that had been taught in the class in my absence and also by his tuition teacher. I didn't want to face humiliation in the class and worked very hard to complete and cover the lessons. Prakash helped me in a big way. I could secure pass marks in all the subjects. Mama managed to get the farming done with the help of Parmeshra and Yusuf and fulfilled my monetary requirements.

After the final examinations, Prakash requested me to join him for a movie. I had never seen a cinema and was scared even to enter the premises of the theatre, as I never had money in my pocket to cater for the cost of the ticket. I always thought that they perhaps would charge even to enter the premises and have a look at the posters displayed at the entrances.

Prakash obviously had offered to pay for the tickets. Mama had advised me not to go for movies as that spoiled and polluted the mind of children and was a sheer waste of money. I was a little confused but inquisitive also to know, after all, what was this movie business like? It was a Sunday; he had come to my place on a bike, on which I too had learned cycling. I offered to pedal as he always had a chance to cycle but I didn't get any chance other than a few times. We left for the movie. It was a weepie-sniffy one, very touching. I could not understand the flashbacks and things happening and asked Prakash to explain. It was very touching. An elephant was killed by one of the characters. How could they kill such a magnificent animal? I kept thinking of the elephant the whole night and even cried after returning to my room. It was a good movie, but I did not really know whether what they showed was a fact or fiction. I took the story to be true and was very upset to see the killing of an elephant. It was the first movie of my life and I wasn't able to forget any bit of it and the feelings that it had aroused in me. It was a great day for me. Moreover, it was totally contrary to the stories told to me by Mama. After all, why had she told me that the cinemas are bad for children? It was very good and I had enjoyed it thoroughly. It was quite educative for me. Might be, Mama advised against seeing a movie because we didn't have money to be spent for such things. This movie remained in my mind for a long time. It had many animals that contributed to the film.

Mama had seen films. Even I had seen some with Mama, she had informed me, but I was too small to remember the films that we had seen together. Then I was an infant. I honestly wrote to her that after the exams we had enjoyed a movie called *Hathi Mere Sathi*. Our final exams were over and results were out. I had passed in all the subjects. I left for the village; I was very excited to share with Mama my experiences of the movie that I had seen. I reached home. Mama had gone very weak, perhaps she didn't look after herself and worried about me. She had not been able to overcome the loss we had from the death of my father.

We were awake for a long time in the night and I narrated to her the story of the film that I had seen. She too enjoyed the story but at the end, she stopped responding to my talk and probably, went to sleep. I too slept with the thought of the dead elephant.

My puppy had a good time as after the death of Ma, Mama used to be scared and kept her inside the house. She always sat near the beam that she had adopted, the very first time I had brought her inside the house. Mama, in fact, felt better with her presence. She barked vigorously at the slightest noise. It alerted Mama and also gave strength to her. After I left home, Mama had someone to give her company.

Now I was in class ten and next year I had to face the Matriculation Board. Mama wished that I at least pass in all the subjects and go to college. I was on the right track and had requested her not to worry about me at all, as I would not bring down her prestige. I was more confident than before and was gradually getting over from the symptoms of depression that had come over me after the death of my father.

I didn't visit any of the houses in the village, as most of the youngsters in the Brahmin and other upper caste communities were busy with the Panchayat election and for the preparation of the same old caste war. This time, two men of the lower castes of our village, too were up against the Brahmin candidates in the Panchayat elections. Ramvilas was the hero of the lower caste and had the full support of not only of the lower caste from our village but also from the other village. He was in a position to influence the election with his support. He had a lot of say amongst the lower caste and could make or break a candidate in the Panchayat election. It was quite evident that with his support only, would the lower caste candidate be elected this time.

Ramvilas was even bribed by the upper caste candidate to support him, but he had decided to stand for the lower caste candidate, as a Sarpanch, and give a jolt to the upper caste. He had made up his own group and was able to even get support of the Naxalites or lower caste extremists active in that area. The group posed a formidable challenge to the booth capturing by the upper caste candidates. Though he was quite young, people were scared to talk to him or confront him on any of the village affairs.

The number of cases of casual sex, that used to be discussed openly amongst the Brahmin and other upper caste, had stopped, as they were scared to talk openly and whatever adventure they indulged in was kept a secret. There were fundamental changes on these accounts in the village, as earlier, it used to be a matter of pride for the upper caste youth or elder to have had sex with a large number of lower caste females. Now they were scared to even discuss with one another.

On one hand, the lower caste females used to be considered as untouchables for the upper caste, as far as working in the houses were concerned; on the other, the upper caste, as and when they got a chance, screwed the same untouchable females. While having sex with them, they would forget that the female they had sex with was an untouchable. They had double standards and used the situation in the village to their advantage. Because of such atrocities, the younger generation amongst the lower caste had defied the diktat of the upper caste elders. Even Babu was gradually made redundant by the lower caste and was not given any respect. He was losing his grip even on the upper caste. It was more so after his wrongdoings with Ma and the incident of fathering a child in a lower caste family by his grandson. The lower caste had decided to eliminate him first, in case he intervened in village politics anymore. Some of the teachers and the clerks, the ones with the radios, who took more interest in the village politics, were now shit scared of the lower caste. They didn't wish to open their mouth at all against the lower caste, as they had to travel early morning or late evening to their place of work, alone at times and were more vulnerable to the lower caste threat of attack.

It was not our cup of tea and we had decided to ignore it completely. It was a very volatile situation in the village. The upper caste and combined groups of lower caste and Muslims were not seeing eye to eye. Many Muslim boys who worked at Calcutta and other metropolitan cities, were the means for collecting arms and ammunition on behalf of the lower caste. Mama was very happy that I was out of village politics and not having any enmity either with the lower caste or the Muslims.

I left for town once again with Ramvilas. He accompanied me to the town with the entire ration for a few months. Mama was quite happy as she could send him anytime she felt like or whenever she wanted to send something for me. It was the last phase of my schooling. I had to pass the matriculation examinations to join college or do something in life.

I admired the Army recruiting team that visited Bhagalpur for the purpose of recruitment. I was not yet eligible as I had not passed matriculation nor had I attained the age of eighteen. I had to wait till I passed high school. I would not mind even joining as a soldier. That was my feeling. I was not very knowledgeable about the army and in the village, people were only aware of couple of ranks like Havaldar, Subedar or Colonel. Most of us did not really know the difference between these ranks in the Army.

Prakash and his parents were against my joining the army, as I was the only child of my mother. I too at times had inhibitions. In case something happened to me, who would look after Mama or what would happen to her. But Mama had been dreaming to see me in the army uniform, and I was not too sure I would be able to become an officer or reach the rank of a colonel.

Time had flown with the normal routine. I had passed in the Matriculation exam with second grade. Mama was very happy. She thanked God for all the help and kindness. Now I was impatient to look for an opportunity to join the armed forces to fulfil the long dream of my mother.

Prakash was after me to join college and continue my studies, till I graduated from a faculty of the Bhagalpur University. I would have easily got admission but I knew we wouldn't be able to afford college expenses and my stay at the town. Mama was already in debt due to my expenses in the town. She could somehow manage expenses to complete my schooling, mainly because Paromita had not been able to change one of the recurring deposits of my father at the bank, that was in Mama's name. She had managed to get it with the help of the clerk, from our village, who worked in my father's office. It was a very petty amount probably, which is why it didn't attract Paromita's eyes and was not transferred in her name. That was all Mama had received after the death of father. There were no hopes of getting family pension or anything else without a long legal battle in the court. Mama had hardly any liability and we could live comfortably on the income that we had from agriculture. All our agricultural land in the village was in the joint name of my grandfather and Paromita knew she wouldn't succeed in that matter. That's why she didn't stake her claim on the landed property that we had in our village and at other places.

I, with the help of Prakash, wrote out an application and sent it to the branch recruiting office of the army. I was given a call for the interview and was selected for their infantry wing. I was damn thrilled and went to meet Mama to show her the selection letter. She could see her dream come true, but she was sad as well, as I had to leave her shortly and go for the training and would not be able to meet her for a long time. I spent a few days with Mama and my puppies at home. They were the happiest days of my life. Everyone at the village was very nice to me. Many of the youngsters in the village admired me and wished to have had a chance like I had. I was becoming an outsider. I was not going to get another chance to stay in the village anymore, as long as I had to serve with the army. I prepared the clothes and other items as per the instructions given with the selection letter and left to report to the training establishment along with other young men selected with me.

We had to report to the parachute regimental centre at Agra. It was a great day for all of us. After a few days only, the basic training started. It was mainly physical training to tone up everyones' body and get us on to the right track. We had no time for ourselves. Our day started very early in the morning and continued till late night. I wrote to Mama every week as she used to be very worried for me. Mama's respect amongst the villagers had grown manifold after I joined the army. She had become like a mother India of the village. Everyone spent a little time with her to know about me. More so, when the police department had sent some of its employees to our house, as a part of their duty for verification of my credentials. It is a routine administrative protocol that is followed by the army to check the credential of its personnel. They too congratulated Mama for her success. There were very few children from that area who had joined the army as a soldier or an officer. I was the one and only from my village. That was a matter of pride for Mama. Even Parmeshra and Ramvilas were very proud of me and gave my example to all their relatives in other villages.

Mama too wrote to me almost every week. Whenever I got time, I read her letters several times. After lunch many of us reached the mailroom to check our personal mail. But we were shit scared of our chief parachute instructor.

We had a chief instructor for 'Basic Parachute Training' who taught us the basics of the parachute jump. He was an Air Force officer, Master Warrant Officer Bhosale. He was very well built at his age and looked physically fit and tough. He was a great disciplinarian and very strict and always had an immaculate turn out. He had joined the Indian Air Force, probably during the British regime. He was one of the best and toughest instructors we ever came across. He even polished the sole of his shoes, and the place between the toe and the heel. One could see his face in his shoes and the leather belt that he wore around his waist. Everyone shivered in his mere presence and never took any chances as long as he stood during the course of training. On one such occasion, I clearly remember, some of the Air Force soldiers laughing at him while the lecture-cum-demonstration was on. He got irritated and yelled, 'You two buggers, fall out!'

All of us were frozen and petrified at his call and wondered who was going to be butchered today. He once again yelled, 'You buffoons, fall out!' Two of the air force Airman came out and stood before him. He asked, 'What made you laugh? Let us all share the jokes. Share the joke with the flight, start rolling.' And the endless front roll began, till one conked out in the hot sun with giddiness. At last he yelled, 'You buffoons, nincompoops, I am like your grandfather. I have spent thirty-five years in the uniform and I must say, all of you were in liquid form when I was in uniform.' Everyone was quiet. He was a very friendly human being and loved and treated us like children. But he never compromised as far as training or discipline was concerned. I finished my training, which was a real tough one. But I have not been able to forget our chief instructor, MWO Bhosale!

Each of us were asked to write to our parents and relatives to visit one of the seven wonders of the world, the famous Taj Mahal in Agra, before we were allotted the respective Parachute Battalions and joined them. We were asked to call a few of our relatives before the final passing out parade was conducted. I too was excited at the thought of bringing my mother and showing her all the places, including the Taj. It was a great opportunity for the trainees. Moreover, it was for the first time that Mama would get a chance to come out of the village after we had arrived there. I too, requested for the free railway warrant entitled to me from the army, for my mother and left with many things that I had bought for Mama. I had not informed Mama about my arrival.

She was in tears to see me in uniform with the parachute sign on the chest. I had grown a little taller and looked muscular, tough and strong. She embraced me and cried for a few minutes. I had grown big and Mama could reach only till my chest. Earlier I used to be till her shoulders. I had saved some money for her and even bought a couple of good saris, oblivious to the fact that it was of no use to her. She was a widow and couldn't have worn the colourful saris that I had brought. She cried as soon as I opened my bag. Finally, she murmured, '*Arre beta*, it won't go waste, it would be used by *bahu*, your wife.' I had bought various other things for her, but had not been able to get her a searchlight and a big torch, that was badly needed to be used in the night. It was of great use for us in the village. I had brought many things famous in Agra, but they were of no use to her. The most important thing that I would have bought for her was a torch. I had forgotten to get it for her, but promised to get her the best one on my next visit.

She told me of the latest developments in the village. 'Babu is dead.' she said. I was relieved and wished to know the details of his death. She was sad to say that he had died a suspicious death. 'He had gone to attend a function at one of his relative's house where he was found dead in the night.' she informed.

I felt relieved and happy to hear about his death, as I had not been able to forget his atrocious and unpardonable behaviour with Ma. I was convinced that his excesses were the sole reason of Ma's death. Otherwise, perhaps, Ma would have been alive to see me in uniform and would have felt very proud of me. There were a few more deaths in the village, Ramvilas was in police custody, and he was suspected of raping a couple of Brahmin and upper caste girls. There were a few lower caste boys suspected to be accomplices of Ramvilas who were also incarcerated. It came as a shock to me. How could Ramvilas do that? He was quite mature and reacted only under provocation. I wished to know more from her. She didn't want me to take interest in the village affairs and ignored it completely.

Many of the upper caste had different and difficult expectations from me. That was clear from the talk that I had with Parmeshra. Parmeshra requested me not to help some of the upper caste to procure firearms and ammo, as I was with the army. The upper caste boys were vying with the lower caste for the procurement of illegal firearms and had planned to meet and discuss the issues with me. It was just not possible and I had decided to acquaint them with the truth. They were frustrated and cursed me for not helping them out to fight the lower caste, being a man in uniform. I was convinced that they had invited these problems themselves.

Parmeshra requested me to help him out to get Ramvilas released from the police lockup. I went along with Parmeshra to visit him at the thana, located miles away from our village. Ramvilas had been beaten up very badly by the person in-charge of the police station, as he himself was an upper caste. He was not in a state to talk to us and gave us a blank look. I could make out that he would turn into a criminal of this area, as it would be difficult for the upper caste to stand by the stories of rape of the girls for various reasons. We returned and advised him to talk to one of the lawyers at the district headquarters. I had very few days with me. I had to return to my training establishment before I was allotted a Battalion. I advised Parmeshra not to worry as he would get bail and would be released shortly, mainly because none of the upper castes were ready to testify to the stories of rape by Ramvilas. Parmeshra was apprehensive that the upper caste policemen might eliminate him in the lockup. I drafted an application on his behalf for the various district administrations and the police officers and sent it by the registered post. Most of the upper castes were unhappy with me; more so, as I had gone to visit Ramvilas at the police lock up.

Many of the upper caste had left the village and settled in the nearby town due to the fear of theft and rape by the Naxalites. It was no more the same village with peace and harmony that it used to have earlier. There were drastic changes on the social front. The lower caste openly showed their strength to the upper caste by looting their crops and allowing their cows and buffaloes to graze there. There was not a vestige of respect for the upper caste anymore and the young generation of the lower caste openly claimed getting married to the upper caste girls. It was a question of survival for the upper caste. The lower caste could do any petty job in the city and earn their livelihood, whereas the upper caste had more expenses because of their old traditions followed during marriages, second marriages, *upnayan sanskars* and deaths in the family. Most of the families had no other income other than agriculture. Their economic condition had collapsed. They had nothing to contribute and could not get together to fight the lower caste. Many of the lower caste had built concrete houses on the income that they had from the land of the upper caste, whereas the upper caste was bankrupt due to old traditions of dowry and other social obligations.

Many of the national level lower caste leaders visiting that area or the nearby town, spat venom against the upper caste and openly abused them. They influenced and instigated the lower caste to destroy the upper castes and loot their property to make them economically crippled. Many of the tribal and lower caste developed wrong notions in their mind and looted the upper castes' crop or properties. I knew things were getting bad to worse and the village was no longer safe for the upper caste families. The basic reason that added to the misery of the upper caste was that they never got united. They never could tolerate their own clan to do well in life and were jealous of one another. I could make out the truth in a local proverb that Mama had said, '*Beta, Brahman, kutta, hathi, yeh hai jaati ka ghati.*' It was quite true to the existing scenario in the village. The lower caste took advantage of the upper castes hatred for one another, and eliminated them completely on social and economic fronts.

I had decided to leave with mother the very next day, She handed over the keys of the house to Parmeshra to look after, as handing over the keys to the upper caste would have created problems and perhaps the lower caste would have looted our house. I requested Parmeshra to look after my puppy, as she had grown old and was not as active as she used to be. I fondled her with love. She could make out we were not going to meet for a long time, as we had met quite often at the rear fence of the house. She gave me a sad look or may be I perceived it that way, as I was moving away for a long period.

It was for the first time that Mama was coming out of the village. I requested her to put on a different sari, other than the white but she refused to budge. I didn't wish to hurt her sentiments by forcing her. Parmeshra came to leave us at the bus stand and was very emotional. He had a tough time stopping my puppy from crossing the canal as she was not able to reconcile with the departure of both of us and followed us. I was touched to see her desperate actions to cross the canal but we had no choice and finally Parmeshra had to scare her away to return. I gave him some money to keep with him. He was touched and prayed for my long life. It was a sad day for him as well. But he was very happy to see the smile on Mama's face. She had gone weak and had never been able to enjoy in her life. While returning, Parmeshra had said, '*Chotan Babu*, next time when you come you must plan to dig a well of our own at the rear of the house as *Malkin* has to go to someone's house for bath and water.' I promised him that next time, whenever I come, I would get enough money for a well of our own in the house. He was very happy.

The bus was about to leave, Parmeshra left. We no longer carried our clothes in the bag made of the old trousers of my father. I had brought one bag and a knapsack exclusively for her. It was quite cheap at Agra. Mama was very happy to put all her clothes in a different and separate bag. She had spent all her life keeping her articles in steel or iron boxes. It was evening time. We had not had anything to eat and were very hungry. I brought many things that she liked.

Mama had never travelled in a train; that too for one-and-a-half day's journey. I had reserved her a seat in the military quota. We had two berths to ourselves. It was something new and an amazing experience for her. I even had a water bottle to carry potable water. We had a nice journey till Agra. We had our vehicles to carry us to the cantonment area.

Many of the soldiers had brought their parents and other family members. The regimental center had organised a few days' stay for all the guests arriving with the soldiers. Mama could see our passing out parade and was thrilled to see her son in the rank and file of the parachute battalion. She also met many other families from south India and was astonished to hear their language. She wished to know and asked me, 'Why can't they speak Hindi and speak only English?'

I replied and made her understand, 'It is not English but Tamil, a south Indian language.'

It was like a foreign language for her. She met many of the south Indian families and enjoyed talking to them even though they didn't understand a word what she spoke or vice versa. It was an amazing experience for Mama. She was astonished to see the outside world. She could never imagine that there existed a world beyond our village and its dirty caste politics. Within a few days of her stay at Agra, her skin had acquired a lustre. She laughed, smiled and talked with everyone. She was an intelligent lady. She could even use a couple of English words within a few days and once I heard her saying to one of the officers' wives, 'Thank you, madam.'

I was thrilled to see Mama and thanked God for providing us with a few happy days together in life after a long time. I had brought her a pair of leather sandals, with a small heel. Mama had never put on any leather sandals and most of her life she had managed with slippers, mostly local ones made and purchased from the roadside or village market. She had given her slippers to me, while I was on the way to join my school at town, whereas she managed at the village without them, till the next crop was sold and she could get one for herself from the village market.

After the formal functions were over, a trip to the Taj was organised by the military authorities. Mama was aware of the history of Taj, as in her early days she had taught in a primary school. She couldn't believe that one day she would be able to see and touch the Taj Mahal that she had read and heard about. We got a joint photograph with the background of Taj. Mama was excited to see the photograph. I requested the photographer to hand it over to me before we left Agra as I was due for posting to one of the battalions of the Parachute regiments. I also requested one of the photographers to take a Polaroid photo that could be handed over to mother instantly. She wished to carry something that she could show to some of our relatives on returning to the village.

Mama was very worried to see the air show organised by the Parachute Training Centre, where she found many of the soldiers coming down from the sky, on to the dropping zone, very near to the place she had occupied a seat. It was a hair-raising experience for the older lot, as they hadn't seen anyone coming down from the sky with a parachute. Many times she stopped breathing to see them coming down from the aircraft. She asked me right after the air show, 'Do you also do the Jump?'

I replied, 'Yes, this is our primary role, and every parachute soldier had to go through this basic training.'

Earth moved beneath her feet. She cried and said, 'Son, I have only one child and the only reason to live my life. If something goes wrong with you, I will die.'

I understood her feeling and said, 'Mama, many of them are the only son or child. You should feel proud of me. Moreover, you only have created this patriotism and feeling for the nation in my heart.' I added, 'Your blessings are with me. Nothing will happen to me. Have faith in God, as long as you are alive and nothing would happen to me.'

Somehow, I managed to divert her attention from the sentimental and emotive topic. I had promised her that I'd make a toilet in the house, along with a well, very soon so that she didn't have to go out for the morning rituals in the open, on the banks of the river at the village. She hugged me. She knew many times our neighbours had stopped her from using their well and it was really embarrassing for Mama to beg them for water. I had planned to save every penny of my salary, till I had accomplished the task of making a toilet and a well of our own and a searchlight for her so that she could stay comfortably at the village. We had finished our sightseeing, including the Red Fort of Agra and Fatehpur Sikri. Mama enjoyed her trip thoroughly.

I wished to show Mama to a doctor. She had been suffering from stomachache for a long time but she didn't speak about it due to the fear of the expenditure that we would have incurred for the treatment. Once I explained that military hospitals are meant for the military personnel and their dependants and it would not charge us anything for the treatment, she agreed. Initially, she didn't believe it and thought I was kidding her. I took her to the military hospital at Agra and showed her to a specialist. Necessary tests were conducted on her. The doctors diagnosed and confirmed that she had developed appendicitis in her stomach. The doctors had also advised her to go for the operation as early as possible. I had no time and had to move to Delhi to join my battalion. I was in two minds and couldn't decide. I had no one at Delhi. I joined my battalion and requested my battalion commander and apprised him with the facts of my life. He was more than generous, and extended all possible help to get my mother admitted at the Army hospital in Delhi and get her operated before she could be sent to the village.

I cried in isolation and thanked God for being so kind to me. Mama was admitted. I was tense, as I didn't know what all she would have to go through before she was operated upon. The commanding officer of the battalion had spoken to a couple of doctors to help me out. He knew that my mother was a widow and I was her only child. It was mentioned in my dossier as well.

After all the formalities were over, she was operated upon at the army hospital in Delhi. The prognosis after the operation was of a speedy recovery. She was very happy and satisfied with the kind of treatment and care that was taken at the hospital. The cleanliness at the military hospital impressed her the most. She recovered very quickly she was given better food than she had ever had at the village.

Every soldier was given a few days leave on joining the battalion. I too got my leave. Mama looked relieved and recovered. She was feeling good. We had our reservation in one of the trains going back to Bhagalpur. I took her around Delhi to show her a few monuments that she had heard about right from her childhood. We visited the Lal Qila, Qutub Minar and Birla Mandir before boarding the train. It was a great day in her life. She enjoyed every moment of her stay at Delhi.

We boarded the train. She was now familiar with the rules and regulations of the train reservation and other journey-related hassles. We reached Bhagalpur and finally, our home. Mama felt as if she had come back after visiting some of the holiest places of her life. She looked much brighter than before. Most of the ladies told her that she looked bright and her complexion had also improved a lot. She talked very proudly about me to many of the villagers and our neighbours.

Many people came to meet us, including Yusuf with his wife and children. Ajra was very pleased to meet me. She had grown big and looked very pretty. She had a very fair complexion and very sharp features. She was shy of talking to me and wished to have a look at my uniform. All of them were damn impressed on seeing my uniform. Yusuf extolled me very highly in front of other villagers and gave my example. Ajra was floored and fascinated to see my uniforms and the muscular body that I had developed due to the rigorous exercises of the basic training. She sat near me, all alone, and wished to know the things we did in our training and the amount of money that I would earn every month. I replied to all her queries and came to know what she had in her mind but it was rather difficult to speak about in a conservative society like ours, more so in the village atmosphere. There would have been chaos and furore had I expressed my feelings to her, and if somehow they were to become public. She too, had a similar feeling and couldn't express it, though her eyes spoke everything. She spent hours together with us before leaving. Ajra was a little emotional. I could make out her heart throbbed faster and her voice trembled. She left my hands hurriedly when she could hear Mama approaching. She was damn scared of Ma and that had carried through to Mama as well. Shc had developed similar fear of Mama.

Parmeshra had not been able to look after my puppy well, as she had left home and didn't return for a long time. I looked for her but she was not traceable. Next day, Mama could locate her on the banks of the river and she returned home with her. She was very pleased to see me and spent most of the time at home. She made a lot of noise on seeing me, as if she was complaining about my leaving her and taking even mother away from her.

Mama was quite confident of me now and more aware of the nature of my job. She knew I was a soldier and now both of us were quite clear that I would never ever be able to become a colonel, as only an officer could become a colonel in the army. It was a very short leave and I had to return to the battalion. I returned with a heavy heart. Mama had come to see me off at the canal. This time also she cried but was happy, as she knew that the separation was inevitable and was for a purpose. She didn't wish to make me weak and was holding onto her tears. I knew once she returned, she wouldn't sleep the whole night and would cry for me. I too, felt very bad leaving Mama, but I had no other mission in life other than making her life comfortable and happy. That was the sole motive of my life. I wished I could keep her with me. I had made a comprehensive list of the utensils and other things needed for Mama to make her life a little easier. Of course, the first and foremost was the well and the toilet. My puppy tried to cross the canal but Parmeshra didn't allow her.

Parmeshra kept asking me, if there were something that could be done for Ramvilas. I myself was very new to the organisation and didn't want to raise false hopes in his mind and informed him that even for becoming a soldier, one had to have certain basic qualifications. I also advised him to focus his attention on the forthcoming Panchayat elections. He was a major and eligible to stand for Sarpanch and had a fair chance of winning, as the population of the lower caste and the Muslims were much more than that of the upper caste. 'He should channel and focus his attention on a fruitful purpose,' I advised.

Ramvilas was about to be released on bail. Mama had handed over set of *kurta pajama* to Parmeshra that she had bought for him at Delhi. He kept talking of Ramvilas and his bail. He was the only son of Parmeshra, though he had two daughters and once again Kusmi was pregnant. I could afford to pay him something. I hadn't done anything for him. It was as good as my duty to help him out in the time of crisis. He had virtually brought me up and we treated him like a family member. I paid him a little money. He asked for a little more as he had to visit to the town a few times, to meet the lawyer before Ramvilas was released on bail. He hugged me and requested me to take care.

I boarded the bus with the memories of my mother. I kept thinking of her throughout my journey and didn't feel like eating anything. Mama had given me *roti* and vegetables of bitter gourd. That was my favourite and it didn't get spoiled easily. I was very upset to leave Mama. I cried many times, covering my face with my handkerchief. I boarded the military compartment of Tinsukia Mail to reach Delhi. I had no reservation. I occupied a place with fellow soldiers and opened my holdall and went to sleep. I didn't feel like talking to anyone, as I was not in a position to share my feelings with anyone. I felt miserable. I didn't eat in the night and went to sleep. Next morning, I felt like eating but didn't want to throw away the *roti* that Mama had given it to me. It had got rancid as it had been cooked more than twenty-four hours ago. I didn't wish to throw it as it was made by Mama and ate it all. I was very hungry and didn't feel the foul smell or bad taste.

I reported to the battalion and met many new people and made many friends. I didn't share my feelings with anyone and every week, wrote letters to Prakash and mother. Prakash had qualified for the IIT (Indian Institute of Technology), at Kharagpur and was in his first year of mining engineering. I regularly wrote to him and received his replies every month or fortnight. I busied myself in the refresher cadre organised by the battalion and other physical activities. I was physically very fit and did well in every aspect of the physical training. My company commander and even the battalion commander liked me. I was one of the better soldiers of the battalion. Everyone liked me, being a soldier possessing all the required traits. We busied ourselves in the routine training programme of the battalion. The routine life of the battalion started. I didn't proceed on leave for a few years, mainly to ensure that I could save enough money to go for the construction of a well and a toilet at my house at the village.

Our letter writing spree continued from both the sides. Ramvilas was released on bail by the District Court, a few weeks after I left the village. Mama kept me posted on all the village matters concerning me. I was aware that the battalion was about to move to the east and it would certainly be nearer to my home but, unfortunately, we moved to the border and that too, to a very remote area. I had decided to go on long leave after reaching the field area, so that I could peacefully oversee the construction of the toilet and well.

We were aware that the battalion had spent a few years in the peace location and was about to be moved to the field area. We were sure that even we would be moved to the operation area in the east. Our battalion was given orders to move to the east, as the situation in the east was not harmonious. Insurgency was at its peak. Rightly so, the Commanding Officer announced the move of the battalion during the *Sainik Sammelan*. We had to move by road and our battalion was kept on high alert. The preparations for the move were on. Everyone was bubbling with the enthusiasm to get a poorvi medal, that is given to the soldiers posted in the field areas in the east. The youngsters were more excited, as they had no ribbons or medals on their chest as a part of their uniform.

It was time to move by road. Many of the vehicles were provided to the battalion by the higher formation. It took a few days to load before we started our journey to the east. Everyone heading the column, was briefed by the Commanding Officer for the night halt and the other formations located on the way, to fall back on, in case of emergencies. Everyone was also told about the route that was to be taken and every commander of the vehicle was provided with the route chart. It was a tiring and uncomfortable journey to move by road, more so as all the soldiers had to travel in the Shaktiman, a transport vehicle provided to the Indian army by the ordnance depot. We were on the move for more than a fortnight before we could reach to our operation area in the east. I had written to Mama regarding our movement somewhere in the east. I had also written that I'd write to her only after we reached our location.

No sooner did we arrive, we busied ourselves in the training programme. We were not really aware of the problems that we were about to face. We took the training programme that was organised as a routine training of the battalion. I had received mother's last letter, written by her in the month of August, wishing me a bright future and a long life as my birthday fell on thirteen September. I was very happy that Mama was all right and had not forgotten my birthday. I received this letter in the month of September. I wrote back to her immediately, as I knew letters took a very long time to reach our forward post in the field area, and even mailouts were protracted when we wrote to someone. Letters from home were the only thing that kept us happy in the field area. We knew that by the time we received another letter from home, it would be October. I wrote to her every week, as she used to be very worried in case she didn't receive any letter from me. We were deployed in the operational area. It was nearing winter and in the hills, Octobers were cold enough to cool the passions of the soldiers.

I was called by the Company Commander. I reached his office, thinking that being a blue-eyed boy of the Company Commander, he might offer me some special task during the forthcoming operation. I was surprised to find even the Commanding Officer of the battalion in the Company Commander's tent. No sooner I arrived, he asked me to enter inside his office. I greeted loudly and saluted with real *josh* to impress him and stood at ease. The Company Commander asked, 'Who all are there in your family?' Before I could have replied anything, the Battalion Commander asked me to occupy a seat. I became suspicious. There was something fishy, else none of the Battalion Commanders would offer a chair in his office to a young soldier, who had hardly a few years of service in the battalion. I had just finished three years and a few months in the battalion. The Battalion Commander was holding a piece of paper in his hand and asked me, 'Is there anyone else other than your mother at home.'

I replied, 'No sir.' The earlier Battalion Commander had met my mother and the rest was written in my dossier. They had verified that there was no one other than my mother at home and neither had she anyone to fall back upon. Once again, he asked me, 'Who is Parmeshra?'

It was too much of a excruciating suspense. Before they could have asked any other question, I took out the last letter that I had received from her and pleaded while putting it on their table, 'Sir, what is wrong? How do you know Parmeshra?'

I told them that he is the person who looks after all our property and crops in the village. I could make out there was something wrong. Both of them were looking into each other's eyes.

The Company Commander said, 'We are sorry to inform you that your mother expired last month, two days after she must have written this letter to you.'

A bombshell dropped on my head. My mouth remained open due to lack of words. I didn't know what to speak and what to inquire from them. I didn't believe my ears.

The earth moved beneath my feet. I was desolated with the news of Mama's death. All was dark before my eyes. I had nothing to say or talk. It was past twenty days since she had died. We had received the telegram sent by Parmeshra after almost fifteen days. There were no details as to how she had died. My reason for living was lost. Earth had become a foreign planet for me. There was nothing on this planet to keep me alive as my motive for living was gone. I had written four letters, after I had received her last letter and was waiting for her reply that was due anytime now.

The Commanding Officer said, 'You may like to proceed on leave.'

It was futile. 'Sir, for what?' I replied. If she had died last month itself there was nothing left for me to do. What would I gain by going on leave to know the reason how she had died? It was all over. I did not proceed on leave. Tears were pouring from my eyes. I didn't allow a word of sorrow to come out of my mouth. My uniform became damp with tears. The Commanding Officers hugged me and requested me to go on leave and complete the formalities of cremation and other rituals. I didn't find it necessary to visit the village where I had no one waiting for me. All I had was my puppy in the village. She would not be able to share the burden of the loss I had gone through. I knew they must have cremated her on the banks of the river at the village itself, that could be seen from the terrace of our house. No one would have felt the need of taking the dead body of Mama to the crematorium located at the bank of the Ganges at Bhagalpur, where Ma and father were cremated. I didn't know what Parmeshra must have done with her body.

The Company Commander tried his best to pacify me to take a few days leave and proceed home to complete the formalities. That would also assuage my mental tension and shock that I had undergone. I was not too sure of myself. What would happen to me in case I left the battalion? Therefore, I decided otherwise and did not proceed on leave.

I came back to the cadre class that was on. As soon as I arrived, the instructor could make out there was something wrong as my eyes were swollen. I had lost contact from my body. A different feeling arose in me. I had become totally numb. My life was not worth living. Her death had left me with a terrible sense of desolation and stupor. I had become an untouchable on this earth. At least an untouchable was touched and liked by someone, but I had none to look forward for. I had become worse than a dog. I had to live only for myself.

I was reminded of the prediction of the pundit, who had said after the death of my father that I had an extra tooth in to my mouth and I was very unlucky for my parents. My mother could never live her life happily. Right after a few years of my birth, we were living an isolated and difficult life though Mama had at least given me many things in life by sacrificing her happiness. But she could never live happily. How did she die? I was in deep thought when the instructor interrupted me and asked, 'What has happen to you? What did the Battalion and Company Commander tell you?'

All I could say, 'Sir, I lost my mother.'

He advised me to go to my tent and relax for some time. I thought it to be a better option and moved towards my tent. One of the soldiers, Pramod, who hailed from

Lucknow, was close to me and was sent by the instructor to look after me till I was more in control. I moved out of the class. The Company Commander ordered the instructor to send two of the boys to look after me till I came out of shock.

I cursed myself for the extra tooth in my mouth. I too started believing that it must be the reason for the death of my parents. I hadn't felt so bad when I had heard about the death of my father. But now it was unbearable. I didn't know what to do as my power of thinking had gone numb. My hands and feet had given up. I was totally broken. I didn't want to live a dog's life in this planet. It was a meaningless life for me. I had decided to end my life. I looked for an opportunity where I could sacrifice my life for a better cause in the battalion and get rid of this dog's life once and for all. I had decided to volunteer for any eventuality that might arise in the battalion where I could get a chance to lay down my life for the battalion or the nation. I could not speak and had become dumb. Even though I tried to speak something, I couldn't. I was granted a few days leave. I wished to spend them in the battalion itself. I even cursed God for being so cruel to me. I was in trauma and no one could have shared it. I had two options with me, either to finish my life or live a waif's life. It took quite a long before I could reconcile a bit and started my routine life in the battalion. One and all knew my plight and sympathised with me.

Chapter VII
SOLDIER

A few months passed. I had not been able to overcome the shock of my mother's death and was very nostalgic. It had left an indelible mark on my mind and heart. I was treated very gently in the battalion. Everyone sympathised with me due to the unfortunate incident that had occurred in my life. I was gradually becoming normal and never took any leave after the death of my mother. It was few years since I had gone on leave. I had no place to go on leave. Even the villagers thought that I had killed myself after the death of mother, as they were aware that I loved her very much. Moreover, Parmeshra had sent me a couple of letters after getting it written by someone who could write in the village, as he could neither read nor write. I hadn't written any letter to anyone, not even to Parmeshra. Even Prakash had got tired of writing to me, as I never replied to any of his letters after Mama's death. It was more than three years. I had not taken any leave and moved out of the battalion.

The Commanding Officer and my Company Commander were deeply worried about my personal life. They too sympathised with me. They wished to know whether I had any other relative who they could contact and send me on leave for a change. They also wished to change my Army Group Insurance to his or her name, after Mama's death as she was my next of kin in all the dossiers and even otherwise in my life. It was a mandatory requirement for them. I told them that I had no one else whom I could trust other than Parmeshra and Yusuf. They still must be thinking of me, and I was sure, must be looking after my agricultural property and would give me the account of each and every penny that they must have earned from the sale of the crops. They were stunned and removed the name of my mother as next of kin from my dossier. I, in fact, had requested them to put the name of the battalion as the next of kin. He was shocked to hear me and could appreciate my feeling. I never even took any advances from my pay that was due to me. They didn't know how to react to this situation. My salary credit had increased beyond expectations, as I had not sent any money to anyone nor I had taken any advance, barring a few times. Everyone in the battalion had become like a member of my family and treated me very nicely.

Our battalion was given a specific role of fighting insurgency in the east. We had just finished our annual training program and routine parachute jumps for the year and had returned to our field location. The Battalion Commander ordered the battalion to move to the thrust area of the battalion, before the real order to cordon off, search and attack on the insurgent, were ordered. It was a very difficult terrain and equally difficult to fight the insurgents in those areas. The insurgents had used booby traps to safeguard their hideouts. The company commander wished to send a patrol party to gain the information on the booby traps and the safe passage for the movements of the insurgents. They could use that as a probable escape route. He had asked for a few volunteers for this task. The platoon commander wished to take me along as one of the members of the patrol party.

It was a pitch dark night. We were closing in towards the enemy hideouts. Our platoon commander himself was a young lieutenant and bubbling with enthusiasm. He asked us to halt and he himself moved forward with another soldier. They moved very close to the hideouts of the insurgents. They were quite excited on their success and in the bargain, the platoon commander stepped on a booby trap and was killed instantly. The soldier accompanying him was shot at while he wished to retreat to the rendezvous area. We too opened fire on the insurgents and killed many of them and moved forward towards their hideout. We had activated the radio wireless set and informed the company commander for reinforcements to capture the insurgents before they changed their locations. We were eleven and six of us were killed on the spot. While moving forward, I too stepped on to one of the anti personal mines and injured my right leg. I had no pain and kept crawling forward towards the hideouts of the insurgents. Three of us had reached very near to the hideouts and had close encounters and firing with the insurgents. Many of the insurgents were killed on the spot before the reinforcement arrived. Two of us were still alive and looked for any kind of support. They were not able to locate us till the time I was in senses. Thereafter, it went all blank. I didn't know what happened.

Once I regained my senses, I was at the base hospital at Siliguri. My condition was serious and the doctor advised the Commanding Officer to arrange for our evacuation to the base hospital in Delhi. Both of us were evacuated to the base hospital in Delhi. The Commanding Officer had decided to save our lives. He was ready to do anything for us. He spoke to the higher formations and decided to evacuate us to Delhi on priority.

For the first few days, I was not at all aware what was happening to me. I was not even aware whether I was taken to Delhi or some other hospital nearby. My whole body had become numb due to the sedatives injected in me. I was not aware whether I had my foot joint on to my body or was already amputated. I remained in hospital for many days. I wished for death. It was painful. My fellow soldier had lost both his legs below the knees. I was not too sure of my legs as the doctor had to once again operate on me due to some complications in the last operation. I was in severe pain and requested the doctor to remove the full leg from my body. Once it was already cut, why to leave the rest? Better to get rid of the rotten part once and for all. The doctor was very sympathetic, but helpless. He didn't know how to react. Both of us were very young and below thirty. All the doctors were trying to save our limbs as much as they could. They had done enough R & D on my foot but ultimately, couldn't save it from amputation.

I thanked God for taking away my mother from my life, as she wouldn't have been able to bear to see me without a leg and would have killed herself. She had been planning to look for a match and get me married in a few years' time. She had dreamt of many things. She would have someone in her house whom she would never treat the way she had been treated in that house. It was good that she didn't see me in this condition, where I couldn't even go to the toilet without support. My life was finished. I didn't want to live and become a lifelong burden on others. The doctors had informed me that I was in hospital for six months. But it looked as if I had just been admitted. I was at the same hospital and same ward where Mama had been admitted for her operation. I had visited her several times there when she had been operated for appendicitis.

Many of the officers and other ranks visited us at the hospital. Our commanding officer was elevated and one of our battalion officers took the reigns of the battalion. Both of them came to meet me in the hospital. I had improved and could walk independently with the help of crutches. I was asked to report to the artificial limb centre for army personnel at Pune. I moved along with other soldiers to Pune to get my prosthetic half-right leg that had been amputated. They took the final measurements and asked us to collect our legs after six months. All the soldiers had returned to their respective units. All of us were given a special support instead of the heavy crutches. I was happy to return to my unit that was like my home and family, though I was good for nothing for the battalion. In fact, I had become a liability.

We reported to the unit. Both of us were given a grand welcome. The other soldier was asked to put in his papers as he had lost both his feet and could hardly do any work for the battalion. The doctors at the military hospitals had recommended boarding him out of the army on medical grounds. Even at the court of inquiry, the board of officers had recommended his release with some compensation and medical pension. We had received our kits from the artificial limb centre, Pune, and were fitted with prosthetics. He was pained when he heard of his future. He was no good to his family, as he had lost both his legs. The military's medical pension couldn't have compensated for his loss and his sacrifice for the nation. The petty amount that a soldier gets after losing his limb, is not sufficient to look after the whole family, lifelong. I was not worried about the financial aspect, as I had no one to support but he had his parents and three children. He shared his feelings with me as we had become quite close to each other as we stayed at the same hospital and suffered in the same military operation against the insurgency. His papers for release were forwarded to the record office by the battalion.

That gave me a severe jolt and made me very upset. In case the doctors recommended boarding me out of the army, where would I go? I was utterly bereft. This bothered me day in and day out. The battalion that was now like my home and I wished to die for, it too had become an outside world for me overnight. It was about to be snatched away by destiny. This fear haunted me as and when any officer called me, I used to be nervous and jittery.

My life in this world had become worse than for my puppy. At least I had been with her to ensure that she could get inside her home, her beam. But for me, there was no place to go. I was of no good to the battalion or the nation for which I had put everything at stake. If they did not have any feelings and discarded fellow soldiers out of the battalion, what could I expect from anyone else in the country or outside the battalion?

After the death of Ma, my puppy had no problems sitting near the beam, as she could not get beneath the beam. She was too big to get under the beam so she sat near the beam, putting her mouth under it. I had no home of my own. Wherever I tried to make my home, it was snatched away by destiny. I couldn't fight with my destiny.

The Commanding Officer had asked the Subedar Major to look after me and assign only light duties to me. I was put in the dispatch section and could not participate in any of the activities of the battalion, not even in the parachute jumps. Though a couple of times I was permitted, but it was difficult for me, after coming down on the ground, to manage things. No one wished to take a risk. In case I would have died in the process, the Battalion Commander would have had a tough time answering the higher formation, as I was with permanent medical category and was not allowed anymore to go for jumps. As far as the active services were concerned, I was a redundant soldier and couldn't participate in any such activities.

I could pull along with the battalion for a few years, but it had become increasingly difficult for me to stay at the battalion, as many soldiers cursed me for not doing anything and enjoying life. It was gradually becoming suffocating for me. I pondered and mulled long enough before I decided to hang my spurs once and for all. I asked for an interview with the Battalion Commander and requested him to get me released on medical grounds. It was impossible for me to remain idle and do some piddling work. I would have been entitled to medical compensation and pension but I was not at all worried about my financial aspect. I completed the formalities of release and within a few months, the dates had arrived to report to the regimental centre at Agra. The regimental centre was the place, where rest of the formalities relating to pension and compensation were to be done.

All the colleagues gave me a send-off party and a few of them came to see me off at the railway station. I felt the same as my puppy had felt, when Ma had thrown it out of its home. There was no difference between my puppy and me. Both had a similar fate; both of us were good for nothing in this materialistic world. As long as I was healthy and I could do something for the battalion, even the battalion commander took care of me, but today, I was a redundant soldier, I was no good for the battalion or the army or the nation. I treated my puppy better than the way other humans treated me. Perhaps, I had no expectation from my puppy and primarily we had developed a relation of caring and sharing. It was not a relation of give and take on which most of the human relations are based. As long as one could contribute to the interest of the battalion or nation, his interests were looked after. No sooner is one not in a position to contribute, he is redundant, and no one cares for him. I was not the only soldier who lost his limb for the cause of the battalion or the nation. There are many hapless soldiers who lose their limbs, but what happens to them thereafter? They spend their life in isolation and darkness. He remains no good for the family, society or the nation. I had not only accepted these hard facts, but also experienced it during my stay at the battalion, after losing my limb. Though it is very easy to sermonise, it is very difficult to accept such hard facts.

I was told by the Subedar Major, to come to the battalion as and when I felt like. It was rather a joke for a person with one leg. I boarded the train for home. I had to return home almost after a decade. I was not aware what had happened to my puppy. She must have died and at the time of her death also, she must have remembered me. I was not too sure of any of the humans of the village, whether they ever remembered me other than Parmeshra and Yusuf. I didn't know whether anybody would even recognise me or not.

At the regimental centre, I met many other soldiers. They were more than thrilled to remove the uniform. They had reported to the pension establishment, after completion of their contractual mandatory service, to qualify for the military pension, from where they would go home with a lot of money and carry something or other for all their relatives and children. Most of them were on a shopping spree. They laughed at me to find me sad on leaving the army. I didn't want to share my feelings ever with anyone.

I had decided to follow what the great poet Rahim had said,

Rahiman niz man ki bayatha,
man hi rakho goy,
Sun ithalaeyen log sab,
bantin na lahiye koi.

Though I don't know exactly what Rahim meant, but one thing I had understood from it was not to share one's feelings and shed tears before anyone, as no one could understand and share another's feeling. All they could do was to laugh and make fun of me and my amputated foot.

There was nothing worse than what I had already gone through. I could remember a *sher* told by some one that Mama had told me not only once, but several times.

Us shaks ke gam ka
koi andaz lagaye,
Jis shaks ko roten hue
dekha na kisi ne.

They didn't know the feeling and the flames I had concealed in my heart. I had a good amount of money on my credit balance on account of my pay and allowances, as I had never taken even a day's leave after my mother's demise. I had left all my personal belongings at the battalion as I would not have been able to carry any heavy luggage. Moreover, it was of no good to me. After all, what I would have done with these earthly things carrying them all the way to my village?

I approached once again, the same photographer at Agra who had photographed us, when Mama had visited Agra on our passing out parade at the Parachute Training Centre. He was unable to locate the negative and requested me to come after two days. I promised to pay him a good amount if he could provide me with a good laminated copy of our photographs. He had agreed. He could make out that I had some special relation with Mama and maybe she was no more. Though I had not opened my mouth, my eyes could convey him all as they had become wet with the thoughts of Mama. I approached him after a few days and he could locate the negatives of the photograph, taken before the Taj, of Mama and me. I requested him to prepare two laminated copies, each of a different size and a few smaller copies of the photographs. I paid a little advance and promised to pay him the rest on delivery. I had finished all the formalities for the pension and related matters and was planning to move back to the village.

In the evening, I visited the Taj and touched the place where Mama had touched and seen the flowers inscribed on the marble. I sat at the place where she had sat with me for hours together. I could feel the same wind that blew, the day I had Mama with me. I could see the gaps between the stones on the walkway where my boot had got stuck and I was about to fall. Mama had held my hand firmly. I had both my feet intact at that time, and I needed Mama's help. How would I be able to live the rest of my life without her and that too with one leg? The Taj had testified to a few happy moments of my life that I had spent with her. I smiled as I was reminded of one of the genuine doubts that Mama had asked me regarding the Taj Mahal. 'Chotu, did Shah Jahan and Noor Jahan or Mumtaj really exist?' she had asked. I had laughed and replied, 'Obviously, if they didn't how come this Taj came into existence? This is the testimony to their existence?' I was in deep thought, when a photographer approached and requested me to go for a lifetime memory at one of the wonders of the world. I was indeed thankful to the photographer and the Taj for giving me at least a photograph of Mama, otherwise perhaps, I would have been deprived of even that. I ignored him and moved on as thereafter I didn't want any memories in my life. These were the few reminiscences that I had of her. I collected the photographs and brought a couple of clothes for Parmeshra and Yusuf and left for the village.

I reached the bus stand, from where we generally alighted for the village. Nothing much had changed. The road was almost the same. The basic difference was that the last time when I had visited this bus stand, I could walk on my feet. I could also help Mama getting down from the bus, as the step of the bus was quite high and one had to really struggle to get off. But this time I myself needed help to get off the bus. People gave a strange look at my feet, more so because it was conspicuous from my walk that I limped. Another problem that I was about to face, was walking with the artificial leg on the *kuchha* bullock-cart tracks and the narrow embankment of the fields. It was difficult for me to walk over the divider of the fields either with crutches or with the artificial leg. I needed both to walk comfortably. I didn't know how to negotiate the embankments of the fields; the short cut walkway track to the village was very difficult to negotiate with the crutches. Its width was not sufficient to help the placing of the crutches. I sat on the ground with the only rucksack that I was carrying, with hardly any clothes in it. I removed my artificial leg and stored it in my rucksack and also folded my trouser upwards. It took hell lot of time for me to reach the village. Most of the people working in the fields and passing by stood watching me walk as if I was performing in the circus. I attracted everyone's attention. I sat on the *kuchha* track, before entering the village and put my prosthetic foot on to my right leg. It was something different and new for the villagers. Everyone goggled at me.

No sooner did I enter the *Chamar toli* of the village, many children and elders followed me. I felt as if I was the Pied Piper of Hamlin, who had come to take away all the rats and children out of the village. Some of them asked, 'Who are you? Whose guest are you? Which village do you belong?'

I was flooded with various questions by the various people in the local lingo that they spoke. I ignored their questions and moved on. I was not surprised to hear the questions by my own villagers. I had to give my identity to the people, where I had spent my childhood. I had become a stranger in my own village. No one recollected who I was. I straightway went to Parmeshra's house, with the herd of humans following me, like we followed the snake or monkey charmers as a child.

He was having his lunch from an aluminium pot. He was foxed to see me. He could not recollect who I was! I was very tired and sweating profusely. It was very difficult to walk with one leg with the support of crutches on the *kuchha* track, that also for miles together. Moreover, I was well built and had put on a lot of weight due to lack of any physical activities, as my movements were totally restricted due to the loss of limb.

I sat on the floor and could see Kusmi coming out with a small baby in her lap. She had covered her face with sari on seeing an unknown person in their house. Many children and elders had been following me right after I had entered the village. All of them were surprised to see me entering a lower caste house. A whole lot of lower castes had gathered before his house to see a man with an artificial foot. It was for the first time that the villagers must have seen a person with an artificial limb. I was an enigma to be watched and scrutinised in the village. I was like a snake or bear charmer that came to the village with a *damru* in hand, collecting the children and the elders for the show. In my own village, I had become an unknown person and an object of entertainment.

Parmeshra came out of his house. It was a big house with concrete; not the *kuchha* mud house with thatched roof that I had seen last when I had left the village. I was confused to see the changes in his lifestyle and living standard. He came out and stood before me. He had lost a few teeth and looked much older than I had seen him last. His cheeks had hollowed and he had developed wrinkles all around his face and neck. That gave me a precise idea of the time I had spent away from the village and the death of my mother. He could recollect me instantly and pulled my hands to embrace me in his arms. He cried on seeing me. He had real tears in his eyes. He cried loudly. Many of the lower caste females and even men wiped their numb eyes as they too had tears in their eyes to see Parmeshra crying. By now, they were fairly clear about the facts and reality of my life. Kusmi and the rest of the villagers kept watching the scene outside his house.

He immediately exclaimed, 'Kusmi our *Chotanbabu* has come. Get fresh cold water from the well.'

I wiped the sweat from my forehead and once again sat on the half concrete wall outside his house. He had not seen my feet. Neither had he any idea of my disability. Kusmi returned with a full bucket of water from the well, a *lota* of mixed metal was washed with mud, right before me, and a full *lota* of water was offered to me. I was really thirsty. The water had the same taste that it had the day I had left the village. This water reminded me of my village days when I used to be offered water by Mama or Ma. Parmeshra was very upset to see the people gathered around his house and proudly said, 'Please leave. He is not an animal, he is my *Chotanbabu.*'

The elders could understand about me, but I could see the little ones and young ones giving me strange looks. They had not been able to guess who I was. Many of the elders came and sat near me. Parmeshra ran to locate a chair for me. While I was busy talking to the people, he arrived with the chair and made me sit on the chair. He also asked me a point blank question, '*Chotanbabu*, They are saying you have artificial leg, that you have put on before entering the village.'

Kusmi was in tears. She couldn't think that a child who had played in her lap could lose his limbs. I didn't answer and asked about mother. There was pin drop silence. No one was able to speak anything. Parmeshra avoided the topic and said, 'First you relax. We will talk about it later.'

I took out the packet of the kurta pajama that I had brought for him from Agra and a tin of jam and toffees and handed them over to Kusmi. She was having a child in her hand. I couldn't guess its identity. Many of the Brahmin and other upper caste boys came to see and ascertain my identity. They were rather shocked to know my identity. Many of them were of the impression that I was dead and, in fact, they had taken back few acres of our land adjacent to their land from Parmeshra. They couldn't do so with the land that was with Yusuf Mian, as it was located nearer to the Muslim-dominated village and it was rather difficult to dictate to Yusuf. He was a man who had displayed unflinching loyalty to our family right from his childhood and wouldn't have given up so easily.

Parmeshra collected the key of my house and moved with me to take me to the house. The village had completely changed. Most of the houses in the lower caste *para* were of concrete or of bricks with thatched roofs, whereas there was not much of a change in the houses in the *tola* of the upper caste, barring a few of them. Parmeshra could make out that whatever the villagers had told him was true and I could not walk properly without the support of crutches or the artificial limb with single crutches. I could see Parmeshra's face. He couldn't bear the thought of my losing a limb, and was curious to know and see what had happened to me. Kusmi followed us. Parmeshra took out the chair that my grandfather once sat, and placed it on the veranda while Kusmi cleaned the house. It gave me a feeling of utter desolation.

Nothing had changed. The beam was lying at the same place but the owner of that beam who had made it a house was not visible. This beam was the first house of my puppy. It remained at the same place but its inhabitant had gone forever. It was the same case with my house. It remained the same but the inhabitants of it had left it forever. It was no more a house; just an earthly entity that stood there as a testimony of my earlier generation who had lived there.

I walked inside the house and went straight to the room where I had shared my bed with Mama, right from childhood all along till I left the village. Albeit apathy and neglect were conspicuous, but Parmeshra had tried his best. He couldn't have done better, as I was almost forgotten and written off by the villagers. It was known as dark room as there was only one window that also remained closed due to the fear of snakes entering the house. Mama never opened the rear windows of the room. I opened the window to see things properly. The bed was rolled up, the cot remained at the same place. Parmeshra had not entered or allowed anyone to enter this room. It was reasonably dark in the room. The torch that I had provided to her, when I had visited her after class tenth examination, was lying under her pillow. I lifted the torch. It was not glowing, I tried opening the rear cover to see the condition of the Eveready battery that I had asked her to use. I could not open the cover.

The bed smelt of the aroma of mother's body. I had not been able to forget the aroma of her body that I had been used to right from my childhood. Even in the dark I could make out whether she was on the bed or not. Parmeshra opened all the windows and doors of all the other rooms and corridor. I could clearly see all the letters even the last one that I had written to her from Chungthang – a place on the China border. It was nicely kept under her pillow. I picked it up, removed the dust that it had collected over a period of time, and smelled it. This too could bring me near mother – the mere smell of her hands.

Mama must have cried after reading most of my letters, as I could see the stains left by the teardrops on the letter. Many of the words were washed away with her tears. I opened the cover. It was the registered letter cover especially printed for registered post. I had used that cover to send her fifty rupees for her expenses. I could not save more than twenty rupees every month as the salary that I used to get then was not very high. I picked up the envelope and took out the letter. I cried. My hands became numb to find that very fifty rupees neatly folded in the cover along with my letter. I had a typical way of folding the letter and mother had not upset the crease of the folding and had retained the creases made by me. I could smell mother. I could feel her in the room I was unable to make my heart understand that it was an illusion. She didn't exist and would never return. I felt as if I have come on leave to spend a few weeks with her, and she would yell any time, offering me a glass of water, lay food for me or ask me to change my clothes.

Many grains stored in the sack and terracotta pots had got rotten, in the house. I could see the pot of *toor* dal that she used to keep exclusively for me, after grinding it at home. It was then taken from the land that Yusuf cultivated. That piece of land was famous for the cultivation of the best quality of *toor* dal in our area. Mama always retained it exclusively for me and prepared it the very first day I joined her at the village.

Parmeshra had not allowed anyone to open the room, as he wanted to preserve her memories and keep everything as it was, before she had died and also keep safe any expensive things that she might have in her box. Though all those were of no good to me, I was really touched the way he had handled mother's affairs. There were no cows in the premises. I decided to open her boxes and see the things only after cleaning the house thoroughly.

Kusmi had brought a pot full of milk and asked if I would like to have a cup of tea or something to eat. I came out and sat on my grandfather's chair. Parmeshra still respected me as before. I had not found any change in his attitude. I did not know how they could make a reasonably good house and even have a tractor.

Things had drastically changed. I sat on the chair in the veranda and could see one very small puppy moving out of the ruined *tabela*, the cowshed that was in ruins as there was no one to look after the animals and its residence. It was a cute looking puppy. It couldn't be more than few weeks old. Perhaps my puppy was of the same age when I had brought her to the house, after washing all the mud in the rainwater. I picked her up in my lap and could see similar patches on her face and ears. It must be a third or fourth generation of my puppy. I walked over towards the *tabela*, the cowshed to see from where this puppy had come out. Parmeshra could see the same Chotu once again in me and led me to the piles of brick arranged by him years ago. I could see the bricks lying where I had made the first house for my puppy.

Parmeshra stopped me entering the corral, and said, '*Chotanbabu*, please don't enter this *tabela*. This is the place where *Malkin* was bitten by the pit viper. It was night time. *Malkin* had gone to feed the cow for the last time in the night. It was her bad luck that she couldn't see as she was not holding the lantern. She had kept it outside the corral. She perhaps mistook the snakebite for some thorn, before she started feeling uneasy and rushed towards my house. By the time she reached my house, she was in a bad shape and about to collapse,' he said. 'She couldn't even communicate properly what had happened to her,' he continued. 'I could make out she was bitten by a snake and made arrangements to carry her to a hospital at the town. There were no educated people or the teacher or the clerical variety to accompany us. I could not save the *Malkin*, and the owner of the family, who had saved my life, when I was bitten by a snake. We reached very late to the hospital and she died early in the morning,' he narrated in tears, the story of mother's death.

My hands trembled with the mere thought of the suffering she must have undergone before she died. I felt ashamed of myself, being a son who could do nothing for her. Perhaps, had I been around, I would have been able to save her life.

Parmeshra once again made me sit on the chair and wiped his tears with the *gamcha* that he had on his shoulder. He said, 'I have committed another sin by not taking *Malkin's* body to the town on the banks of the Ganges, for cremation and had cremated her at the riverside crematorium, at our village.' He continued, 'I had requested the pundit to light the funeral pyre of *Malkin*.'

I looked at him and said, 'That would not have made any difference even if you would have lit the funeral pyre of mother. In any case, it was the dead body of a *lavarish* – body of a person that had no one to care for.'

He put his hands over my mouth and said, '*Malik*, please don't speak like that. She was our *Malkin* and I tried my best to save her life.'

Before I could have asked him about mother's *Asthi Kalas*, he himself said, 'I have buried the earthen pot of *Malkin's Asthi Kalas* in the courtyard of the house. Only the pundit and I know about it.'

I was very happy to know about it. I requested him to show me the place where he had buried it. It was properly cemented. I decided to take it out, only after discussing with the pundit and to take it to the Ganges where the ashes of all our ancestors were submerged. I was not in a position to take it to Benaras where Mama had arranged to submerge the *Asthi Kalas* of my father. I hugged Parmeshra and conveyed my appreciation for preserving the *Asthi Kalas* of mother till date. I bent down and paid my obeisance at the place and cleaned the surface with my hands. Parmeshra was very emotional by nature and started crying. Even Kusmi cried all the while we discussed this topic.

It was all over for me. I had decided my future plans. I asked Parmeshra about the details of Ramvilas and other people in the village. It was a pleasant surprise to know that Ramvilas stayed in the city and was appointed as the district president of one of the national parties. There were very fair chances that he might get elected as an MLA, on the ticket of that party. I knew the way things were moving in the village and the way hatred between the various castes were growing. It was bound to give birth to many such local leaders from the lower castes. He was elected as the Sarpanch of the area before. There were many upper caste boys from the village who worked in his office. He had employed many of the village boys with his influence in the coalmines under Coal India Limited and other industries in the area. His power and influence was unquestionable. He is the potential future of our country.

'He was about to hold an election rally organised to protest against the deforestation of land and illegal mining by the upper castes along with one of the national leaders visiting that area.' Parmeshra informed.

I asked. 'Which place are they going to organise the rally?

He replied, 'At Godda, *Chotanbabu*, you too must attend. I will request Ramvilas to arrange for a jeep for you. Nowadays, a jeep can enter the village through the bullock-cart tracks. It is totally dry.' I could see the pride in his eyes.

They were the people beaten by the upper caste for suspected petty thefts of their goats or cows in this village. Today, they were united and had brought down and trampled the entire false ego and traditions of the upper caste to dust. Kusmi was the proud mother of a potential MLA or, perhaps, a minister.

I could see the hatred in Parmeshra's eyes for the upper caste. Probably, it was not for me as I was good for nothing or no threat to anyone of them.

Kusmi had given birth to four other children after I had left. In fact, she too was pregnant when Ramvilas' wife delivered. Both Kusmi and her daughter-in-law delivered the same year. The child Kusmi carried in her lap was not of Ramvilas but her own. This was not very uncommon or out of place to find in the village, both mother and daughter or daughter-in-law carrying at the same time. It was not only confined to the lower caste but it was common amongst all the castes in the village. The teacher and clerks had left everyone behind, as they had a little extra money to support and could offer their offsprings Bournvita or Dabur Chavanprash. They had left behind everyone. They had the maximum number of children and their wives carried even when their daughters or daughter-in-law also carried.

Parmeshra and Kusmi were a little apprehensive of doing petty work in an upper caste house. Though they could do so out of decency, but it was not for ever. They themselves had a few of the lower caste women working for them. He offered to help me on this, as long as I stayed in the village. I was not very surprised and was amazed as to why they had not been able to accept these facts and speak the truth so far.

Finally the truth was out. He promised to pay me the amount of income that he had enjoyed over a period of time, after mother's death. I could make out I had become an outcaste by even the lower caste. I didn't have anything to cook or any other place where I could have my food. Parmeshra offered to continue sending food to me, as long as I wished. I requested him to send information to Yusuf if he could meet me, as I wouldn't have been able to travel to his village, though after Ma's death I had been to his house with Mama several time. Parmeshra left along with Kusmi.

I sat outside the house and didn't know what to do and how to plan my life, all alone in this world. I had a fair amount of money to lead a normal life that a clerk or a teacher could lead in this village. I cleaned the whole room where I used to sleep with Mama, and had slept with her the last day I had come to leave her on returning from Delhi, after her appendicitis operation. I took out her only photograph and arranged it in one of the better rooms of the house, where Ma lived. I removed her *Charkha* and placed the photograph of both Ma and Mama. I had no photograph of my father. If at all Mama had one, that must have been lying in her tin boxes.

I had not been able to make a well or a toilet or even get her a searchlight, as I had promised. Had I been able to provide her with a searchlight, probably she would have been alive today. I was the real cause of her death. First of all, that extra tooth in my mouth and secondly, I hadn't been able to hand her a searchlight or a better quality torch, that was available at the military canteens at a reduced price. I was the real cause of my Mama's death. These thoughts were killing me from within and made me very upset.

I had great problems going to the riverside for defecating and morning ablutions, for the first few days as many children from the village followed me till I vanished behind the bush. Subsequently, I had decided to return before they woke up like Ma or mother used to do. I now had a searchlight and was sure that I wouldn't die of snakebite. Moreover, I had only one leg. That meant the risk of snakebite had reduced by fifty per cent.

Chapter VIII

AJRA – THE LOST LOVE

It was very early in the morning. I was returning from my morning ablutions. I could see in the twilight, a shadow moving on the divider of the fields towards the village. I had decided to go to the banks of the river, before the children of the village woke up and followed me to see how I eased myself and struggled due to one leg. I had great difficulty on the banks of the river. It was a major operation for me. I couldn't sit properly to ease myself and children and even some of the elders observed me, standing on a high ground and laughed. I had no other way but to ignore or avoid them. It was very embarrassing and irritating, but since many of the elders too enjoyed and laughed watching me, it was rather difficult to stop the children from making remarks. Moreover, whenever or wherever I came across any children, they addressed me as *Aye Langda,* meaning a man without a leg. I was addressed in the village as *Langda Sepoy*. Initially, it hurt me a lot, as my own countrymen and especially the villagers who were all fully aware of my predicament, addressed me as *Langda*, what to talk and expect from others! Yes! This is the medal or *tagma,* a retired and hurt soldier gets in this country by their own countrymen. I had reconciled with the world and didn't take it to heart at all and forgave them for their ignorance.

The man walked faster on the grass glistening with morning dew. I had to be very careful before placing every step on the grass covered with cold dew. The dew that I had enjoyed all through my life in the village, as I had moved about on bare feet, till Mama had given me her slippers, before I had left for the town for schooling. That shadow was clearer than before in the fast approaching first light. The birds' movements on the Peepul were vigorous. It twittered about the Peepul tree taking off and returning again. It was their home where they could roost and freely move in or out, without any restrictions. This peepul had stood there for many years, perhaps even before my grandfather was born. It was a witness to all the events that took place, year after year in the village. Perhaps, even our grandfather must have watched many cobras eating the baby birds, while rest of the birds like mynahs, parakeets, parrots and others chirped to scare it away and attacked it with their beaks. I was not the only one acquainted with the natural phenomena of nature that took place at times on the peepul tree. Generation after generation had passed to observe the natural phenomena that took place here.

By now, I had entered the mango grove and the tree under which I had performed the rituals of Ma and father's death. My one foot and the crutches made noises while I moved, disturbing the old, yellow dry leaves on the ground. The shadow had not entered the mango grove yet, and probably had not been able to hear the noises that I made. It was about to catch up with me. I stood for a while under the tree to have a rest, as I could not walk continually. I turned around to have a look. The shadow was closing in faster.

I stood under the tree. It was one of the trees that had seen many young and old ones completing the last rites of the death of their near and dear ones. I moved on. The shadow had come quite close to me. He was not able to see me properly and gave a strange look and moved on. He left me behind. I could make out who he was. There were not much of a change in his walk and height, as it was in my case. I took time to reach home. It was open. I never locked the house right from the day I had arrived. There was nothing in the house that one could steal. Moreover, I had got over the fear of all this and had very little attachment for earthly things. I had seen life and death very closely. That had transformed my life, and I had transcended above all these rituals of life like caste, creed, name, fame and wealth after Mama's death. There were absolutely nothing that attracted me on this earth. Whatever little desire I had to live was only for Mama. That also was ultimately snatched by the Almighty. All these had become useless for me. I had realised that there were hardly any difference between a soldier and a tree – both of them live for others.

I arrived at the entrance of the house, and I could see the person peeping inside the house and yelling for someone. He had not climbed the veranda. He knew he was an untouchable for this house. How could he enter? A small piece of tile was lying on the ground and it made a cracking sound as it came under the steel cap of the crutches. The shadow turned around. I knew he was Yusuf, a very fair old man with a lot of wrinkles on his face. He just wore a *kurta* over a lungi in checks.

He was not too sure of my identity. It was a fairly bright morning now. I moved closer to him. I gave a warm call, '*Yusuf Mian, main apka Chotanbabu*.'

He came closer. He was now smaller to me in height. He held my crutches and cried, 'What is this? What has happened to you? Where were you all these days? Many people said you are dead!' Tears filled his eyes. He embraced me in his arms, whispering many things. I felt like a small baby and was reminded of the days when I sat on his lap and at times was lifted on to his shoulders. I had once cleaned my nose with his lungi, Mama had scolded me, but he had never said anything and once again cleaned all the phlegm of my nose properly with his lungi.

My relation with him was filial and fraternal. I could see tears rolling down his eyes. I wiped it with the hand towel that I always carried with me to hold the crutches. He helped me to climb on to the veranda. He didn't want to come up.

I requested him and told him, 'Yusuf Mian, Parmeshra has grown big. I am left with no one of my own in this village. If you too will not enter my house, I will lose another tree that could provide me with its shade.'

He understood and climbed on to the veranda. I brought the chair out of the room and requested him to sit. He took a few minutes before occupying it. He had never visited alone. Perhaps this was the first time I had seen Yusuf Mian coming to our house all alone and asked him, 'Where is Ajra?'

He was stunned. His face became red. He looked perplexed. Deep despondent lines could be seen on his face. *Did I ask him anything that I shouldn't have asked,* I thought. 'She must have grown very big.' I said. He didn't reply at all. I once again asked, 'Where is Ajra?'

He cried and said, '*Chotanbabu* she is in hell.'

I couldn't understand what he meant. I once again put my hands over his thighs and requested him to tell me the facts. What he told me was disgusting. There were no justifications for such things in the time of modern era and humanity. The story of Ajra was disgusting as well as pathetic.

In his village, there was a haji, a well-to-do farmer, who came back after pilgrimage to Mecca and Medina. After his return, the muezzin of the village called a meeting of the Muslims on a *Jumma* day after Namaj, and requested them to offer their daughters in marriage to the haji saheb, as that would pave a path to heaven. Yusuf, being one of the poor farmers of that village, was under tremendous pressure to offer his daughter to the haji saheb. He perhaps was one of the Muslims in that village who survived on the agricultural income from the land owned by the Kafirs. That was not liked by many of the fundamentalist of his clan and they wished to eliminate him.

He had two daughters, Ajra and Farida. Ajra was his elder daughter; we were, in fact, brought up together. On our every visit to his house or his to ours, we had seen her growing into a pretty girl. Yusuf tried his best but couldn't avoid the pressure of the clergies of his village. They had threatened to discard him from the Muslim society. He succumbed to the pressure of the well-to-do Muslims of his village and sacrificed his lovely daughter. It was a real cruelty against a minor girl child, but there was no one to support or raise their voice against the strong powerful lobby of the clergies and the hajis of the village.

Finally Ajra, then aged about fifteen or sixteen, the daughter of the poorest Muslim, Yusuf, was offered in marriage to the eighty-year-old haji, whose grandchildren were much older than Ajra. Yusuf cried and called for help but couldn't resist. Ajra, being a child, didn't know what was happening to her. She too cried once she realised what had happened to her but it was too late. She was sacrificed to the old traditions of the Muslims. She was victimised on the name of Islam.

After a few years, Ajra gave birth to three sons from the grandchildren of haji saheb. In other words, the grandchildren of the haji saheb produced their own father. It was pathetic.

He cried before me profusely. I solaced him and asked, 'Where is she now?'

He replied, 'With me. I have to look after her. After the death of the haji she was blamed for having relations with other men and was thrown out of their house.'

I was shaken by this story. I had thought I was the only victim of the curse of nature, but there were many. I was not the only soul who suffered from the cruelties of the society or nature. I could remember Ajra, a very pretty child with toffees in her hand sitting in the lap of her father. I had met her last, when she had grown into a pretty lass bubbling over with youth. Her bust was almost bursting forth from her tight salwar kameej. Mama was able to guess that I had been looking at her breast and arch and the cleavage of her back. If I had loved any girl in my life that was her. I confessed it, but it was rather late in life for anything.

Yusuf was a broken man with an enormous liability on his shoulders. His son was even younger to Ajra's elder child. He had apprehension about my future plans for the land.

'I have kept some money from the income that I had over a period of time,' he said, 'but *Chotanbabu*, I wouldn't be able to return it in one go.'

I admired the truthfulness and moral courage in a man of his calibre. I put my hands once again on his thighs and said, 'I haven't asked you at all about the money, and also promise you to help if you wish to go for pilgrimage to Mecca and Medina yourself.'

'Inshallah!' he whispered, astounded. He was stunned to hear my offer. Tears rolled down his eyes off the chin. He got off the chair and hugged me and said, 'You are my son. My wife was right when she said that nothing would have happened to you and you would return to the village. She always prayed and offered Namaj for your long life and safety. She never believed that you are dead as everyone in the village.'

He had suffered at the hands of the clergies and the only option Yusuf Mian had was to go for the pilgrimage himself to safeguard his interest. That would have also assuaged his rage for the clergies. I had a fair amount of money as I had no liabilities at all, and had hardly spent anything while in the battalion. I asked Yusuf to continue cultivating and retain even my share of fifty per cent till he could go for Haj. I also assured him I'd pay a little additional cash whenever he planned for that. I also offered to meet Ajra and his other family members whenever he visited next. He agreed to bring them whenever he planned his visit to our village. Yusuf left more than satisfied and was saddened to see my condition – I needed help to even put on knickers. I handed him the pajama kurta that I had brought for him from Agra. He was not ready to accept, as he had never put on a pajama and wore lungis all his life. I had insisted that he leave the house in the new set of kurta and pajama to surprise his wife. He looked different and handsome.

It was time for the rally against the deforestation of land, organised by the tribals and the other lower castes of that area with the help of the lower caste national leaders active in national politics. Ramvilas visited the village before the rally was organised at Godda, a nearby district town under which our village fell, mainly to request all the people to join the rally. His effort was to gather the maximum crowd to give a jolt to the upper caste of that area and show off the strength of the lower castes. They had also arranged for tractors and some jeeps to transport the people. I could hear the noise of the jeeps and the revving of their engines. The *kuchha* track was very sandy when it was dry, and was slushy in the rainy seasons. It was either way problematic for the vehicles to reach the village. Parmeshra informed Ramvilas that I had returned to the village minus one leg.

Ramvilas arrived at my place, after a few hours, once he had finished with the villagers. I was sitting on the steps of the veranda and talking to my little new puppy. It was a way to pass time and it also gave me a feeling of nearness to its mother or to its great grandmother, that my puppy might have been. I had once again developed a fascination for it.

I couldn't recognise Ramvilas. He looked much fairer than before and sported a beard and wore a spotless pair of white Khadi pajama kurta. He had put on lots of weight and looked handsome. His vernacular had not changed much and he used the same rustic language. He was the same Ramvilas, the boy who had carried my ration many times to the town or the bus stand, when I studied at the school. His eyes had the same look as before. He greeted and did namaste to me in the typical netaji style. He showed the characteristics and attributes of a leader and was in hurry and didn't have much time. He was very sympathetic to me and assured me of any financial help that I needed, and also a job in the city in any of the central government organisations I wished to join.

He also boasted of his generosity to the villagers, as he had offered jobs and other indirect employment, not only to the lower caste but also the upper caste boys. Babu's grandson worked at his office. He had also offered many jobs to the upper caste boys of the village as personal assistants or in household work like cooks, caretakers, drivers of the lower class national leaders. A couple of the upper caste boys, were employed in the railways and Coal India as sweepers and peons. He had fulfilled the dream of the national Dalit leaders, who advocated time and again, to revolt against the upper caste and ensure their humiliation, by making them sweep the floor and lift offal at their house.

The younger generation of the lower caste had always dreamt of forcing the upper caste youths to work for them and do the lowest job of lifting offal and sweeping their office or home. They achieved their aim. Many of the upper caste took up the petty job of working in the lower caste leader's kitchen, house and offices as peons. The lower caste had an advantage as they had job reservation, if they did such a job. Whereas, even though the upper castes were forced by destiny to do a similar job in the houses and offices of the lower caste presidents, ministers, members of parliament, governors, bureaucrats and other MLAs, they were deprived of any such privileges. Instead, the children of the lower caste presidents, members of parliaments or MLAs, got the benefit of the reservation created by the Government of India, mainly on the basis of caste. The upper caste lost their false tradition, ego and opportunity as well. This was a well-planned strategy of the lower caste national leaders, which was started as petty village politics and was later implemented at the national level.

Ramvilas, whose parents worked all through their life in my house, even offered me a job, ostensibly because of my amputated leg, but the actual reason was the satisfaction of his ego. I had been able to read the ego in his eyes and face, though he pretended to be genuinely worried for my future in the village. In any case, I was not worried, as I had nothing to do with Ramvilas or his job. I had enough of income, with no expenses other than for my food. That way even my little new puppy could manage on its own.

There was a pleasant surprise for me. Yusuf Mian had arrived with the whole family. I requested Parmeshra to arrange for their lunch. Ajra was in Burka. She removed it only after her mother advised her to do so. She had three children to support. All her children had very little age gaps amongst them. After seeing her children, it gave me a fair amount of idea about the time that had elapsed after I had met her last. Ajra's mother was surprised to see my feet and had a closer look. Ajra was in tears to see me. She didn't have the courage to touch my amputated foot.

I once again showed Ajra my small puppy but this time I didn't hold her hand. She too had gone back fifteen to twenty years in time, and was perhaps remembering the days when I had shown her my little puppy and she had run to her father crying because my puppy had scared her. My heart throbbed faster. I had many things to communicate and talk to her but couldn't. She too wished to talk of many things, but she knew it was too late in life for her. She still looked as pretty as ever. She was still at the peak of her youth and looked much younger than I. She looked a few times into my eyes. I could see the same affection in her eyes. She was feeling pity for me. Her mother asked me many things to ascertain and read my mind about the future, but I myself was not too sure of anything; what support could I have given to anyone. I had a good time with all of them, Parmeshra and Kusmi could see the affection for Ajra, in my eyes but they too knew it was too late. Kusmi discouraged me to go closer to her. She took me aside and said, giving her sectarian view, '*Chotanbabu*, you are a Brahmin. How can you touch or love a Muslim girl with three children?' I didn't say anything and completely ignored her.

I had not been able to forget Ajra and vividly remembered the day, when she had drawn a moustache on me, while I was fast asleep in the night, with the smoke dust collected on the earthen pot, used for cooking, while Mama and I had visited their house. Yusuf Mian had warned her not to repeat it in future; even Mama had laughed and enjoyed seeing my face with the big moustache. When I had visited their house after my tenth class examinations, both of us had got under a blanket and talked on the *machan* – a hut made on to the field to look after the crop of maize or sugar. She had held my hand and kept it on her *Pupu*. I too liked touching it but didn't know what was happening to me. I had a different feeling. Before that I had no carnal knowledge and hadn't experienced anything similar. I had also touched her *Phu* and realised that whatever the elder daughter of Pratima had told me, was the truth. Everyone grew hair on their *Phu*. I had not developed any then but Ajra had.

She had caught my hands and had inserted one of my fingers in her *Phu*. She had closed her thighs tightly and moved her lower part slowly. She had even touched my *Phu* and had whispered, '*Masha Allah,* you have grown big.' My *Phu* had become erect after she had fondled it. She never used to wear a panty like Pratima's daughters. My finger had become fully wet with a gummy liquid in her *Phu*. I felt warm inside her and was very excited. I pushed my finger fully inside as much as I could. She closed her eyes and caught me very firmly and bit me on my lips. She prised her tongue inside mine and I sucked her like a lollypop. We had become one, merged with one another and moved out of this planet with sublime pleasure. We had moved much away from everyone. It was a great experience. I was unaware of my existence on the earth and had forgotten about everything else. It was the best thing made by the Almighty, that I had ever experienced in my life. She had taught me to catch the tip of the *Phu* or rub the tip of it on the pillow or shake it with the hands till it sprinkled some liquid. I was confused. She tried, but nothing came out of it other than a few drops of liquid like honey. She had whispered, 'You are safe', and had touched my *Phu* with hers for a long time.

We had enjoyed this game many times even in the night, sleeping on the floor on the bed made of hay, but didn't know whether what we were doing was wrong or right. One thing was sure, it was enjoyable and Ajra enjoyed more than I did. Most of the time, she took the lead as I used to be damn scared of Mama, as I was once caught playing *Dekha-Dekhi* by her.

Ajra used to close her eyes and press her *Pupu* to my head, putting my face in the cleavage of her *Pupu* and I could feel her nipples touching my ears. Her creamy white nipples pointed straight towards me. There was no sagging at all of her *Pupu*. It used to be a wonderful feeling for me. I had touched and seen her *Pupu* in broad daylight while she had her bath, at a place covered with the wooden twigs of *toor*. She was taller than me and had even developed big

Pupus. They didn't look big, while her clothes or *Dupatta* covered them, but they were big while I touched her with my hands. Her nipples became harder and darker when I touched and fondled them.

It was nice meeting the people who could share my pain and feelings and sweet memories of the past. We all spent the whole day on the terrace and then spent some time in the village. Even her children enjoyed the outing before they returned to their village, wishing me goodbye and good luck.

I was deeply worried, as I had nothing else to do other than think about Mama and her *Asthi Kalas*. Many times I used to sink into depression. I knew I wouldn't be able to survive in the village, as it lacked even the basic amenities like water and electricity. I requested the pundit to take some time out to accompany me to the town to submerge the *Asthi Kalas* of mother in the Ganges at Bhagalpur, as I couldn't go to Benaras. That would have meant a long-term planning as well as being unmanageable for me, as I held the crutches in one hand. I wouldn't have been able to hold the earthen pot containing the *Asthi Kalas* and managed all alone.

The pundit was more than pleased to accompany me to town, as he was aware his day wouldn't get wasted and he would get paid for the services rendered to me. In any case, he had nothing better to do and waited for someone's death or some other opportunity to keep himself busy. I handed over my new little puppy to Parmeshra and requested him to look after it till I returned to the village. I left along with the pundit. He got fed up of me as I couldn't keep pace with him, and time and again he had to wait for my arrival. After every kilometre or so, I needed a few minutes rest before resuming the journey on the *kuchha* animal track. He too realised, it was difficult to deal with a handicapped person and regretted his decision. It was for the first time, that I had moved out of the village when Mama had not come to see me off till the outer canal. I crossed and sat for a while to remember Mama's face, which always guided me and was my reason for living. I turned my face to see if I could see Mama waving her hands and wiping her tears with the corner of her sari.

The pundit couldn't understand the sentiment involved, and kept nagging me to hurry up as we might miss the bus to the town. There were a couple of buses that plied on this route, unlike earlier, when we had only one old bus converted from an auctioned Dodge truck. I was sure it wouldn't leave on time until and unless they packed the bus more than its capacity, like a cattle train or lorry moving to an abattoir. We managed to reach the bus stand well ahead of time. The pundit wished to have something to eat, mainly the sweets that were sold near the bus stand. I never had the habit of eating junk food. Moreover, I had decided to eat only after I submerged the ashes in the Ganges. I had in my mind to check if I could meet Prakash in the town. It was a long time since I had met him. We reached the town, late in the evening and we wished to stay in any hotel for the night, as the rituals were only possible the next day. The pundit had one of his relatives in the town. He requested me for some money for his food, and left after promising to meet me the next day, near the same banyan tree that was near my place of stay and at the crossroad of the crematorium.

I asked the rickshaw to take me to where Prakash had his house. I had put the *Asthi Kalas* pot in the bag to ensure that people didn't know what it was. The people with such jobs are treated as untouchables and no one dares come near them. I walked a few steps and asked one of the children playing on the street to look for Prakash. To my surprise, he was Prakash's son. He ran to his house and called his father. Prakash didn't have any trouble in recognising me and was very excited to see me. I went upto him and whispered in his ear the reason for my travel to the town. He was shocked. He was not aware of Mama's death. He offered to accompany me to the crematorium and extend all possible help, as his office was closed for a few days. He worked in the planning and designing of the Central Coalfields Limited at Ranchi.

No sooner had I turned back to reach the rickshaw, he asked me the reason for my limping, 'What is wrong with you?' I did not go into the details and informed him that I had left the army on medical grounds. He advised me to take up a job in the handicapped or ex-service men quota, in Coal India Limited. He also promised to offer all assistance. His parents were very sad and surprised to see and know about me.

We had a long chat at the hotel. He left to return the next day and meet me under the banyan tree. I reached the banyan tree very early in the morning. The pundit had not arrived, nor had Prakash. I waited for a long time. The sun was about to rise in the sky, birds were making hell of a noise on the banyan tree. The milkmen were out on the streets, the newspapermen were out with their cycles. The *tanga*, was plying to take the people to the railway station, to catch first passenger train passing Bhagalpur railway station. Many of the pundits and other people moved towards the Ganges, for their routine daily dip along with their relatives, visiting them from the village, mainly to have a dip in to the river to have the salvation from the sins earned by them.

At the temples, the loudspeakers were blaring the Hanuman Chalisa by Hari Om Sharan as well as the Ramayana. I was about to set off slowly as it was not very far from that place. I could hear the horn of a vehicle approaching very fast towards the banyan tree. It was Prakash in his ambassador car to carry me till the banks of the Ganges. I informed him that the pundit had not arrived yet and we had to wait till he joined us.

We sat inside the car and waited for his arrival. He arrived very late. The sun was quite high up in the sky. The barber who had sat under the tree and gave us haircuts, had installed his mirror and was ready with his first customer. I approached and spoke to him. He couldn't recollect me. I gave the reference of my father's dead body and he remembered. He asked, '*Beta*, why have you come now?' I didn't tell him anything. He could make out something was wrong. I showed him the earthen pot. He could understand the situation more than I would have explained to him. But he was still a little confused and wished to know a little more. I told him that I had lost my mother ten years back. He couldn't believe me and thought I was making fun of him. He was surprised to see the condition of my feet but didn't ask the reason. It was nothing new for me, as I knew everyone sympathised with the lame or handicapped but did nothing for them.

The pundit was in hurry. He smelled of pyorrhoea and *Nira*, toddy, a country liquor that he had had a few minutes before. I didn't ask him the reason for being late, as the smell from his mouth was manifesting the reasons for the delay. Prakash was stunned to see the pundit I had brought with me. He didn't speak but conveyed everything through his eyes. No sooner did we arrive on to the banks of the Ganges, our pundit swung into action and started the rituals. I was unable to stand in the water with one leg. Prakash helped me in reaching till shoulder level water. I submerged Mama's remains in the Ganges. The last rites of mother were completed. Prakash had tears in his eyes. My foot had gone numb. Mama's face was right before my eyes. She had lived the life of Sita in the Ramayana. She had lived life of rejection all through. She had hopes from her child, but even he had failed to look after her. All these thoughts were killing me from within. I had decided to be stoic and not allow my eye glands to release any drops of tears from my eyes. I cried from my heart and carried on a conversation within me, between my heart and mind. 'Mama... for whom do I have to live? Why and how could you leave your Chotu all alone on this earth, making him a waif? Mama, I love you and miss you...'

I refused Prakash's offer to join any of the offices for work, and took up a voluntary job of teaching the children in one of the primary schools run by a missionary, near my village. They knew me to be a staunch Hindu Brahmin and never forced me to join the choirs singing during assembly, that was organised in the morning. I stood at the end of the row to listen and repeat them in my mind every morning. I had no identity of being a Brahmin, or an upper caste. All I remembered, time and again after seeing my amputated leg, was that I was a soldier and perhaps would die as a soldier, as everyday of my life without a leg was a struggle. There were no restrictions anymore even for my puppy, as it stayed with me in the same campus and in the same room beneath my bed. My little puppy perhaps had got its home and reasons for living but I didn't... a soldier's life continued...